DARK FLAME
THE IMMORTALS

Alyson Noël is the author of many books for
teens, including *Saving Zoë, Art Geeks and
Prom Queens,* and *Evermore, Blue Moon* and
Shadowland, the first three books in The
Immortals series. She lives in Laguna Beach,
California, where she is at work on the next
book in The Immortals series.

'This young adult novel ponders immortal love and the knowledge that "revenge weakens and love strengthens." Fans of the Twilight series should love it' *Orange Coast Magazine*

'Get ready for a wild ride that is filled with twisting paths and mystery, love and fantasy' *The Book Queen (5/5 stars)*

'Readers who enjoy the works of P. C. Cast and Stephenie Meyer will love this outstanding paranormal teen-lit thriller' *Midwest Book Review*

'*Evermore* will thrill many teen fantasy-suspense readers, especially fans of Stephenie Meyer's Twilight series . . . Noël creates a cast of recognizably diverse teens in a realistic high-school setting. Along with just the right tension to make Ever's discovery of her immortality – should she choose it – exciting and credible' *Booklist*

'Beautiful main characters, tense budding romance, a dark secret, mysterious immortals – what more could you ask from this modern gothic romance?' *Justine Magazine*

DARK FLAME

THE IMMORTALS

Alyson Noël

MACMILLAN

First published in the US 2010 by St. Martin's Press

This edition published in the UK 2010 by Macmillan Children's Books
a division of Macmillan Publishers Limited
20 New Wharf Road, London N1 9RR
Basingstoke and Oxford
Associated companies throughout the world
www.panmacmillan.com

ISBN 978-0-330-52061-4

DARK FLAME by Alyson Noël. Copyright © 2010 by Alyson Noël, Inc.
By arrangement with the author. All rights reserved.

The right of Alyson Noël to be identified as the
author of this work has been asserted by her in accordance with the Copyright,
Designs and Patents Act 1988.

1 3 5 7 9 8 6 4 2

A CIP catalogue record for this book is available from
the British Library.

Printed and bound in the UK by CPI Mackays, Chatham ME5 8TD

FOR ROSE HILLIARD –
BECAUSE SHE'S AN ABSOLUTE DREAM
TO WORK WITH AND I COULDN'T
HAVE DONE IT WITHOUT HER!

'I BEHELD THE WRETCH –
THE MISERABLE MONSTER
WHOM I HAD CREATED.'

MARY SHELLEY, FRANKENSTEIN

ONE

"What the fug?"

Haven drops her cupcake, the one with the pink frosting, red sprinkles, and silver skirt. Her heavily made-up eyes searching mine as I glance around the busy plaza and cringe. Instantly regretting my decision to come here, foolish enough to think a trip to her favorite cupcake place on a nice summer day would be the best place to break the news. Like that little strawberry cake would somehow sweeten the message. But now I'm just wishing we'd stayed in the car.

"Inside voice. *Please.*" I aim for a light delivery but end up sounding like a cranky old schoolmarm instead. Watching as she leans forward, tucks her long, platinum-streaked bangs back behind her ear, and squints.

"Excuse me? But are you for real? I mean, here you drop a major bomb on me—and I mean *major*—as in my ears are still ringing and my head is still spinning and I kind of need you to repeat it just to make sure you really did say what I think—and your only concern is that I'm *talking too loud? Are you kidding me?*"

I shake my head and glance all around, slipping into full-on damage control mode as I lower my voice and say, "It's just—nobody can know. It's *got* to remain secret. It's *imperative*," I urge, realizing too late that I'm talking to the one person who's never been able to keep anyone's secret, much less her own.

She rolls her eyes and slams back in her seat, muttering under her breath as I take a moment to study her closely, dismayed to see the signs already present: her pale skin is luminous, clear, practically poreless as well, while her wavy brown hair with the blond streak in front is as shiny and glossy as a high-end shampoo ad. Even her teeth have gone straighter, whiter, and I can't help but wonder how this happened so quickly, with only a few sips of elixir, when it took so much longer for me.

My eyes continue to graze over her as I take a deep breath and dive in. Forgoing my usual promise not to eavesdrop on my friend's innermost thoughts, while I strain to get a better look, a glimpse of her energy, the words she's not sharing—sure that if snooping ever was warranted, it's now.

But instead of my usual front-row seat, I'm met by a rock-solid wall that bars me from entering. Even after I casually slide my hand forward and tap my fingertips against hers, feigning interest in the silver skull ring she wears, I get nothing.

Her future is hidden from me.

"This is just so—" She swallows hard and looks around, taking in the bubbling fountain, the young mom pushing a stroller while yelling into her cell phone, the group of girls exiting a swim shop with armfuls of bags—looking just about anywhere but at me.

"I know it's a lot to take in—*but still*—" I shrug, knowing I've got to make a better case but not quite sure how to do it.

"*A lot to take in?* Is that how you see it?" She shakes her head and drums her fingers against the armrest of her green metal chair as her gaze slowly sweeps over me.

I sigh, wishing I'd handled this better, wishing I could do something to make it go away, but it's too late for that. I've no choice but to deal with this mess that I made. "I guess I was hoping that's how *you'd* see it." I shrug. "Crazy. I know."

She takes a deep breath, face so still, so placid, it's impossible to read, and I'm just about to speak, just about to start begging forgiveness, when she says, "Seriously? You made me an immortal? Like—*for reals?*"

I nod, stomach a jumble of nerves as I sit up straighter and pull my shoulders back, bracing for the blow that's surely headed my way. Knowing that whatever she gives, be it verbal or physical, I've no choice but to take it. I deserve nothing less for wrecking her life as she knows it.

"I'm just—" She sucks in her breath and blinks several times, her aura invisible, offering no clue to her mood, now that I've made her like me. "Well—I'm in a total state of shock. I mean, seriously. I don't even know what to say."

I press my lips together and drop my hands to my lap, worrying the crystal horseshoe bracelet I always wear as I clear my throat and say, "Haven, listen, I'm so sorry. *So— very—very—sorry.* You have no idea. I just—" I shake my head, knowing I should cut to the chase but feeling like I need to explain my side of things—the impossible choice I was forced to make—how it felt to see her so pale, so helpless, teetering on the verge of death, every shallow breath quite possibly her last—

But before I can even begin she leans toward me, eyes wide and fixed on mine. "Are you *insane?*" She shakes her head. "You're actually *apologizing,* when I'm just sitting here, so psyched, so totally gobsmacked, I can't even imagine how I'll ever repay you!"

Huh?

"I mean, this is just *so* fugging cool!" She grins, bouncing up and down in her seat, face lighting up like a thousand-watt bulb. "It's seriously the coolest fugging thing that's ever happened to me—and I owe it all to *you!*"

I gulp, nervously glancing around, unsure how to react. This is not what I expected. Not what I prepared for. Though it's pretty much exactly what Damen warned me about.

Damen—my best friend—my soul mate—the love of my lives. My amazingly gorgeous, sexy, smart, talented, patient, and understanding boyfriend who knew this would happen and begged to come along for this very reason. But I was too stubborn. Insisting I do it alone. I'm the one who *turned* her— I'm the one who made her drink the elixir—so I'm the one who should explain. Only it's not going at all like I thought. Not even close.

"I mean, it's like being a vampire, right? Minus the blood-sucking?" Her sparkling eyes eagerly search mine. "Oh, and without all the coffins and sun avoidance too!" Her voice rises with glee. "This is *so* amazing—like a dream come true! Everything I've ever wanted has finally happened! I'm a vampire! A beautiful vampire—but without all the gruesome side effects!"

"You're not a vampire," I say, voice dull, listless, wondering how it got to this point. "There's no such thing."

Nope, no vampires, no werewolves, no elves, no fairies—just immortals, whose ranks, thanks to Roman and me, are quickly multiplying . . .

"And how can you be sure of that?" Haven asks, brow raised.

"Because Damen's been around a lot longer than I have," I say. "And he's never met one—or met anyone who's met one. We figure the vampire legends all stem from immortals, only with a few big distortions—like the bloodsucking, not being able to go out in sunlight, and the whole being allergic to garlic thing." I lean toward her. "It's all been added on for extra drama."

"Interesting." She nods, though her mind is clearly elsewhere. "Can I still eat cupcakes?" She motions toward the dented strawberry mess, one side caved in, flattened against its cardboard container, while the other side remains fluffy, begging to be eaten. "Or is there something else I'm supposed to—" Eyes going wide, giving me no time to reply before she slaps the table and squeals, "Omigod—it's *that juice,* isn't it? That red stuff you and Damen always drink! That's it, huh? *So,* what are you waiting for! Hand it over already, let's make it official—I can't wait to get started!"

"I didn't bring any," I say, seeing her face drop in disappointment as I rush to explain. "Listen, I know you think it sounds really cool and all—and some of it is, there's no doubt about that. I mean, you'll never grow old, never get zits or split ends, you'll never have to work out, and you might even grow taller—who knows? But there's other stuff too—stuff you need to know—stuff I have to explain in order to—" My words are halted by the sight of her jumping out of her chair so quickly and gracefully she's like a cat—yet another immortality side effect.

Hopping from foot to foot as she says, "Please. What's to know? If I can jump higher, run faster, never age or fade away—what else could I possibly need? Sounds like I'm good to go for the rest of eternity."

I glance around nervously, determined to curb her enthusiasm before she does something crazy—something that'll draw the kind of attention we cannot afford. "Haven, please. *Sit.* This is serious. There's more to explain. *A lot* more," I whisper, the words harsh, brutal, but having no effect whatsoever. She just stands there before me, shaking her head and refusing to budge. So drunk on her new immortal power she skips past defiant and heads straight for belligerent.

"*Everything* is serious with you, Ever. *Every—single—thing* you say and do is just *so* dang serious. I mean, *seriously,* you hand me the keys to the kingdom then demand I stay put so you can warn me about the dark side? How crazy is that?" She rolls her eyes. "Come on, unclench a little, would ya? Let me try it out, take it for a test drive, see what I'm capable of. I'll even race you! First one to make it from the curb to the library wins!"

I shake my head and sigh, wishing I didn't have to do it, but knowing a little telekinesis is in order. It's the only thing that'll put an end to all this and show her who's really in charge around here. Narrowing my eyes, I focus hard on her chair, driving it across the pavers so fast it buckles her knees and forces her to sit.

"Hey—that hurt!" She rubs her leg and glares.

But I just shrug. She's immortal, it's not like she'll bruise. Besides, there's plenty more to explain and not enough time if she continues like this, so I lean toward her, making sure I have her full attention when I say, "Trust me, you can't play the game if you don't know the rules. And if you don't know the rules, someone's bound to get hurt."

TWO

Haven hurls herself into my car, scrunching her body tightly against the door and propping her feet on the seat. Frowning and glaring and mumbling—a full litany of complaints leveled at me—as I pull out of the lot and onto the street.

"Rule number one." I glance at her, pushing my long blond hair out of my face, determined to ignore her openly hostile gaze. "*You—can't—tell—anyone.*" I pause, allowing the words to sink in before adding, "Seriously. You can't tell your mom, your dad, your little brother Austin—"

"Please." She shifts, crossing and uncrossing her legs, tugging at her clothes and jiggling her foot in a way so antsy, so squirmy, it's clear she can barely stand to be contained here with me. "I barely talk to them anyway." She scowls. "Besides, that's a repeat. You already sang that one loud and clear. So, come on, keep it moving, let's just get 'em over and done with, so I can get out of here and start my new life."

I swallow hard, refusing to be either rushed or swayed, gazing at her as I stop at a light, determined she understand the full importance of this when I add, "And that includes Miles. Under no circumstances whatsoever can you tell him."

She rolls her eyes and fiddles with her ring, twisting it around and around her middle finger, clearly tempted to flip it at me. "Fine. Can't tell anyone. Got it," she mumbles. "Next, please!"

"You can still eat real food." I make my way through the intersection, slowly picking up speed. "But you won't always want to, since the elixir pretty much fills you up and provides all the nutrients you need. But still, in public anyway, it's important to keep up appearances, so you have to at least *pretend* like you're eating."

"Oh, like you?" She looks at me, brow arced, lip curled into a smirk. "You know, how you sit there at lunch, tearing your sandwich to shreds and crumbling your potato chips into tiny little bits and thinking no one notices? Is that what you've been doing all this time? *Keeping up appearances?* Cuz Miles and I just thought you had an eating disorder."

I take a deep breath and focus on driving, keeping my speed light, refusing to let her get to me. Like the karma Damen's always going on about—claiming that all of our actions cause a reaction—this is where my action has led me. Besides, even if I could go back and do it over again, I wouldn't change a thing. I'd make the exact same choice as before. Because no matter how awkward this moment may be, it's still better than attending her funeral, any day of the week.

"Omigod!" She looks at me, her mouth dropping, eyes going wide, voice all high and squeaky when she says, "I think—I think I heard that!"

My eyes meet hers, and despite the fact that the top is down, despite the fact that the Southern California summer sun is beating straight down on us, my skin goes instantly chilled.

This is not good. Not good at all.

"Your *thoughts*! You were thinking something about being glad you didn't have to go to my funeral, *right*? I mean, I actually *heard* your words in my head. That is *so* cool!"

I immediately raise my shield, barring all access to my mind, my energy, everything, all of it. More than a little freaked by the fact that she was able to do that when I can't read hers, and I haven't even had a chance to show her how to shield herself yet.

"So you guys weren't kidding, were you? About the whole telepathy thing? You and Damen really do read each other's minds."

I nod, slowly, reluctantly, as she surveys me with eyes that shine brighter than ever. What was once your everyday, basic shade of brown, often hidden by crazy-colored contacts, is now a brilliant swirl of gold, topaz, and bronze—yet another immortality side effect.

"I always knew you guys were weird—but this takes it to a whole new level. And now I can do it too! Jeez, I wish Miles was here."

I close my eyes and shake my head, striving for patience and wondering how many more times I'll have to repeat this, when I brake for a pedestrian and say, "But you can't tell Miles—*remember*? We've already been over that."

She shrugs, my words glancing right off her, as she twirls a chunk of glossy brown hair around and around her index finger, smiling as a black Bentley pulls up right beside us with some kid from our school behind the wheel.

"Fine. *Fine!* Seriously, I won't tell him. Chillax already, would ya?" She zeros in on our classmate, smiling and flirting and waving, even going so far as to blow a series of air kisses at him, and then laughing when he does a double take. "The secret's safe. I'm just used to telling him when exciting stuff happens, that's all. It's a habit. I'm sure I'll get over it. But still, you gotta admit, it's pretty dang cool, right? I mean, how'd you react when you first found out? Weren't you totally psyched?" She looks at me, smiling when she adds, "No pun intended."

I frown, pushing the gas harder than I meant to, the car lurching forward as my mind travels back to that very first day—or, at least the first time Damen tried to break the life-altering news out in the parking lot at school. But I wasn't up for listening then. And I was pretty much as far from *excited* as it gets. Then, the second time he insisted on explaining our long and tangled past, I was still on the fence. I mean, on the one hand I thought it was pretty cool that we could finally be together after centuries of being kept apart. But on the other, it was a lot to take in. A lot to give up.

And while at first we thought the choice was all mine— that I could continue to drink the elixir and embrace my immortality—or ignore it completely, live out my life, and succumb to my death at some point in the far distant future—now we know better.

Now we know the truth about an immortal's demise.

Now we know about the Shadowland.

The infinite void.

The eternal abyss.

The place where immortals linger—soulless—isolated— for all of eternity.

A place we need to steer clear of.

"Um, hel-*lo*—earth to Ever?" She laughs.

But I just shrug. It's the only answer I plan to give.

Which only prompts her to lean toward me and say, "Excuse me, but I so don't get you." Her eyes rake over me. "This is like the best day of my *entire* life and all you want to do is focus on the negatives. I mean, hel-*lo*? Psychic powers, physical prowess, ageless youth, and beauty—does it mean nothing to you?"

"Haven, it's not all fun and games, it's—"

"Yeah, yeah." She rolls her eyes and slams back in her seat, pulling her knees to her chest as she wraps her arms tightly around them. "There are rules—a downside. Roger that, loud and clear." She frowns, gathering her hair to the side and twisting it around and around into a glossy brown coil. "But jeez, don't you ever get tired of it? Of always being so burdened, so weighted down by the world? It's like, you have the best life ever. You're blond, blue-eyed, tall, fit, gifted, oh, and to top it all off, the sexiest guy on the planet just happens to be madly in love with you." She sighs, wondering how I can possibly be so blind to her truth. "I mean, let's face it, you've got the kind of life other people can only dream of— and yet, you make it look like the road to Suck City. And honestly, I'm sorry to say it, but I think that's crazy. Cuz the truth is, I feel fantastic! Electrified! Like a lightning bolt's surging through my body from my head to my toes! And no way am I joining you on your journey to Sad Land. No way am I slinking around campus in fugly hoodies and sunglasses with an iPod practically implanted in my head like you used to do. I mean, at least now I know why you did it, to avoid all the voices and thoughts, *right*? But still, no fugging way am I living like that. I plan to embrace it—with *both* arms. I also plan to kick some serious Stacia, Honor, and Craig butt if they so much as bother me or my friends!" She leans forward, elbows on her knees as she narrows her gaze. "When I think of all the crap they put you through and how you just rolled over and took it—" She purses her lips. "I don't get it."

I look at her, knowing I can just lower my shield, think the answer, and she'd hear the words in my head, but knowing it'll resonate a lot more if it's spoken out loud, I say, "I guess because it all came at such a high price—the loss of my family—never getting to cross—" I pause, halting the words from escape. Not quite ready to explain about Summerland, that glorious mystical dimension between the dimensions, or the bridge that takes all mortals to the *other* side—or at least not just yet anyway. One thing at a time. "It's just that I'll always be *here*. I'll never get to cross *over* and see my family again—" I shake my head. "And, well, for me anyway, that feels like a pretty big penalty."

She reaches toward me, her sad puppy dog look displayed on her face, before quickly pulling away. "Oops, sorry! Forgot how you hate to be touched." She crinkles her nose as she tucks a windblown chunk of hair behind her multipierced ear.

"I don't hate to be touched." I shrug. "It's just sometimes— well, it can be pretty revealing, that's all."

"Will it be like that for me too?"

I look at her, having no idea what *gifts* she has in store. She's already so far ahead of the curve, on just one bottle of elixir, who knows what a full case will bring?

"I don't know." I shrug. "Some of it happened because I died and went to—"

Her eyes narrow, straining to read my thoughts but not getting very far, thanks to the shield that I built.

"Well, let's just say I had a near-death experience. It tends to change things." I pull onto her street.

She looks at me, gaze fixed, intense, fingers idly picking at a small tear in her leggings as she says, "Seems like you're kind of cherry-picking the things you want me to know." She raises her brow, daring me to deny it.

But I don't. I don't do anything but close my eyes and nod. So tired of lying and covering up all the time. It feels good to admit to a few things for a change.

"Can I ask why?"

I lift my shoulders and take a deep breath, forcing my gaze to meet hers. "It's a lot to take in all at once. Some of it needs to be experienced to understand—while other stuff—well, a lot of it can wait. Though there are still a couple things you need to know."

I park on her drive and fumble through my bag, handing over a small silk pouch, just like the one Damen gave me.

"What's this?" She pulls the strings and digs her finger inside, coming away with a small cluster of colorful stones, held together by thin gold strands, and hanging from a black silk cord.

"It's an amulet." I nod "It's—it's important you wear it all the time. Pretty much every day from now on."

She squints, swinging it back and forth, watching as the stones catch and reflect in the sunlight.

"I have one too." I pull mine out from under my tee, revealing my own cluster of stones.

"How come mine's different?" She glances between them, comparing, contrasting, trying to decide which is better.

"Because no two are the same—we all have different—needs. And wearing these will keep us safe."

She looks at me.

"They hold protective qualities." I shrug, knowing I'm treading into murky waters, the part Damen and I disagreed about.

She tilts her head and scrunches her face, unable to read my thoughts but well aware I'm holding back. "Protect us from *what* exactly? I mean, we're immortal, right? Which, if I'm not mistaken, pretty much means we'll live forever, and yet, you're telling me I need *protection*? To be kept *safe*?" She shakes her head. "Sorry, Ever, but that just doesn't make any sense. Who or what could I possibly need to be protected from?"

I take a deep breath, assuring myself I'm doing the right thing, the only thing, despite what Damen may think. Hoping he'll forgive me as I say, "You need to be protected from Roman."

She shakes her head and crosses her arms, refusing to believe. "Roman? That's ridiculous. Roman would never hurt me."

I gape, hardly believing my ears, especially after everything I've just told her.

"Sorry, Ever, but Roman's my *friend*. And not like it's any of your business, but we're actually well on our way to becoming *more* than friends. And since it's no secret you've hated him from day one, it's really not all that surprising to hear you saying this now. *Sad*, but not surprising."

"I'm not making it up." I shrug, striving for a calm I can't even summon. Knowing that raising my voice, trying to force her to see things my way, will never work on someone as stubborn as her. "And yeah, maybe you're right, maybe I don't like him, but considering how he tried to kill you and all—well, call me crazy, but I think that's a good enough reason. I even have witnesses—I wasn't the only one there, you know!"

She squints, fingernails tapping against the door handle as she says, "Okay, so let me get this straight, Roman tries to poison me with some messed-up tea—"

"Belladonna—also known as deadly nightshade—"

"Whatever." She waves it away. "The point is, you claim he was trying to kill me, and yet instead of calling nine-one-one you just stroll on over to see for yourself? I mean, what's up with that? Obviously you didn't take it very seriously, so why should I?"

"I did try to call—but it was—*complicated*." I shake my head. "It was a choice between—between something I really need—and you. And as you see, I chose you."

She looks at me, eyes wide, mind calculating, not saying a word.

"Roman promised to give me what I need if I just let you die. But I couldn't do it—and so—" I gesture toward her. "Now you're immortal."

She shakes her head and gazes around, focusing on a group of neighborhood kids driving a jacked-up golf cart up and down the street. Keeping quiet for so long I'm just about to speak when she says, "Sorry you didn't get what you want, Ever, really I am. But you're wrong about Roman. There's no way he'd let me die. From what you said, he had the elixir standing by, ready to go in case you chose differently. Besides, I think I know Roman just a *little* better than you, and the fact is, he knows how unhappy I've been, about the stuff going on with my family—" She shrugs. "He probably just wanted to make me immortal to spare me from that, but didn't want to sire me since there's a lot of responsibility that goes with it. I've no doubt that if you hadn't made me drink, he would've stepped in. Face it, Ever, you made the wrong choice. You should've just called his bluff."

"There's no *sire*," I mumble, inwardly rolling my eyes at myself. Out of that whole entire litany, that's what I choose to focus on? I shake my head and start over. "It's not like that—not even close—it's . . ." Voice fading as she looks away, fully convinced of one thing—she's right and I'm wrong. And since I tried to warn her about all the dangers—about *him*—Damen can't possibly fault me for what I say next.

"Fine, believe what you want, just do me a favor. If you're going to insist on hanging with Roman, then all I ask is that you always wear your amulet. Seriously, don't *ever* take it off—not for anything—and—"

She looks at me, brow raised, door half open, desperate to get out of this car and away from me.

"And if you're serious about repaying me for making you immortal—"

Our eyes meet.

"Then Roman has something I really need you to get."

THREE

"How'd it go?"

Damen opens the door before I can knock. His gaze deep and intense as he follows me into the den where I drop onto his plush velour couch and kick off my flip-flops. Careful to avoid his eyes as he lands on the cushion beside me, usually all too eager to spend the rest of eternity just gazing at him—taking in the fine planes of his face—his high sculpted cheekbones, lush inviting lips, the slant of his brow, his dark wavy hair, and thick fringe of lashes—but not today.

Today I'd prefer to look just about anywhere else.

"So, you told her?" His fingers trail along the side of my cheek, the curve of my ear, his touch filling me with tingle and heat despite the ever-present energy veil that hovers between us. "Did the cupcake provide the distraction you hoped it would?" His lips nip at my lobe before working their way down my neck.

I lean back against the cushions, closing my eyes in a feigned bout of fatigue. But the truth is, I don't want him to *see* me, to observe me too closely. Don't want him to sense my thoughts, my essence, my energy—that strange, foreign pulse that's been stirring inside me for the last several days.

"Hardly." I sigh. "She pretty much ignored it—guess she's like us now—in more ways than one." Feeling the weight of his gaze as he studies me intensely.

"Care to elaborate?"

I scrunch down even lower and toss my leg over his, my breath slowing as I settle into the warmth of his energy. "She's just—so far advanced. I mean, she has the whole look, you know? That eerie, flawless, immortal look. She even heard my thoughts—until I blocked them." I frown and shake my head.

"*Eerie?* Is that how you see it—*see us?*" Clearly distressed by my words.

"Well—not really *eerie*." I pause, wondering why I phrased it like that. "More like—*not normal*. I mean, I doubt even supermodels look that perfect all the time. Not to mention, what are we gonna do if she grows four inches practically overnight like I did? How do we possibly explain that?"

"Same way we did with you," he says, eyes narrowed, cautious, more interested in the words I'm not saying than the ones that I am. "We'll call it a growth spurt. They're not that uncommon among mortals, you know." His voice lifts in a weak attempt at levity that doesn't quite work.

I avert my gaze, taking in the crowded bookshelves filled with leather-bound first editions, the abstract oil paintings, most of them priceless originals, knowing he's onto me. He knows something's up, but I'm hoping he can't sense just how far it goes. That I'm just saying the words, going through the motions, not really invested in any of this.

"And so—does she hate you like you feared?" he asks, voice steady, deep, the slightest bit probing.

I peer at him, this wonderful glorious creature who's loved me for the last four hundred years and continues to do so no matter how many blunders I make, no matter how many lives I mess up. Sighing as I close my eyes and manifest a single red tulip that I promptly hand over. Serving not just as the symbol of our undying love, but also the winning wager in the bet that we made.

"You were right—you win." I shake my head, remembering how she reacted just like he said. "She's thrilled beyond belief. Can't thank me enough. Feels just like a rock star. No—scratch that, *better* than a rock star. She feels like a *vampire* rock star. But you know, the new and improved kind—without all that nasty bloodsucking and coffin sleeping." I shake my head and smile in spite of myself.

"A member of the mythical undead?" Damen cringes, not liking the analogy one bit. "I'm not sure how I feel about that."

"Oh, I'm sure it's just a side effect of her recent goth phase. The thrill will die down eventually. You know, once the reality sinks in."

"Is that how it is for you?" he asks, finger just under my chin, making me look at him again. "Is the thrill dying down—or perhaps even—*gone*?" His gaze deep, knowing, attuned to every shift of my mood. "Is that why you find it so hard to look at me now?"

"No!" I shake my head, fully aware that I've been caught and desperate to refute it. "I'm just—*tired*. I've been feeling a little—*on edge* lately, that's all." I nuzzle closer, burying my face in the hollow of his neck, right next to where the cord for his amulet rests. That *edgy* prickly feeling I've been carrying for days, tempering, melting, as I inhale his warm musky scent over and over again. "Why can't every moment be like this?" I murmur, knowing what I really mean is: Why can't *I* always be like this—*feel* like this?

Why is everything changing?

"It can." He shrugs. "There's really no reason why it can't."

I pull away and meet his gaze. "Oh, I can think of at least two very good reasons."

Nodding toward Romy and Rayne, the twin terrors we're now responsible for as they bound down the stairs. Identical in their straight dark hair with razor-slashed bangs, pale skin, and large dark eyes—but complete opposites in their dress. Romy wearing a pink terry cloth sundress with matching flip-flops, while Rayne's barefoot and dressed in all black, with Luna, their tiny black kitten, riding high on her shoulder. The two of them shooting Damen a happy, warm smile and glaring at me—business as usual, and pretty much the only thing that *hasn't* changed around here.

"They'll come around," he says, wanting to believe it and wishing I would too.

"No they won't." I sigh, fumbling for my flip-flops. "But then, it's not like they don't have their reasons." I slip on my shoes and look at him.

"Leaving so soon?"

I nod, avoiding his gaze. "Sabine's making dinner, Munoz is coming over—it's a whole *bonding thing.* She wants us to get to know each other better. You know, less student teacher, more future nonblood relations." I shrug, realizing the instant it's out that I should've invited him. It's incredibly rude not to include him. But Damen's presence will only mess with my *other* evening plans. The ones he may suspect but can't possibly witness. Especially after making his feelings on my foray into magick so abundantly clear. Tacking on an awkward, "So—*you know* . . ." and leaving it to hang there, dangling between us, since I've no idea where to take it from there.

"And Roman?"

I take a deep breath as my eyes meet his. The moment I've been avoiding is now here.

"Did you warn Haven? Tell her what he did?"

I nod. Recalling the speech I practiced in the car all the way over, about how Haven could be our best chance to get what we need from Roman. Hoping it'll sound better to his ears than it did mine.

"And?"

I clear my throat, allowing myself that, but nothing more.

He waits for me to continue, the patience of six hundred years stamped on his face, as I open my mouth to launch into my speech, but I can't. He knows me too well. So instead, I just lift my shoulders and sigh, knowing words are unnecessary, the answer's displayed in my gaze.

"I see." He nods, his tone smooth, even, without a trace of judgment, which kind of disappoints me. I mean, I'm judging me, so why isn't he?

"But—it's really not like you think," I say. "It's not like I didn't try to warn her, but she wouldn't listen. So I figured, what the heck. If she's going to insist on hanging with Roman, then what's the harm in her trying to snag the antidote while she's at it? And I know you think it's wrong, believe me, we've been over that, but I still don't think it's all that big a deal."

He looks at me, face calm, still, betraying nothing.

"Besides, it's not like we actually have any real proof that he would've let her die. I mean, he had the antidote all along, he knew what I'd choose. But even if I did prove him wrong, how do we know he wouldn't have given her the elixir himself?" I take a deep breath, hardly believing I'm borrowing Haven's argument, the same one I balked at just a few moments earlier. "And then—maybe he even would've tried to turn the whole thing around! You know, tell her we were prepared to let her die and end up turning her against *us*! Did you ever think of *that*?"

"No. I suppose I didn't," he says, lids narrowed, concern clouding his face.

"And it's not like I'm not gonna monitor the situation cuz I totally am. I'll make sure she's safe. But she does have free will, you know, it's not like we can choose her friends for her, so I figured, you know, when in Rome . . . and all . . . so to speak . . ."

"And what about the romantic feelings Haven holds toward Roman? Did you consider that?"

I shrug, my words containing a conviction I don't really feel when I say, "She used to have *feelings* for you too if you'll remember. She seemed to get over that pretty quickly. And don't forget about Josh, the guy she was convinced was her soul mate who got booted over a kitten. And now that she's in a position to have pretty much whatever or whoever she wants—" I pause, but only for a moment, not long enough for him to interject. "I'm sure Roman will lose his allure and slide way down on her list. I mean, I know she can seem kind of fragile, but she's actually a lot tougher than you think."

I stand, signaling an end to this conversation. What's done is done and I don't want him to do or say anything that'll make me doubt my stance on Haven and Roman's relationship any more than I already do.

He hesitates, gaze moving over me, taking me in, then rises in one, quick, languid move as he grasps my hand and leads me to the door, where he presses his lips against mine. Lingering, fusing, pushing, melding, the two of us drawing this kiss out for as long as we can, neither one willing to break away first.

I press hard against him, the contours of his body barely dimmed by that ever-present energy veil that hovers between us. The broad expanse of his chest, the valley of his torso—every inch of him conforming so tightly to me it's nearly impossible to tell where he ends and I begin. Wishing this kiss could do the impossible—banish my mistakes—this strange way I feel—chase away the dark angry cloud that follows me everywhere these days.

"I should go," I whisper, the first to break the spell, aware of the heat rising between us, that incendiary pull, a painful reminder that, for now anyway, this is as far as it goes.

And just as I've settled into my car and Damen's gone back inside, Rayne appears, Luna still perched on her shoulder, twin sister Romy at her side.

"Tonight's the night. Moon's moving into a new phase," she says, eyes narrowed, lips grim. No other words necessary, we all know what that means.

I nod and shift into reverse, ready to back down the drive, when she adds, "You know what to do, right? You remember our plan?"

I nod again, hating the fact that I'm in this position, knowing that as far as they're concerned, I'll never live this one down.

Backing out of the drive and onto the street, their thoughts chasing behind me, burrowing into my mind, as they think: *It's wrong to use magick for selfish, nefarious reasons. There's karma to pay, and it'll come back times three.*

FOUR

The first thing I see when I pull into the drive is Munoz's silver Prius. Which, to be honest, pretty much makes me want to turn around and go just about anywhere else. But I don't. I just sigh and pull into the garage instead. Knowing I've no choice but to face it.

Face the fact that my aunt/legal guardian is falling hard for my history teacher.

Face the fact that it's a heckuva lot better to sit around the *dinner* table than the *breakfast* table, which, if things continue to progress at the rapid pace that they are, then it's just a matter of time before it's: *Good-bye Mr. Munoz, hello Uncle Paul!* I've *seen* it. It's as good as done. Now I'm just waiting for them to realize it too.

I slip through the side door, tiptoeing lightly, hoping to make it up to my room without being seen so I can have some time to myself—time that I desperately need in order to set some things straight.

Poised and ready to dash up the stairs when Sabine pokes

her head around the corner and says, "Oh good, I thought I heard your car in the garage. We're going to eat in about half an hour, but why don't you come in and visit a bit beforehand."

I peer over her shoulder in search of Munoz, but thanks to the wall that separates us from the den, all I can see are a pair of leather man-sandals perched on the overstuffed ottoman, appearing so relaxed and casual it's as if they don't belong anywhere else but that very spot. Switching my gaze to her and taking in the sweep of her shoulder-length blond hair, the flush at her cheeks, her sparkling blue eyes, and renewing my vow to be happy that she's happy—even though I'm not exactly thrilled with the reason behind it.

"I'm—I'll be down in a bit," I say, forcing a smile. "I'm just gonna wash up—and stuff . . ." My gaze drifts back to Munoz, unable to tear it away no matter how disturbing the view. I mean seriously, just because it's summer doesn't mean I should have to look at faculty feet in my own house.

"Okay, well, don't take too long." She starts to turn, hair swinging over her shoulder as she adds, "Oh, and I almost forgot, this came for you."

She swipes a cream-colored envelope off the side table and offers it to me. The words MYSTICS & MOONBEAMS printed in purple on the top left corner, my name and address in Jude's angular scribble scrawled across the front.

I just stand there and stare, knowing I could grab it, place my hand on the front, and intuit the contents without ever having to unseal it. But the thing is, I don't want to touch it, don't want anything to do with it, the job I once held, or Jude, the boss who, as it just so happens, played a significant role in pretty much all of my lives. Reappearing again and again, always managing to claim my affections until Damen showed up and swept me away. A centuries-old love triangle that ended the second I saw his Ouroboros tattoo last Thursday night.

And even though Damen claims that lots of people have them—that its original meaning wasn't at all evil, that Roman and Drina just made it that way, I can't take the chance that he's wrong.

Can't take the chance that Jude's not one of *them*, when I'm pretty dang sure that he is.

"Ever?" Sabine tilts her head, shooting me her usual look that says: *No matter how many books I read on the subject, adolescents may as well be aliens.* A look I know all too well.

A look that prompts me to snatch the envelope right out of her hand, careful to handle it by its edges as I smile weakly and tackle the stairs. Hands shaking, body thrumming, as the contents reveal themselves to be a paycheck I definitely earned but have no intention of cashing, along with a brief note asking if I'll please let him know if I've no plans to return so that he can hire another psychic to replace me.

That's it.

No: *What the heck happened?*

Or: *Why did you go from nearly kissing me to tossing me across your yard and into the patio furniture?*

But that's because he already knows. He's known all along. And while I may not know just what he's up to, he's clearly up to *something.* He may be ahead of the game for the moment, but unbeknownst to him, I'm about to catch up.

I toss the envelope toward the trash, figuring my lack of response should be answer enough. Directing it in a complicated choreography of loops and circles and one very perfect, spot-on figure eight, before bringing it down with a soft, barely heard thud and heading into my walk-in closet where I retrieve the box from the top shelf—the one that holds my supplies—everything I need to undo what I've done.

The time is right—providing for a fresh new start, the perfect opportunity (the *only* opportunity according to Romy and Rayne) to break the spell I unwittingly cast when I accidentally summoned the dark powers to aid me. The moon is now waxing, which means the goddess is rising, making her ascent, as Hecate, the one I mistakenly called upon before, plummets to the underworld where she'll mark her time until a month from now when it all comes full circle again.

I reach into the box, retrieving the candles, crystals, herbs, oils, and incense I'll need, taking a moment to organize them neatly and placing them in the order in which they'll be used. Then I shed my clothes and lower myself into the tub for my ritual bath, bringing along a sachet filled with angelica for protection and hex removal, juniper for the banishing of negative entities, and rue to aid in healing, mental powers, and the breaking of curses, along with a few drops of petitgrain oil that promises to banish evil and remove all negativity. Sinking all the way down 'til my feet hit the far edge and the water fills up around me, grabbing a few clear quartz crystals from the ledge and plopping them in too, as I chant:

> *I cleanse and reclaim this body of mine*
> *So that my magick may properly bind*
> *My spirit reborn, now ready for flight*
> *Allowing my magick to take hold tonight.*

But unlike the last time I indulged in a soak, I don't envision Roman before me. I don't want to see him until I'm ready, until it's absolutely necessary. Until it's truly time to undo what I've done.

Any earlier is a risk I can't take.

Ever since the dreams began, I can't trust myself.

The first night I woke in that cold, clammy sweat with images of Roman still dancing in my head, I was sure it was just a result of the horrible night that I'd had—learning the truth about Jude—turning Haven by giving her the juice. But the fact that they've returned every night since, the fact that he intrudes not just in my night dreams but in my daydreams as well, the fact that they're accompanied by this weird, foreign pulse that's constantly strumming inside me—well, it's pretty much convinced me that Romy and Rayne are right.

Despite my feeling perfectly fine just after the spell was complete, later, when everything began to unravel, it became pretty clear that the damage I'd done was nothing short of major.

Instead of binding Roman to me—I bound myself to him.

Instead of him seeking me out in order to do my bidding—I'm shamelessly, hopelessly, seeking him.

Which is something Damen can *never* know. No one can know. Not only does it prove his earlier warning about the downside of magick, insisting that it's nothing to be toyed with, and that amateurs who immerse themselves too quickly often wind up in way over their heads—it may be the end of his patience with me.

It may be that last and final straw.

I take a deep breath and sink even lower, enjoying the way the water laps at my chin, as I soak up all the healing energies that the stones and herbs are meant to provide, knowing it's just a matter of time before I rid myself of this unholy obsession and put everything right. And when the water begins to cool, I scrub every square inch of skin, hoping to wash away this new tainted version of me in order to recover the old, then I climb out of the bath and straight into my white silk hooded robe. Tying the sash snugly as I head back into my closet and reach for my athame. The same one Romy and Rayne criticized, claiming it was too sharp, that its intent should be to cut energy not matter, that I'd made it all wrong—urging me to burn it, melt it down to a stub of metal, and hand it over to them so they could complete the banishing ritual, not trusting such a complex task to a misguided novice like me.

And though I agreed to burn it before them, running the blade through the flame again and again in a sort of magical sanctification, I shrugged off the rest of their plan, convinced they were just seizing the chance to make an even bigger fool of me. I mean, if the real problem, as they claimed, was my weaving a spell on the night of the dark moon, then what difference could a simple knife make?

But this time around, just to make sure, I add a few additional stones to its handle, adorning it with Apache's tear for protection and luck (which the twins are convinced I'll need plenty of), bloodstone for courage, strength, and victory (always a good combination), and turquoise for healing and strengthening of the chakras (apparently my throat chakra, the center of discernment, has always been a problem for me). Then sprinkling the blade with a handful of salt before running it through the flame of three white tapers, I call upon the elements of fire, air, water, and earth, to cast away all dark and allow only light—to push out all evil and summon the good. Repeating the chant three times before calling on the highest of magical powers to see that it's done. This time sure that I'm calling on the *right* magical powers—summoning the goddess instead of Hecate, the three-headed, snake-haired, queen of the underworld.

Cleansing the space as I walk three times around it, incense held high in one hand, athame in the other, pulling up the magick circle by visualizing a white light flowing through me. Starting at the top of my head and working its way through my body, down my arm, out the athame, and into the floor. Weaving and curving and circling around and around, encouraging thin strands of the brightest white light to entwine and grow and reach ever higher until joining as one. Until I'm wrapped in a silvery cocoon, a complex web of the brightest, most shimmering light, that completely seals me in.

I kneel on the floor of my clean, sacred space, left hand held before me as I trace the blade down the length of my lifeline, sucking in a sharp intake of breath as I plunge the tip deep into my flesh and a great swell of blood rushes out. Closing my eyes and quickly manifesting Roman sitting cross-legged before me, tempting me with his irresistible, deep blue gaze and wide inviting smile. Struggling to get past his mesmerizing beauty, his undeniable allure, and straight to the blood-soaked cord tied snug at his neck.

A cord soaked with my blood.

The same cord I placed there last Thursday night when I created a similar ritual—one that seemed to work until everything went tragically wrong. But this time, everything is different. My intent is different. I want my blood back. I intend to *unbind* myself.

Hurrying through the chant before he can fade, singing:

> *With this knot that I untie*
> *Banish this magick before thine eye*
> *Where once this cord was bound and tight*
> *I now reverse it to set things right*
> *Your hold no longer potent, now loosed on me*
> *I unbind this cord and set myself free*
> *Let it harm none as I send it away*
> *This very change to take hold today*
> *This is my will, my word, my wish—so mote it be!*

Squinting against the gale force wind that whirls through my circle, pushing the walls of my web to their limits as a flash of lightning strikes and thunder cracks loud overhead. My right palm raised, open, ready—my gaze locked on *his* as I mentally loosen the knot at his neck and summon the blood back to me.

Back to where it originated.

Back to where it belongs.

Eyes widening in excitement as it arcs straight toward the center of my wounded hand, the cord around his neck lightening, whitening, until it's as clean and pure as the day it began.

But just as I'm ready to banish him for good, free myself of this unholy bind, that strange foreign pulse, that hideous intruder, snakes through my insides with such force, such determination, overtaking me so quickly, I can't stop it.

The monster inside me now fully awakened, rising, stretching, with its insistent, throbbing hunger demanding to be met. Causing my heart to crash violently, my body to shake— and no matter how hard I struggle against it—it's no use. I'm a hostage to its longing—captive to its desires—I'm of no consequence whatsoever. My only purpose is to meet all its needs—to see that it's done.

Watching helplessly as the cycle repeats once again. My blood surging forth, soaking the cord at Roman's neck 'til it sags, red and heavy, dripping a thick trail of me down his chest. And no matter what I do—no matter how hard I try—there's no stopping it.

No stopping the undeniable lure of his gaze.

No stopping my limbs from yielding toward his.

No stopping this spell that binds me to him.

His body like a magnet that seeks only me, closing the small space between us in less than a second. And now, with our knees pressed tightly together, our foreheads flush—I'm defenseless—powerless—unable to curb this unbearable yearning for *him*.

He's all I can see.

All that I need.

My entire world now whittled down to the space between his gaze and mine. His moist, inviting lips just a razor's width away, as this bold, insistent intruder, this strange, foreign pulse, urges me forward, willing us to mesh, unite, join as one.

My lips push toward his, moving closer, ever closer, when from somewhere down deep, somewhere I can't quite reach, the memory of Damen, his scent, his image, flickers inside. No more than a brief flash of light in the midst of all this dark—but still enough to remind me of *who* I am, *what* I am—my *real* reason for being here.

Just enough to allow me to break free of this horrible dreamscape and shout, *"No!"*

I leap back, removing myself from him—from *this*. Moving so quickly and violently the web collapses around me as the candles extinguish and Roman dissolves from my sight.

The only trace of what just occurred is my crashing heart, bloodstained robe, and the words still reverberating in my throat.

"No, no, no, no, no, oh, God, please, no!"

"Ever?"

I gaze around the closet, fingers frantically clutching at my white silk robe now stained beyond repair, hoping she'll just go away—give me some space—or at least enough time to figure this out—

"Ever—you okay in there? Dinner's just about ready, you might want to make your way down!"

"Okay—I'll . . ." I close my eyes, quickly banishing my robe and manifesting a simple blue dress in its place. Having no idea what to do now, where to go from here. Though one thing is clear—I can't tell Romy and Rayne—they already witnessed my last flubbed attempt, and I'll never live this one down. Besides, they're too close to Damen, and they'll never forgive me.

"I'll be there in a sec, really!" I say, sensing her energy from the other side of the door debating whether or not to bust in.

"Five minutes!" she warns, voice resigned. "Then I'm coming in to get you myself!"

I close my eyes and shake my head, shoving my feet into some flip-flops while combing my hands through my hair. Taking great care to ensure everything appears clean and pristine on the outside, because inside, there's no doubt that things just took a major turn for the worse.

FIVE

I slip out the side gate and onto the street, the soft lilting sounds of Sabine and Munoz laughing and enjoying the last of their wine by the pool drifting behind me as I break into a run. Careful to temper the pace, going neither too fast nor too slow, reluctant to attract any undue attention from anyone who might see.

It was bad enough having to explain it to Sabine. Especially after having just gulped down three-quarters of a barbecued chicken breast, a lump of potato salad, an entire corn on the cob, and a glass and a half of soda—none of which I was the slightest bit interested in, and which, in the end, only seemed to raise a whole new suspicion.

Her voice all raised and squeaky, gone completely high alert when she said, *"Now?* But it'll be *dark* soon—and you just *ate!"* Her ever-watchful gaze sweeping over me, as a new possibility formed in her brain—*exercise bulimia!*

Having ruled out anorexia and just plain old bulimia to explain my odd behavior and even odder eating habits—she's now onto something new, leaving no doubt that a trip to our local bookstore's self-help aisles will be squeezed into her weekend's agenda.

And I wish I could explain it to her, sit her right down and say, "Relax. It's not at all what you think. I'm immortal. The juice is all I need to get by. But right now, I've got a little spell-casting problem to fix so—*don't wait up!*"

But that's never gonna happen. It *can't* happen. Damen was clear about keeping our immortality a secret. And after seeing what's happened when it's gotten into the wrong hands, I have to say I agree with him one hundred percent.

But keeping it a secret has been one of my greatest challenges, and that's where the jogging comes in. I am now, officially (or at least where Sabine and Munoz are concerned), a person who slips into a T-shirt, sneakers, and shorts and goes for an evening run.

A nice healthy excuse for getting out of the house and away from Munoz, whom I can't help but like as a person, even though I never wanted to get to know him as a person.

A nice healthy excuse for getting away from an aunt who's so kind and considerate and helpful toward me that I can't help but feel like the world's worst niece for all of the trouble I've caused.

A nice healthy excuse to get away from two wonderful, kindhearted people so I can indulge in a much darker, not at all healthy, obsession.

One that's got a hold on me.

One I'm determined to beat.

I make a swift left onto the next street, noticing how the cars, the pavement, the sidewalks, the windows are all dappled with that burnished gold that the tail end of magic hour brings—the result of the first and last hour of sunlight when everything appears softer, warmer, bathed in the sun's reddish haze. My muscles pumping, feet moving faster, picking up speed, even though I know better, even though I try to slow down—it's too dangerous, too risky, someone might see—and yet I keep going. Unable to stop it. No longer the one who controls me.

Aiming for my destination like an arrow on a compass, my entire being is focused on one single point. Cars, houses, people—everything around me is reduced to a single, orangey blur as I close street after street. My heart crashing hard against my chest—but not from the run or the exertion, because the truth is, I've barely broken a sweat.

This live wire inside me is all about the proximity.

The simple fact that I'm near—

Getting closer—

Almost there.

Like a siren song propelling me toward uncertain ruin, and I can't seem to get there quickly enough.

The second I see it, I stop. My gaze narrows as everything around me ceases to exist. Staring at Roman's door as I will the beast to retreat. Renewing my resolve to overcome this strange, foreign pulse now beating in me, wanting only to slip inside, casually, easily, and confront him once and for all so we can put an end to all this.

Forcing myself to take long, deep breaths as I summon the strength that I'll need. Just about to take that very first step when I hear my name called from a voice I'd hoped never to hear again.

He saunters toward me, head cocked to the side, as cool and casual as a summer's breeze. His left arm heavily bandaged and wrapped in a navy blue sling, stopping just shy of me, purposely positioning himself out of my reach, when he says, "What are you doing?"

I swallow hard, relieved to feel the pulse lessening, receding, and yet startled to realize my first instinct isn't to run, isn't to finish the job and put the rest of him in a sling too—but to *lie*. To make any excuse that I can to explain my heated, gaping, practically salivating presence, right outside Roman's store.

"What're *you* doing?" I squint, lids narrowed to slits as I harshly take him in. Knowing it's hardly a coincidence to find him here too. After all, they're good friends, members of the same immortal rogue tribe. "Oh, and nice prop, by the way." I gesture toward his supposedly banged-up arm, which probably provides a pretty good cover for those who don't know any better. Too bad I do.

He looks at me, shaking his head and rubbing his chin, voice steady, calm, *almost* convincing, when he says, "Ever, are you okay? You're not looking so good—"

I shake my head and roll my eyes. "Nice try, Jude, I'll give you that." Fielding his *what the heck are you talking about* look with, "Seriously. Faking concern for me, faking an injury, you're prepared to go all the way with this, aren't you?"

He frowns, head tilted in a way that allows a few chunks of golden brown dreadlocks to fall over his shoulder and land just a few inches shy of his waist. His deceptively cute and friendly face all scrunched and serious when he says, "Trust me, I'm not faking. Wish I was. Remember when you picked me up like a Frisbee and tossed me across your yard?" He motions toward his arm. "*This* is the result. A crap load of contusions, a fractured radius, and some seriously messed-up phalanges—or at least that's what the doctor said."

I sigh and shake my head. I've no time for this charade. I need to get to Roman, show him that he can't control me—means *nothing* to me—show him who's boss around here. Sure that he's somehow partly responsible for what's happening to me, and needing to convince him to give me the antidote and put an end to this game.

"While I'm sure it all looks and sounds very believable to most people, unfortunately for you, I'm not most people. I know better. And the fact is, you *know* I know better. So let's just cut to the chase, okay? *Rogues don't get hurt.* Not for long anyway. They have instantaneous healing abilities, but then you already knew that, didn't you?"

He looks at me, brows merged in confusion, as he takes a step back. And the truth is, he really does look perplexed, I'll give him that.

"What're you talking about?" He gazes all around, before focusing back on me. "*Rogues?* Are you serious?"

I sigh, fingers drumming hard against my hip when I say, "Um, hel-*lo*? *Evil members of Roman's tribe?* Ring any bells?" I shake my head and roll my eyes. "Don't pretend you're not one of them—I saw your tattoo."

He continues to stare, that same confused, gaping expression still stamped on his face. And all I can think is: *Good thing he's not an actor, he's got really crummy range.*

"Um, hel-*lo*! The *Ouroboros? On your back?*" I roll my eyes. "I *saw* it. You *know* I saw it. You probably *wanted* me to see it—or why else would you convince me to get into the Jacuzzi with—" I shake my head. "Whatever, let's just say it pretty much told me everything I needed to know. Everything you apparently *wanted* me to know. So feel free to drop the game anytime now, I'm all clued in."

He stands before me, good hand rubbing his chin as his eyes search the area as though looking for backup. *Like that's gonna help him.* "Ever, I've had that tattoo for ages—in fact, I—"

"Oh, I'll bet." I nod, refusing to let him finish. "So tell me, how long ago did Roman turn you? Which century would it have been? Eighteenth, nineteenth? C'mon, you can tell me. Even though it was a long time ago, I'm sure you never forget a moment like that."

He rubs his lips together, encouraging those matching dimples to spring into view, but it doesn't distract me; that sort of thing no longer works. Not that it ever really did.

"Listen," he says, struggling to keep his voice low, steady, though his aura tells all, taking a sudden turn toward murky and fragmented, revealing the full extent of his nervousness. "*Honestly,* I have no idea what you're talking about. Seriously, Ever, in case you can't hear it, this is coming off as pretty insane. And the truth is, despite all of that, despite all of *this*"—he tugs on his sling—"I'd really like to help you—but—well—you seem pretty much beyond all of that with the *rogues* and the *turning* and"—he shakes his head—"but let me just ask you this—if this Roman dude's as bad as you say, then why are you lurking outside his store looking all charged and heated like a dog waiting for its owner?"

I glance between him and the door, cheeks flushing, pulse racing, well aware I've been caught in the act, but not about to admit it.

"I'm not *lurking*—I'm—" I press my lips together, wondering why on earth I'm defending myself when he's clearly the one who's up to no good. "Besides, it's not like I can't ask you the same question since, I hate to break it to ya, but you're standing here too." My eyes rake over him, taking in the bronzed skin, the slightly crooked front teeth—most likely kept that way on purpose, to throw people off—people like me. And those eyes—those amazing blue/green eyes—the same eyes I've gazed into for the last four hundred years. But no more. Not since I learned he's one of *them*. Now we're officially through.

He shrugs and rubs his sling protectively. "Nothing sinister, just headed home, that's all. If you'll remember, we close early on Saturdays."

I narrow my gaze, not fooled for a second. It's all very plausible. *Almost* believable. But not quite.

"I live up the street." He motions toward some unknown place in the distance, a place that probably doesn't even exist. But I don't follow his hand. My gaze stays on his. I can't afford to drop my guard. Not even for a second. He may have fooled me before, but now I know better. Now I know what he is.

He takes a step closer, slowly, cautiously, careful to maintain a safe distance still just outside of my reach. "Maybe we can go grab a coffee or something? Go someplace quiet, where we can sit down and talk? You look like you could use a break. What do you say?"

I continue to study him. He's persistent, I'll give him that. "Sure." I smile, nodding in assent. "I'd just *love* to go someplace quiet, grab a seat, drink some java, and enjoy a nice, long *chat*—but first, I need you to prove something."

His body goes tense and his aura—his *fake* aura—wavers, but I'm not buying it.

"I need you to prove you're not one of *them*."

He squints, face a cloud of concern. "Ever, I don't know what you're—"

His words cut short by the sight of the athame now clutched in my hand. Its jewel-encrusted handle an exact replica of the one I used just a few hours before, figuring I'll need all the luck and protection the stones can provide, especially if this goes the way that I think.

"There's only one way to prove it," I say, voice low, gaze locked on his, taking one small step forward that's soon followed by another. "And I'll know if you cheat—so don't even try. Oh, and I should probably warn ya—I can't be responsible for what happens once I prove that you're lying. But don't worry, as you well know, this'll only hurt for a second—"

He sees me moving, lunging straight for him, and even though he tries his best to dance out of my way, I'm too quick, and I'm on him before he even realizes it.

Seizing his good arm and slicing my athame right through his skin, knowing it's just a matter of seconds before the blood stops gushing and the wound fuses together again.

Just a matter of time until—

"Oh God!" I whisper, eyes wide, throat dry, watching as he falters, stumbles, and nearly loses his balance.

His eyes darting between me and the gash on his arm, both of us watching as the blood seeps through his clothes and pools onto the street in a growing puddle of red. "Are you *crazy?*" he shrieks. "What the *hell* have you done?"

"I—" My mouth hangs open in shock, unable to form any words, unable to tear my gaze away from the gaping gash that I made.

Why isn't it healing? Why's it still bleeding? Oh, crap!

"I'm—I'm so sorry—I can explain—I—" I reach toward him, but he moves away, clumsily, unsteadily, wanting nothing more to do with me.

"Listen," he says, sling pressed to the wound, trying to ebb the flow, but it only makes a much bigger mess. "I don't know what your deal is, or what's going on with you, Ever, but we're done here. You need to walk away—*now!*"

I shake my head. "Let me take you to the hospital. There's an emergency room just down the street—and I'll—"

I close my eyes, manifesting a plush towel to hold against the wound until we can get some professional help. Noticing how pale and unsteady he's gone, knowing we've no time to waste.

Ignoring his protests, I slide my arm around him and lead him toward the car I just manifested. That strange insistent pulse quieted for now, but still forcing me to glance over my shoulder just in time to see Roman watching from behind the window, his eyes shining, face creased with laughter, as he flips the sign over from OPEN to CLOSED.

SIX

"How is he?"

I toss my magazine on the small table beside me and stand. Careful to address the nurse instead of Jude, since one quick glance is all it takes to see that both of his arms are now heavily bandaged, his aura's turned red with rage, and if the angry, cruel look in his narrowed eyes is any indication, he clearly wants nothing more to do with me.

The nurse stops, her gaze traversing the sixty-eight inches between my head and my toes. Scrutinizing me so closely I can't help but cringe—can't help but wonder just what exactly Jude might've told her.

"He's going to make it," she says, voice sharp, businesslike, not the least bit friendly. "Cut went all the way to the bone, even made a groove in it, but it was clean. And if he takes his antibiotics, it'll stay that way. He'll be in a fair amount of pain, even with the meds I gave him, but if he takes it easy, gets plenty of rest, it should be healed in a matter of weeks."

Her gaze moves to the door and I follow it. Just in time to

see two uniformed members of Laguna Beach's finest heading right toward me, their eyes darting between Jude and me, and stopping when the nurse nods affirmatively.

I freeze, swallowing past the lump in my throat as I pull my shoulders in, shrinking under the glare of Jude's dark, hostile gaze. Knowing I deserve every last bit of his anger, deserve to be handcuffed and hauled away—*but still*—I didn't think he'd actually do it. I didn't think it would come to this.

"So, anything you want to tell us?" They stand before me, legs spread wide, hands on hips, eyes hidden between mirrored lenses, taking me in.

I glance between the nurse, Jude, and the cops, knowing this is it. This is what it's come to. And despite all the trouble I'm in, all I can think is: *Who will I pick for my one phone call?*

I mean, it's not like I can ask Sabine to wave her lawyer's wand and get me out of this one—I'll never live it down, and it's not like I can explain it to Damen either. Clearly this is one dilemma I have to deal with alone. . . .

And I'm just about to clear my throat, just about to say something, *anything*, when Jude jumps in and says, "I already told her"—he nods toward the nurse—"it was a home repair gone wrong. Didn't know my limits. Guess I'll definitely have to hire a handyman now." He forces a smile, forces his gaze to meet mine. And even though I want to smile right back, nod in agreement, and play along, I'm so shocked by his words, at his defending me, it's all I can do just to stand there and gape.

The cops sigh, obviously unhappy about being called out for nothing, but making one last attempt when they look at Jude and say, "You sure about that? You sure there isn't more to it? Kind of crazy to take on a home repair when you're down to one hand . . ." Their heads swivel between us, obviously suspicious but willing to let it go if he is.

"I don't know what to tell you." Jude shrugs. "It may be crazy, but it was purely self-inflicted."

They frown—at him, at me, at the nurse—and then they mumble something about if he decides to change his story and slip a card into his pocket. And the moment they're gone the nurse clutches her slim well-aerobicized hips, scowls at me, and says, "I gave him something for the pain." Her gaze busy on mine, clearly not buying a word of Jude's story, clearly pegging me as an insanely jealous, completely crazed, psycho girlfriend who nicked him in a fit of rage. "It should kick in soon, so I don't want him driving—not that he can in that condition—" She nods toward his arms. "And make sure he gets this prescription filled." She holds up a small slip of paper, about to hand it to me, before she thinks better and yanks it right back. "We want to ward off any chance of infection, but the best thing he can do now is to go home and rest. He'll probably fall right to sleep, so I expect you to leave him alone and let him do just that." She frowns, her gaze like a challenge.

"I will," I say, but I'm so freaked by her scrutiny, by the police, by Jude's defending me, the words come out like a squeak.

Her mouth quirks to the side, obviously reluctant to leave Jude in my care or to hand the prescription over, but she has little choice.

I follow Jude outside, over to my manifested Miata, an exact replica of the one I usually drive. Feeling awkward, nervous, barely able to look him in the eye.

"Just pull out here and make a right," he says, voice low, groggy, giving no indication of what he's truly thinking or just how he might feel about me. And though his aura appears to be softening, there's still a good bit of red clinging to its edges, a fact that pretty much speaks for itself. "You can drop me at Main Beach. I'll take it from there."

"I'm not dropping you at Main Beach," I say, taking the opportunity to study him as I brake at a light. And even though it's dark out, there's no missing the hollows under his eyes, the sheen of sweat on his brow, two unmistakable signs that he's suffering a great deal of pain—thanks to me. "Seriously, that's just—ridiculous." I shake my head. "Just tell me where you live and I promise to get you home safely."

"Safely?"

He laughs, a sort of ironic chuckle that comes from somewhere down deep, his two messed-up arms resting on his lap as he says, "Funny, you've used that word twice in the last five minutes, and to be honest, I'm feeling pretty much anything *but* safe around you."

I sigh, gazing into a starless night sky, pressing lightly on the gas and foregoing my usual lead foot since I don't want to alarm him any more than I already have. "Listen," I say. "I—I'm sorry. *Really and truly—sorry.*" Gazing at him for so long, he nods nervously toward the street.

"Uh, *traffic?*" He shakes his head. "Or do you control that too?"

I avert my gaze and try to think of what to say.

"It's up here, on the left. The one with the green gate. Just pull into the drive and I'm good to go."

I do as he says, braking just shy of a garage door that's the exact shade of green as the gate, immediately killing the engine, which prompts him to say, "Oh no." He looks at me. "No need for that. Trust me, you are *not* coming in."

I shrug, reaching across him, wanting to unlock his door the old-fashioned way instead of the telekinetic way, noticing how he winces when my arm veers too close to his.

"Listen," I say, back in my seat. "I know you're tired, and I know you probably want to get as far from me as you possibly can, as quickly as you can, and I can't say I blame you. I mean, if I were you, I'd feel the same way. But still, if you could just spare me a few more seconds of your time, I'd really like a chance to explain."

He mumbles under his breath, gazing out the window for a moment before shifting toward me in a way that allows for his full, undivided attention.

And knowing I have to move fast, that he's prepared to allow me a few seconds and no more, I say, "Listen, it's like this—I mean, I know it sounds crazy, and I really can't go into all the details, but you have to trust me when I say I had really good reason to think you were one of *them*."

He closes his eyes for a moment, brows squinched with pain, looking at me when he says, "A rogue. Yeah. You've made your point, Ever. Made it *abundantly* clear, remember?" He glances between his injured arms and me.

I scrunch my nose and rub my lips together, knowing this next part probably won't go over any better, but still forging ahead when I say, "Yeah, well, you see, the thing is—I thought you were *evil*. Seriously. It's the only reason I did what I did. I mean, I saw your tattoo—and—I have to say it was pretty convincing—well, except for the fact that it didn't flash or blink or anything like that—but *still*, that, coupled with the fact that Ava called, and, well, some other stuff I can't exactly get into, but anyway, all of that made me think that you—" I shake my head, knowing I'm not getting anywhere with this and choosing to just drop it, abandon it for something that's been niggling at me ever since we left the hospital. "You know, if you're so mad at me, if you hate me *so* much, then why'd you help me back there? Why'd you lie to those cops and take all the blame? I mean, I'm the one who hurt you, we both know I did it, heck, even *they* knew I did it. But still, you totally blew your big chance to get me cuffed and hauled away and thrown into the slammer when you lied on my behalf. And to be honest, I just don't get it."

He shuts his eyes again and tilts his head back, his pain and fatigue so palpable I'm about to call it off, about to tell him never mind, just go inside and get some rest, when he levels those amazing green eyes right on mine and says, "Listen, Ever, here's the thing—as crazy as it sounds, I'm a lot less interested in *why* you did it, than *how* you did it."

I look at him, fingers gripping the steering wheel, unable to speak.

"How you tossed me like a Frisbee across your backyard—"

I swallow hard, eyes fixed straight ahead, not saying a word.

"And how one moment you were standing before me, hands empty, no pockets in sight—and the next thing I know you're wielding a double-edged, jewel-handled knife—that—by the way—seemed to disappear just after you attacked me—am I right?"

I take a deep breath and nod. There's no use lying now.

"And then there's the small fact that you started this car without a key—and I think we both know it's not that kind of car—that this particular model definitely requires one. And let's not forget about the first day when I found you in the store, despite the fact that the door was locked, not to mention how quickly you found *The Book of Shadows,* which was also protected by a lock. So, forget all the rest, forget the apologies and explanations and all of that nonsense, what's done is done, there's no going back. All I want now is for you to explain the *how*. That's all I'm really interested in."

I glance at him, swallowing hard, unsure how to proceed. Attempting a feeble joke when I say, "Okay, but first, tell me, have those pain meds kicked in yet?" Chasing it with this horrible laugh that only succeeds in making him mad.

"Listen, Ever, if you ever decide to get honest, you know where I live. Otherwise—" He tries to open the door, tries for the big, bold, dramatic exit, but with both arms bandaged, it's not as easy as it seems.

So I jump from my side to his, appearing beside him well before he can blink and hoping he doesn't view it as a threat to his masculinity when I say, "Here—allow me."

But he just stays seated, sighing and shaking his head as he says, "And then of course, there's *that*—"

Our eyes meet and I suck in my breath.

"The way you move as quickly and gracefully as a jungle cat."

I stand there, silent and still, unsure what comes next.

"So, you gonna help me or not?" he asks, raising a single spliced brow.

I nod, going through the motions of opening his door and offering my arm for support, sensing how weakened he is the moment he leans his weight onto me.

"Can you get the front door too?"

"Of course." I nod, looking at him. "Just hand over the keys."

His eyes graze over me. "Since when do you need a key?"

I shrug, heading down the narrow, softly lighted path that

leads to his door, taking in an amazing array of vibrant pink and purple peonies when I say, "I had no idea you had such a green thumb."

"I don't. Well, not really. Lina planted everything. I just maintain it. We grow most of the herbs for the store right here." He motions toward the door, obviously tired of this, tired of me, eager to just get inside and be done with all this.

So I close my eyes, *seeing* the door open before me until I hear that unmistakable *click* and wave him right in. Then I stand there like an idiot, performing this ridiculous little half wave, like I just dropped him off after a really nice picnic. Reluctant to move even after he shakes his head and motions me in, requiring a firm, verbal invite before I venture any farther.

"You gonna attack me again?" His gaze sails over me, filling me with a wave of nice, languid calm.

"Only if you get out of hand." I shrug.

"Was that a pun?" He squints, his lips curving ever so slightly.

I laugh. "Yes, and a really bad one at that."

He leans against the doorjamb, looking me over slowly, leisurely, taking a long deep breath before he says, "Listen, I hate to admit this, especially to you of all people, since you've pretty much emasculated me enough for one lifetime, but I might need a little help getting set up. The meds are kicking in and I wasn't much good when I was sober and one-handed, so I can't imagine how I'll fare now. It'll only take a minute, two at the most, and then you can get back to Damen and on with your night."

I frown, wondering why he just said that. Switching on the lights and closing the door behind me as I follow him inside, gazing around the small cozy space, amazed to find myself inside a real, authentic Laguna Beach cottage. The kind with old brick fireplaces and large picture windows. The kind you don't see in these parts anymore.

"Cool, isn't it?" He nods, reading my face. "It was built in 1958. Lina picked it up cheap, a long time ago, before all the money and reality shows rolled in."

I head for the sliding glass door that leads to a nice brick patio that leads to a steep grassy slope, a set of stairs, and a slightly moonlit ocean beyond.

"She rents it to me cheap, but my dream is to buy it someday. She says she'll only sell if I promise not to turn it into yet another Tuscan-style duplex. As if." He laughs.

I turn away from the window and wander into his kitchen, flicking on a light and opening a few cupboards until I find the one containing a set of drinking glasses. Looking around, searching for a bottle of water, only to find him standing so close I can make out each individual fleck in his eyes.

"Isn't it easier to just *manifest it*?" he says, voice thick, low, deep.

I gaze at him, not sure what I'm bothered by more, his intimate proximity, the longing in his tone, or the way he was able to sneak up on me.

"I—I thought I'd just get it the old-fashioned way—if that's okay? Guaranteed to taste the same," I mumble, the words clumsy on my lips, hoping he's too hopped up on pain medication to see just how much his nearness is affecting me.

He continues to stand there, gaze steady, giving nothing away. Voice groggy and deep when he says, "Ever—what *are* you?"

I freeze, fingers gripping the glass so hard I'm afraid it

might break in my hand. Focusing on the tiled floor, the small table to the right, the den just beyond, anywhere but at him. The silence hanging so thick between us, I only want to break it when I say, "I—I can't tell you."

"So, it's not just the book then, it's—*something else.*"

My eyes meet his, immediately recognizing my blunder, how I basically just admitted I'm not at all normal when I could've just blamed it on magick instead. But the truth is, he wouldn't have bought it. He knew something was up from the first day we met, long before he ever lent me that book.

"Why didn't you tell me *The Book of Shadows* was written in code?" I say, eyes narrowed, putting him back on the defensive again.

"I did." He breaks the gaze and moves away, annoyance stamped on his face.

"No, you told me it was written in the Theban code and that it had to be intuited to be understood. But what you failed to mention is that it's actually protected by a code—a code that has to be cracked in order to see what's *truly* inside. So what gives? Why didn't you tell me about that? It's a pretty major detail to leave out, don't you think?"

He leans against the tiled counter, shaking his head when he says, "Excuse me, but am I under suspicion again? Because, correct me if I'm wrong, but I was under the impression that when you sliced me open, you pretty much determined I was one of the good guys."

I fold my arms and squint. "*No,* I determined you're not *a rogue.* I never said you were *good.*" He looks at me, striving for patience, but I'm far from done yet. "You also failed to mention how you got the book—how it ended up in your hands."

He shrugs, gaze fixed, voice steady, measured, when he says, "I told you—I got it from a friend, a few years back."

"And does this friend have a name—like maybe *Roman*, perhaps?"

He laughs, though it comes out more like a grunt. His annoyance ringing loud and clear when he says, "Oh, I see, you're still convinced I'm part of his *tribe*. Well, excuse me for saying so, Ever, but I thought we were through with all that?"

I fold my arms across my chest, allowing the glass to dangle from my fingers. "Listen, Jude, I'd like to trust you, really I would. But the other night when—" I pause, realizing I can't really continue that thread. "Well, anyway, Roman said something about the book once belonging to him, and I really need to know if that's where you got it—if he somehow sold it to you?"

He reaches toward me, the few fingers that still actually work snatching the glass right out of my grasp. "My only connection to Roman is through you. I don't know what else to tell you, Ever."

I squint, scrutinizing his aura, his energy, his body language, adding it all up as he heads for the sink, and coming to the conclusion that he really is telling the truth, not hiding a thing.

"Tap?" I ask, seeing him glance over his shoulder at me. "It's been a while since I saw someone do that. Not since I left Oregon."

"I'm a simple guy, what can I say?" He takes a hearty swig, draining it completely before turning to fill it again.

"So seriously, you didn't know about the book?" I follow

behind, watching as he heads for an old brown couch where he promptly plops himself down.

"To be honest, pretty much everything you've said since I ran into you has been a mystery. None of it makes any sense. Normally, I'd just give you the benefit of the doubt and blame the meds, but I seem to remember you talking crazy long before it resulted in that."

I frown, dropping onto the chair just opposite him and propping my feet up on an elaborately carved antique door he uses as a coffee table. "I'm—I wish I could explain it—I feel like I owe you that much. But I can't. It's—it's too complicated. Stuff that involves—"

"Roman and Damen?"

I squint, wondering why he just said that.

"Just a guess." He shrugs. "But from the look on your face, a successful one."

I press my lips together and gaze around the room, taking in tall stacks of books, an old stereo, some interesting art, but no TV. Neither confirming nor denying his statement when I say, "I have these powers. Stuff that goes way beyond the psychic stuff you already know about. I can make things move—"

"Telekinesis." He nods, eyes closed now.

"I can make things appear."

"Manifestation—but in your case—*instant*." He opens one eye to peer at me. "Which makes me wonder—why the book? You've got the world at your feet. You're beautiful, smart, blessed with all kinds of powers at your disposal, and I'm betting your boyfriend's hiding some gifts of his own . . ."

I look at him. That's the third time he's mentioned him, and it bugs me just as much as it did the first time around. "What's your deal with Damen?" I ask, wondering if he's on to us, if he somehow senses something about the long and convoluted past the three of us share.

He shifts, swinging his legs up onto the cushions and propping his head against a pillow. "What can I say? I don't like him. There's just—something about him. Can't really put my finger on it." Turning his head to look at me when he adds, "That *wasn't* a pun, and you *did* ask. And if there's anything else you wanna know, now's your chance. These meds are kicking in big time, starting an *unbelievable* buzz, so you might want to catch me before I fade out, while I'm still able and willing to talk fast and loose."

I shake my head, having already gotten all the answers I needed when I nicked him on the sidewalk a few hours before. But now, maybe it's time I share a few truths of my own—or at least lead him toward the truth and see if he drinks.

"You know, there's a reason why you and Damen don't care for each other—" I venture, biting down on my lip, not yet decided just how far I'll take it.

"Ah—so it's mutual." His gaze meets mine, holding it for so long, I'm the first to break away. Studying the threadworn rug at my feet, the scarred wood table before me, the large citrine geode propped up in the corner, wondering why on earth I started this, and just about to speak when he says, "No worries." He struggles to kick the blanket over his feet but doesn't quite make it. "No need to explain, no need to—worry. It's just your everyday, garden-variety guy thing. You know, the kind of primal competition that takes place whenever there's one absolutely amazing girl and two guys who desperately want her. And since only one of us can win—excuse me—since only one of us *has* won—I'll just wander back to my cave, bang my club against the wall a few times, and lick my wounds where no one can see." He closes his eyes, voice lowered when he adds, "Trust me, Ever, I know when to cry uncle. I know when to bow out, so don't you worry. There's a reason I'm named after the patron saint of lost causes—I've done it many times before, and . . . I . . . "

His words fade as his chin sinks to his chest, so I get up from my chair and move toward him, grabbing the plush, tangled throw at his feet and carefully arranging it so it covers him completely. "Get some sleep," I whisper. "I'll fill your prescription tomorrow, so no worries there. You just stay here and rest." Knowing he's drifting off, moving on to some other place, but wanting to assure him nonetheless.

Tucking the blanket under his feet when he says, "Hey, Ever—you never answered—about the book. Why'd you want that book when you already have everything you could ever possibly want?"

I freeze, gazing upon the guy I've known for so many centuries, so many lives, who's managed to show up yet again. Knowing there must be a reason, that from everything I've seen and experienced so far, the universe isn't nearly as random as it seems. But the thing is, I don't know the reason. In fact, I don't know much of anything anymore. All I know is they couldn't be more different. Jude's calming presence is the exact opposite of Damen's sultry mix of tingle and heat. Like the yang to his yin. Opposites to the purest degree.

I finish tucking him in, waiting until he's drifted off again before I head for the door, saying, "Because I don't have everything I want. Not even close."

SEVEN

"I *knew* there was something up** with you guys all along. Especially *you*." She points at Damen. "Sorry, but no one's *that* perfect."

Damen smiles, opening the door wide and motioning us inside, his deep dark gaze holding mine like a lover's embrace, showering me with a deluge of telepathic red tulips meant to provide the courage and strength I'm obviously gonna need.

"And just so you know, I saw that," Haven says, heavily ringed fingers clutching her leather-clad hips, eyes darting between us, before shaking her head and charging into the foyer.

Damen looks at me, brows raised, but I just shrug. Haven's gifts are only just starting to surface. Mind reading is just the beginning.

"Wow, I can't believe you live like this!" She twirls around and around as she takes it all in—the elaborate chandelier hanging from the tall, domed ceiling, the plush Persian rug at her feet—two priceless antiques dating back several centuries that were almost lost for good when Damen went through what I now refer to as his "monk phase"—back when he was sure his extravagant, vain, narcissistic past was directly to blame for all the troubles we face. Determined to rid himself of all worldly goods, until the twins came to stay and the FOR SALE sign came down, wanting to provide them with all the extra comforts and space that he could. "You could throw the most *awesome* parties just right here in the entry!" She laughs. "Is this part of being immortal? Living in fancy digs like this? Because if so, sign me up!"

"Damen's been at it awhile—" I say, unsure how to explain his multimillion-dollar manse, since I've yet to get to the part about the ancient art of instant manifestation, along with picking all the right ponies at the track—and not sure that I will.

"Well, how long has Roman been at it, cuz his place is nice and all, but it's nothing like this."

Damen and I look at each other, unable to communicate with our usual telepathy now that we know she can hear, but still mutually deciding to ignore the question. Determined to keep the details as vague as we can, for as long as we can. Delaying the inevitable day when she discovers the real truth behind all of this, not to mention what really happened to her good friend Drina.

We follow her through the kitchen and into the den, only to find the twins plopped on either end of the couch. Each of them reading their very own copy of the same book, with Rayne munching on a bar of chocolate, while Romy dips into a big, buttery bowl of popcorn.

"So, are you guys immortal too?" she asks, causing

Romy and Rayne to look up, Rayne with her usual scowl, while Romy just shakes her head and returns to where she left off.

"No, they're—um—" I glance at Damen, eyes pleading for help. Having no idea how to explain the fact that while they're not technically immortal, they have been hanging out in an alternate dimension for the last three hundred years, and now, thanks to me, can't seem to return.

"They're family." Damen nods, shooting me a look that tells me to just play along and follow his lead.

Haven stands in the middle of the room, brow raised, face squinched, obviously not buying a word of it. "So, you're trying to tell me you've kept in touch with your family for—" She narrows her gaze, looking him over, trying to determine just how old he is, then shrugging in defeat when she says, "Anyway, that must make for some *very interesting* reunions, to say the least."

I glance at Damen, seeing he's fully prepared to let that one go, but still hoping to save it, I jump in and say, "What he means is, they're *like* family. They're—"

"Oh, please!" Rayne tosses her book onto the table and glares, at me, at Haven, but not Damen, of course. "We're not family, and we're not immortal, okay? We're witches. Refugees from the Salem Witch Trials. And don't ask any more questions because we won't answer them. That's more than you need to know anyway."

Haven looks at us, eyes wider than I ever would've thought possible, gawping at all four of us freaks as she says, "Jeez. I mean, can this get any weirder?"

I shrug, exchanging a look with Rayne, making it clear she should've kept that one under wraps, and watching as

Haven settles onto an overstuffed chair, eagerly glancing between us as though anticipating some kind of confidential password reveal, a grand indoctrination, a secret initiation of some sort, and not even trying to hide her disappointment when Damen heads into the kitchen, only to emerge a moment later with a small box full of elixir he promptly hands to her.

She peers into the box, tapping the lid of each bottle with the tip of her black-painted nail, gazing at us in confusion when she says, "That's it? *Seven?* Only a one-week supply? I mean, you're not serious, are you? How am I supposed to survive on just this? You trying to kill me before I even have a chance to get started?"

"Duh, you're immortal—they *can't* kill you." Rayne shakes her head and rolls her eyes.

"*Duh*, yes they can. That's why Ever makes me wear *this*." Haven snakes her amulet out from under her black lace top and waves it in front of Rayne's face.

But Rayne just groans, crossing her skinny, pale arms across her sunken chest when she says, "Please, I know all about that. Take it off, get a punch to the wrong chakra and you're toast. Leave it on and you live happily ever after and after and after. It's not rocket science, you know."

"Jeez, is she always this grouchy?" Haven asks, laughing and shaking her head.

And just as I start to say *yes,* glad to have an ally for a change if nothing else, I watch as she gets up from her chair and plops down beside Rayne, mussing her hair and tickling her feet in a way that makes them instant best friends. And just like *that,* I'm back to being the outcast again.

"You don't need to drink it every day," Damen says, determined to get this back on track. "In fact, you could last the next hundred and fifty years without so much as a single sip, perhaps even longer, who knows?"

"Well, if that's the case, then why do you sip it like your life depends on it?" Haven asks, removing Rayne's feet from her lap as she takes us both in.

Damen shrugs. "I guess because it kind of does at this point. I've been around awhile, you know. A long while."

"How long?" Haven leans forward, pushing her platinum-streaked bangs off her face and gazing at him with two heavily made-up eyes.

"*Long*. Anyway—the point is—"

"Wait—you're joking, right? I mean, you're seriously not gonna tell me your real age? What are you—like one of those thirty-somethings who pile up the twenty-ninth birthdays well into their eighties? I mean, sorry, Damen, but how vain are you?" She laughs and shakes her head. "Trust me, when I'm old, I plan to shout it from the rooftops. I can't wait 'til I'm a porcelain-skinned one hundred and eighty-two."

"It's not vanity, it's—*practicality*," Damen snaps, and when I look at him, I realize he's flustered, but probably only because it *is* a little bit vanity, he just doesn't want to admit it. As much as he's tried to rid himself of all the fancy clothes, hair-grooming products, and handmade Italian leather boots, a hint of vanity remains. "Besides, you *can't* flaunt it, you *can't* tell anyone. I thought you and Ever talked about that?"

"We did," Haven and I both say, our voices blending as one.

"So, there should be no question. You just stick to your normal cupcake-eating routine, keeping your behavior as normal as possible, careful not to draw any—"

"Unnecessary attention to myself." Haven shakes her head

and rolls her eyes in the most exaggerated way. "Trust me, Ever gave me the whole lowdown, warned me of the dark side, the monster under the bed, the one in the closet, not to mention the boogeyman who lives under the stairs, and I hate to break it to you, but I'm not really interested in any of that. I've been ordinary my whole entire life. Ignored, over-looked, practically blending into the walls and treated like I was invisible no matter how crazy I tried to act and dress, and I'm telling you, that kind of anonymity is overrated. I'm totally and completely over it. So if now's my chance to really kick it—to really stand out and be *seen* for a change—well, I'm not about to hold back. I plan to embrace it with all that I've got! So, with that in mind, I'm thinking you can do a lit-tle better than this." She taps the side of the box. "Come on, humor me, hand over the juice so I can give everyone the shock of a lifetime when we start senior year."

Damen looks at me, alarmed, speechless—shooting me a look that says: *She's your creation—your Frankenstein—do something!*

So I clear my throat and turn to her, legs crossed, hands clasped, rearranging my face into a pleasant expression de-spite the fact that I'm every bit as freaked as he is. "Haven—*please*," I say, careful to keep my voice steady and low. "We talked about this—we—"

But not getting very far before she cuts in. "*You* drink it all the time—so why can't I?" She drums her fingers against the box and narrows her gaze.

I pause, unsure how to explain that the juice enhances my powers, powers I prefer she not have, fumbling around for just the right words when I say, "While it may appear that way, the thing is—I don't really need it—not like Damen does anyway.

I just sort of drink it because—well—because I'm used to it. And even though it doesn't taste all that great—I kind of like it. But trust me, it's really not necessary to drink it every day— not even every week—or every year, for that matter. Like Damen said, you can go a hundred years, maybe two hundred, without a single sip." I nod, hoping she'll buy it, not wanting her to know about the surge in power and speed and magical abilities that regular consumption can bring. That would only make her want it more.

"Fine." She nods. "Guess I'll just have to get it from Roman, then. I'm sure he'd be happy to give it to me."

I swallow hard, not saying a word, well aware that she's challenging me. Watching as Luna jumps onto her lap and Haven starts to pet her.

"Hey there, kitty—weren't you supposed to be mine? Is that why you're here now? Because you sense your true owner?" She lifts her up high and nuzzles her chin, laughing when Romy jumps up from her end of the couch and snatches her away. "Relax." Haven laughs. "It's not like I'm gonna steal her or anything."

"You can't *steal* her." Romy glares, lifting Luna onto her shoulder, her favorite place to perch. "You can't *own* her either. Pets aren't possessions, they're not accessories you discard when you decide you no longer want them. They're living creatures that *share* our lives." She looks at her sister, signaling for her to follow as she storms out of the room.

"Jeez—testy!" Haven glances over her shoulder, watching them leave.

But I'm not about to let her brush that off, she's the one who put it out there, now I'm just following up. "Speaking of—how *is* Roman?" I ask, trying to come off as conversational, only vaguely interested, hoping no one else noticed the way my voice just trembled when his name left my lips.

She shrugs, sensing exactly where I'm going with this when she says, "Fine. He's just fine, thanks for asking. But I've got nothing to report. Or at least nothing that would interest *you*." She glances between Damen and me, her lips curling up at the corners as though it's all a big joke, a game she hasn't fully committed to playing, despite the assurance she gave. Switching her focus to her nails when she says, "Jeez, do your nails grow this fast too? I mean, I just cut them this morning and check it out, they're already long again!" She holds her hands up so we can see. "And my hair—I swear my bangs have grown a full half inch in just a few days!"

Damen and I exchange a quick glance, both of us thinking the same thing: *All of this on just one bottle of elixir?* And knowing I've no choice but to tell her, and hoping I can pull it off convincingly, I say, "Listen—about Roman—"

She drops her hands in her lap, cradling the box as she looks at me.

"I've been thinking—" I pause, aware of Damen's gaze, deep, intense, boring right into mine, wondering where I'm headed with this, since I certainly haven't discussed it with him. But the truth is, it's a conclusion I've only just come to myself—a result of all the creepy things that have happened in the past twenty-four hours. "I think you need to avoid him at all costs," I say, eyeing her carefully. "Seriously. If it's money you need, I can totally float you until you find another job, but I don't think you should be working there. It's not—*safe*. And even though I know you don't believe me, even though you think I've got it all wrong, the thing is, I don't. Damen was there too, he can tell you." I glance at Damen, seeing him nod in agreement, but Haven remains unaffected, her face so placid it's like she hasn't even heard. "I can't express it enough," I urge. "Seriously. He's dangerous. A complete and total menace. Not to mention he's—" *Evil and awful, and devastatingly, alluringly irresistible—his voice in my head, his face in my dreams—always there, ever-present—and no matter how hard I try, I can't seem to shake him—can't stop thinking about him—can't stop wanting him—can't stop dreaming about him—*"And—um—anyway, I'd hate to see you get hurt." I swallow hard, my body so ramped up with just the thought of him, with that strange, foreign pulse stirring inside me, I come *this* close to blowing my cover.

But when she looks at me, her brow lifted as though she heard the words in my head, sees what I really am up to, I panic. Privately and quietly panic. Until I remember that my shield is in place. And no matter how powerful she may be, if Damen couldn't hear me, then neither could she.

"Listen, Ever, it's been covered, and now you're just being redundant. I heard you the first time, just like I heard you this time. And if you'll remember, we agreed to disagree. Besides, how you gonna get what you want if I don't cozy up to him?" She glances between us, eyes narrowed, catlike. "Trust me, Roman's hardly a threat, at least not to me. He's so incredibly sweet, and kind, and loving—he's nothing at all like you think. So if you two want to be together"—she wags her finger between Damen and me—"then you'll probably want to stay on my good side. As far as I can tell, I'm pretty much your only shot at this point—*no?*"

Damen steps forward, his eyes sparking, angry, voice low and menacing when he says, "It's a dangerous game that you're playing. And while I realize you're excited about your prospects, thrilled with this new power that's raging inside you, it's all too easy to get in over your head. I know, because I was once like you. In fact, I was the first. And even though it was a very long time ago, I remember it like yesterday. I also remember the long list of mistakes I made, the regrets I accumulated when I let my hunger for power override my common sense and human decency. Don't be like me, Haven. Don't make that mistake. And don't you even consider threatening either Ever or me in any way. We have plenty of options, plenty of means, and we don't need you to—"

"Enough already!" Haven shakes her head as her eyes dart between us. "I'm sick of you both talking down to me all the time. Did you ever stop to think that maybe I can teach you guys a thing or two about how to use all this power?" She rolls her eyes and scowls, answering her own question when she says, "Of course not! It's just, *'Do this, Haven, do that, Haven, we're rationing your elixir because we don't trust you, Haven.'* I mean, come *on*. If you refuse to trust me, then why am I supposed to trust you?"

"It's not you we don't trust," I say, eager to defuse this, calm things down before it gets any more heated. "It's *Roman*. I know you don't want to see it, but he's *using* you. You're just a pawn in this twisted little game that he plays. He sees all your weaknesses and he's using them to pull your strings like a puppet."

"And what weaknesses are those?" She drums her fingers against the box and presses her lips into a thin, grim line.

But before this can go any further, escalate into something we'll all surely regret, Damen holds up a hand and jumps in. "We're not trying to pick a fight with you, Haven. We're trying to protect you. It's for your own good."

"Because I need protecting? Because I'm too dumb to figure stuff out for myself?" Her gaze darts between us, and when Damen sighs in frustration, her eyes grow cold. Then she nods, grips the box tighter, and stands. "I wish I could believe you, but the thing is, I just can't. Because you're the one holding something back, Ever—I can *feel* it. And even though I have no idea what it is, one thing's pathetically clear—you're jealous." Her lip curls when she adds, "Yep, believe it or not, perfect Ever Bloom is jealous of *me*—little Haven Turner." She shakes her head. "How's *that* for a change of events?"

I stiffen but continue to stand there, not saying a word.

"You're used to being top dog around here. The smartest, the prettiest, the most perfect at everything, with the most perfect, smartest, sexiest boyfriend." She smiles at Damen, then shrugs and laughs when he fails to return her smile. "And now that I'm immortal like you, it's just a matter of time until I catch up—until I'm perfect too. And the fact is, you can't stand it. Can't stand the thought of it. But the funny part, the *ironic* part is, in the end, you have only yourself to blame, since you're the one who made me this way. And even though you claim you'd make the same decision all over again, I can't help but think you liked me better before. Back when I was a pathetic, little, attention-starved wannabe—the loser who ate too many cupcakes and made up stuff at anonymous meetings." She shrugs, shoulders rising and falling with such confidence, such arrogance, it's clear she's no longer that girl. "Don't bother denying it, I know those are the *weaknesses* you were referring to. It's pretty obvious how superior you've always felt to Miles and me. Like you were deigning to hang with us until something better came your way—"

"That's not true—you're my best friends—my—"

"Please." She rolls her eyes, clucking her tongue against her cheek in the same way Roman does. "Spare me your heartfelt declarations. The moment the Italian stallion came along"—she nods at Damen—"we pretty much only saw you at lunch, and sometimes not even then, since the perfect little couple was too busy with their perfect little lives, and their perfect little love, to hang with such unperfect dorks like us. We were just the losers you kept on standby—just in case you might need us someday. But now it looks like you're in for a long and lonely summer cuz Miles is headed for Florence, and I made some new friends who aren't the slightest bit intimidated by the new me."

"Haven—this is *crazy*! How can you even say these things?" I ask, as my eyes rake over her, taking her in. Even though she's just as teeny as ever, even though she hasn't grown even the slightest bit, it's like her diminutive stature is somehow more pronounced—more toned, more sinewy, like she's a tiny black panther in black leather leggings, lacy black shirt, and tall spiky black boots. And though she's gotten mad at me before, this time is different—*she's* different. Now she's dangerous, and knows it, and likes it that way.

"*How* can I say it?" she mocks, eyes narrowed into slits. "Because it's *true*, that's how." She dumps the box into Damen's arms, assuming he'll catch it as she heads for the door, glancing over her shoulder to say, "You can keep your elixir. I've got my own source. And trust me, he'll be more than happy to teach me all the things that you won't."

EIGHT

Damen turns toward me, the word *trouble* coursing from his mind to mine.

But I just stand there, so stunned I have no idea where to take it from here.

"I knew she'd be a problem." He shakes his head and drops onto the couch. "She's too fragile, too volatile, she won't be able to handle any of this. She'll be consumed with power before long, just wait."

"*Wait?*" I perch on the armrest beside him. "Are you serious? Wait for *what*? You think it's actually gonna get worse than what we just saw?"

He nods, making a great effort to withhold the *I told you so* gaze. But it's not like it matters. We both know I'm the one responsible for this mess.

I sigh, sliding off the armrest and toppling onto him. Knowing I have to do something—take control of this situation before it gets any worse—but having no idea what that *something* is. Every decision I've made up to this point has only made everything worse. And I'm just so tired—so *drained*—all I want to do is take a nice long peaceful nap where Roman can't enter my dreams.

Roman.

The name reverberating from my mind to his, and when he looks at me, I know it's too late—I know that he sensed it.

"Why'd you change your mind?" He studies me closely, seeking the truth behind the look in my eyes, the words on my tongue. "Why'd you tell her to avoid him?"

"Because you were right," I mumble, hating the lie I'm about to tell. "It was a selfish thing to do—to put her in that kind of danger just so we could benefit—" I shake my head, allowing my hair to fall onto my face in a way that obscures it.

Because the truth is, I'm worried I didn't do it for her.

I'm worried I tried to keep her from Roman, so there'd be more room for me.

I remain like that, face hidden as I struggle to pull myself together, summon up some small glimmer of the old me. Finally lifting my head only to find his brow creased with worry, as his hand squeezes my knee.

"Hey, take it easy," he says, voice soft and low. "Don't be so hard on yourself. So, we've entered a bit of a glitch, we'll get through it. We still have each other, right? That's all that matters in the big scheme of things. As for everything else—we'll find a way—I promise we will."

"Do we?" I look at him, my eyes going wide when I realize what I just said, having meant to say *will we*—meant to question the part about *finding a way* and *not* the part about us having each other.

He looks at me, clearly disturbed by my words. "I thought that was a given. Am I wrong?"

I swallow hard and reach for his hand, watching as the slim veil of energy dances between his palm and mine, holding back the words until I can trust my voice again. "You're not wrong," I whisper. "You're the best thing in my life—the only thing that truly matters." Repeating the words that I know for sure to be true, just wishing I could *feel* them in the same way that I used to.

But Damen's not buying it, he knows me too well—having witnessed a million different mood swings, a gazillion different voice inflections and avoidance techniques over the last four hundred years—and that's just counting mine.

"Ever, is something wrong? You've been acting strange ever since—"

I look at him, my voice sharp, edgy, cutting in when I say, "Ever since I made you drink the elixir that turned our touch lethal?"

He shakes his head.

"Ever since I turned Haven into an immortal?"

He shakes his head again, this time pressing his finger to my lips, quieting me when he says, "I wasn't referring to any of those things. You made the best decisions you could under the circumstances you found yourself in. I've no right to fault you for that. What I was going to say is you've been acting strange ever since you started delving into magick. You seem preoccupied, distracted, like you're never fully present anymore. And I'm worried about you, wondering if you've gotten in over your head, and if so, how I might help."

I look into his eyes, and there's so much hope and tenderness there that I can't bring myself to confess what I've been feeling for Roman. The thought alone is too gruesome. "I admit, I got into a little *bind*. And while I'd rather not go into all the details, it's better now. Romy and Rayne showed me how to undo it, and it's all—*good*. You just have to trust me."

He looks at me, his concern deepening, but still he just nods and says, "If you tell me to trust you, then I'll trust you. But let me know if there's anything I can do."

I reach toward him—my boyfriend—my soul mate—my partner for life. Knowing this is how it's meant to be—that everything I'm going through now is just a rude interruption—a technical difficulty—a brief blip on the screen of our infinite lives. Aware of that horrible insistent hum, thrumming in the background, threatening to take over again, I look him right in the eyes and say, "What do you say we get out of here?"

He looks at me, face softening, eyes lightening, always game for a good adventure. "Any place in particular?" he asks, having no idea what I have in mind but clearly complicit in his gaze.

I nod, squeezing his hand and quietly urging him to close his eyes, as I whisper, "Follow me."

NINE

The second we land, the two of us toppling side by side on the grass, I feel better. Like a million, trillion, gazillion times better. Jumping to my feet and skipping through the field, freed from that horrible trespassing energy—that strange foreign pulse and the thoughts of Roman it brings. All of it reduced to nothing more than a vague and distant memory, as the buoyant grass springs under my feet, and the perfumed flowers shiver beneath the tips of my fingers. Glancing over my shoulder, beckoning for Damen to join me, as a genuine grin lights up my face for the first time in days.

I am regenerated, renewed, able to begin all over again.

He comes toward me, stopping just shy of my reach as he closes his eyes and instantly transforms the vast fragrant fields of Summerland into an exact replica of the Château de Versailles. Placing us in the middle of a hall so grand and opulent it takes my breath away.

The floors are made of the smoothest polished parquet, while the cream-colored walls gleam with a liberal use of gold

leaf. And the ceilings—those insanely high, elaborately fres-
coed ceilings—are punctuated by a succession of glistening
chandeliers, their finely cut crystals shining and glinting from
the flames of burning candles, filling the room with a kaleidoscope of soft, glowing light. And just when I think it can't
possibly get any better, the majestic sounds of a symphony
begin and Damen bows before me and offers his hand.

I lower my gaze, bending into a brisk curtsey, taking the
opportunity to glance down at my dress—its bodice tight and
low, spilling into soft loose folds of the shiniest blue silk that
swirls all the way to the floor. Lifting my gaze to find him
retrieving a slim velvet box from his coat, and gasping in
excitement when he opens it to reveal an exquisite sapphire-
and-diamond-encrusted necklace he clasps around my neck.

I turn, glancing into the long line of mirrors that punctuate
each side of the hall, gazing upon the two of us together, he in
his breeches, blazer, and boots, me in my opulent finery, hair
twisted and curled into the world's most complicated updo—
and I know exactly what he's doing—exactly what he's up to—
he's giving me the happily ever after Drina stole from me.

I gaze around the ballroom in awe, hardly believing I
could've had *this,* could've been part of this world—*his* world.
If my *Cinderella* ending hadn't been ripped right out from
under me, robbing me of my chance to even try the glass
slipper.

If I'd only been allowed to live, he would've given me the
elixir and instantly transformed me from the lowly French
servant named Evaline into *this*—this radiant being staring
back from the mirror. And a hundred and some-odd years
later, we could've danced here together, shared this beauti-

ful night, dressed in our finest and glinting with jewels, right alongside Marie Antoinette and Louis XVI.

But that didn't happen. Instead, Drina killed me, forcing Damen and me to continue our search for each other, again and again.

I gaze at him, blinking back the tears as I place my hand on his shoulder and he cups his arm snugly around my waist, twirling me across the dance floor, our feet moving expertly, my skirts swirling in a dizzying haze of blue. So overcome by the beauty he's created, replicated just for me, I press tightly against him, lips at his ear when I ask if there are any more rooms to see.

And before I know it, I'm whisked down a confusing maze of halls, to the finest, grandest bedroom I've ever seen.

"Now, granted"—he smiles, pausing in the doorway as I try not to gawk as I take it all in—"this isn't the Royal Bed Chamber—Marie Antoinette and I were never *that* close. Though this is an exact replica of the room that I stayed in on my numerous visits—so tell me, what do you think?"

I make my way across the large woven rug, taking in the silk-covered chairs, the abundance of candles, the liberal use of crystal and gold, making a running leap onto the plush, richly draped, canopied bed and patting the space just beside me as though I don't have a care in the world.

Because I don't.

I'm in Summerland now.

Roman can't reach me.

"So, what do you think?" He leans over me, gaze sweeping my face.

I reach up, fingers tracing his high cheekbones, the sharp

line of his jaw, when I say, "What do I think?" I shake my head and laugh, the sound light, joyous, the way it used to be. "I think you're the most amazing boyfriend in the whole entire world. No, I take that back—"

He looks at me, feigned apprehension in his gaze.

"I think you're the most amazing boyfriend on the planet—*in the universe!*" I smile. "Seriously, who else gets a date like this?"

"Are you sure you like it?" he asks, real concern moving in.

I lift my arms, encircling them around his neck as I pull him down to me. Aware of the energy veil that hovers between his lips and mine—allowing for what I'm starting to think of as our now-standard, *almost* kiss. But still happy to take what I can get.

"These were such heady times," he says, pulling away and propping his head on his hand to better see me. "I just wanted you to experience it, get a taste for what it was like, what *I* was like. I'm so sorry you missed it, Ever, we would've had such fun. You would've been the belle of the ball—the most beautiful one"—he squints—"no—on second thought, Marie might not have liked that." He shakes his head and laughs.

"Why?" My fingers play at the ruffles covering the front of his shirt, sneaking their way between the buttons to the expanse of warm chest beneath. "Did she have *designs* on you—as they say? And was this before or after Count Fersen split the scene?"

He laughs. "Before, during, *and* after. It was definitely the place to be—or at least for a while anyway." He shakes his head. "And no, for your information, we were merely good friends, she had no *designs* on me, or none that I noticed at least. I was thinking more in terms of how some beautiful women aren't always so pleased when another one enters the scene."

I look at him, taking in the elegant planes of his face, the lock of glossy dark hair that falls over his eye, thinking how gallant he looks, how noble he is, how this look really suits him, really says who he is, far more than the faded jeans and black motorcycle boots ever did.

"So what'd Marie Antoinette think of Drina, then?" I ask, remembering her in all of her creamy-skinned, emerald-eyed, redheaded glory—a beauty so great it robbed me of breath. Realizing just after it's out that I'm actually having a conversation about Damen's evil ex-wife and not feeling even the slightest twinge of my usual jealousy. And it's not just because of the magick of Summerland, but because I really, truly am at peace with it now.

Though, unfortunately, Damen's not aware of my new outlook, which probably explains why his brow's gone all slanted and his mouth grim. Wondering if I'm really going to start this up again, after he's gone to all the trouble to make this for me.

But I just smile, inviting him to look inside my mind and *see* for himself. I asked only because I was curious, nothing more. There's not a hint of jealousy to be found.

"Drina and Marie didn't quite care for each other," he says, visibly relieved with my change of heart. "I mostly came calling on my own."

I look at him, imagining all of the beautiful single women who must've just swooned the second he walked in the room with no partner beside him—and again, just like before, I feel nothing.

Everyone has a past. Even, it seems, *me*. The only thing

that really matters is that he loves me. Has always loved me. Spent the last four hundred years searching for me. And I think I finally get just how big a deal that really is.

"Let's stay here forever," I whisper, pulling him to me and covering his face with my kiss. "We'll just take up residence in this amazing place, and when we get tired of it—*if* we get tired of it—we'll just manifest somewhere else to live."

"We can do that at home, you know." He looks at me, gaze tender and deep, hand buried in my hair, smoothing the strands. "We can *live* anywhere we want—*have* anything we want—*go* anywhere we want—just as soon as we graduate high school and move away from Sabine." He laughs.

And even though I smile and laugh along with him, I know better.

I can't really have this at home.

Not after the spell that I wove.

And until I can find a way to break it, this is the one and only place I can be like this, *feel* like this. The magick will dissolve the second I make my way back through the portal.

"But in the meantime, there's really no reason to hurry back—*is there?*" He grins, tipping my chin 'til my lips meet his.

He presses against me, his body covering mine, the *almost* feel of his hands on my skin filling me with tingle and heat. The two of us surrendering to the moment, surrendering to the limits we've no choice but to accept. My lips at his ear as I murmur, "No reason I can think of. No reason at all."

TEN

"Ever—*Ever*, wake up! We have to be getting back soon."

I roll onto my back and stretch, extending my arms up high over my head, while arching my back and flexing my toes, moving slowly, leisurely, infused with such languid warmth I'm tempted to just roll over again.

"Seriously." Damen laughs, his lips at my ear, nipping the lobe in that way that makes me giggle. "We've already discussed this, we both agreed we'd return eventually."

I lift one droopy lid, then the other, met by an overload of silk, gilt, and the ruffles from Damen's shirt tickling the tip of my nose—*I'm still in Versailles?*

"How long did I sleep?" I stifle a yawn but not very successfully, seeing Damen hovering over me, an amused look on his face.

"There's no time in Summerland." He smiles. "And trust me, I'll try not to take it personally that you nodded off."

I stiffen, wide awake now and gaping. "Wait—you mean I fell asleep while you—while we—" I shake my head, cheeks heating to a thousand degrees. Hardly believing I actually fell asleep—*while we were kissing.*

He nods, luckily looking more amused than mad. But still I hide my face with my hands, horrified by even the thought of it.

"That is *so* embarrassing. Seriously, I'm *so*—" I shake my head and cringe. Needing no further testimony to how exhausted I've been after everything that's happened in the past week.

He rises from the bed, helping me to stand when he says, "Don't be. Don't be sorry or embarrassed. You know, in a way it was kind of nice. I don't recall that ever happening before and you don't really get to experience many firsts after the first—oh, hundred or so years." He laughs, pulling me to him as his arms wrap tightly around my waist. "Feeling better?"

I nod. That's the first decent sleep I've had since—well, since *you know who* started invading my dreams. And even though I've no idea how long I was out, I feel so much better now, like I'm ready to head back to the earth plane and face all of my demons—or at least one in particular.

"Shall we?" He lifts his brow.

About to close his eyes and make the veil when I say, "But—what about this place? What'll happen to it once we leave?"

He shrugs. "Well, I was going to let it go since we can always manifest it again. You know that, right?" He gives me a strange look.

And even though I know it's easy enough for him to re-create it exactly as is, somehow I want it to stay. I want to know that it's solid and lasting. A place I can return to on a whim, and not just some hazy figment of a really great day.

He smiles, bowing deeply as he answers my thoughts. "And so it is." He takes my hand. "Versailles stays."

"And this?" I grin, fluffing the frills on his cream-colored shirt, causing him to laugh in a way I don't hear nearly enough anymore.

"Well, I thought I'd change for the return trip home—if that's okay with you?"

I cock my head and screw my lips to the side, carefully looking him over as I consider. "But I like you like this. You're so handsome, so gallant—regal, really. It makes me feel like I'm looking at the *real* you, dressed in the period you seem to have liked best."

He shrugs. "I liked 'em all—some better than others, but in retrospect they all had something to offer. And you, by the way, look quite dazzling too." He trails his fingers over my jewels and down the snug-fitting bodice of my dress. "But still, if we want to fit in back home, a costume change is in order."

I sigh, sad to see our eighteenth-century finery replaced by our usual Laguna Beach wear.

"And now—" He nods, tucking my amulet back under the neck of my dress. "What do you say—my place or yours?"

"Neither." I press my lips together, knowing he's not going to like what comes next but committed to being completely honest with him during the few times I can. "I need to see Jude."

He flinches. It's minor, barely visible to the untrained eye, but still, I see it. And I need him to know what Jude already knows: that there's no competition. Never really was. Damen won my heart centuries ago. And he's had it ever since.

"There was an accident." I nod, determined to keep my voice calm, even, and just stick to the facts, no matter how gruesome. And though I could just let the scene flow from my head to his—I don't. There are too many parts I don't want him to see, things he might take the wrong way, so instead I say, "I—I sort of attacked him—"

"*Ever!*" He balks, his expression so shocked it's all I can do not to look away.

"I *know.*" I shake my head, pausing to take a deep breath. "I know how it sounds, but it's not what you think, I—I was trying to prove he was a rogue—but—well—when I learned that he wasn't—that's when I rushed him to the emergency room."

"And you failed to tell me this because—" He looks at me, obviously hurt by my neglect.

I sigh, looking right at him when I say, "Because I was embarrassed. Because I mess up *all* the time and I didn't want you to lose patience with me. I mean, not that I'd blame you—but still." I shrug, scratching my arm even though it doesn't itch, yet another nervous habit of mine.

He places his hands squarely on my shoulders, looking me right in the eye when he says, "My feelings for you are not conditional. I don't judge you. I don't lose patience with you. I don't punish you. I just love you. That's all. Pure and simple." His eyes search my face, his gaze so warm, so loving, clearly upholding the promise of his words. "You have no reason to hide anything from me—*ever.* Understood? I'm not going anywhere. I'll always be here for you. And if you need anything, find yourself in a bind, or in over your head, all you have to do is ask and I'll be right there to bail you out."

I nod, unable to speak I'm so humbled by my amazingly good fortune, feeling so incredibly lucky to be loved by someone like him—even though I'm not always sure I deserve it.

"So, you go take care of your friend, I'll take care of the twins, and we'll meet up tomorrow, okay?"

I lean in to kiss him, quickly, careful to let go of his hand since we're headed in different directions. Closing my eyes long enough to envision the portal before me, that shimmering golden veil that'll lead me back home.

I land at Jude's door, taking a moment to knock a few times, allowing plenty of time for him to answer, before I decide to give up and go in uninvited. Searching every last room in his tiny beach cottage, including the garage and backyard, before locking up and heading straight for the store.

But on my way there, I pass Roman's. And all it takes is one look at the window display—one look at the sign overhead, reading: RENAISSANCE!—one look at the open front door that leads directly to *him*—and just like *that*, the magick of Summerland is gone and this strange foreign pulse, this horrible invader, has taken over again.

I will myself forward, summoning every last bit of my strength to move past it. But my legs are too heavy, unwilling to cooperate, and my breath runs too shallow and comes out too quickly.

I'm rooted. Unable to flee. Overcome by this horrible *need* to find him—to *see* him—to *be* with him. This ugly invader taking over as though my evening of enchantment never happened. As though I was never at peace.

The beast now awakened, demanding to be fed. And despite my best efforts to get out of this place before it's too late—it *is* too late. He's come to find me.

"Well, fancy finding *you* here."

Roman leans in the doorway, all golden haired and shiny teethed, his glinting blue eyes fixed right on me. "You're looking rather—*piqued*. Everything *all right?*" His contrived British accent causing his voice to rise in a way that usually annoys me to no end, but now—now I find it so alluring it's all I can do to stay where I am. Continuing to fight this epic battle now raging inside me—that strange, foreign pulse versus me.

He laughs, head tossed back in a way that clearly displays the Ouroboros tattoo on his neck—the snake coiling, slithering, its beady eyes seeking mine, as its long, skinny tongue beckons me near.

And despite everything I know about good and evil, right and wrong, immortals and rogues, I step forward. Taking one small step toward defeat, that's quickly followed by another. And another. My gaze fixed on Roman—gorgeous, glorious Roman. He's all I can see. All that I need. Only vaguely aware of that small glimmer of me, still in there somewhere— struggling, shouting, demanding to be heard—but it just can't compete. And it's not long before it's silenced by the single-minded pulse now residing inside me—its sights set on only one thing.

His name swells on my lips, as I stand right before him, so close I can make out each individual violet fleck in his eyes, and feel the cool chill that emanates off his skin. The same chill I once found abhorrent, repulsive, but not anymore. Now it's a welcome siren, calling me home.

"Always knew you'd come around." He grins, his gaze slowly taking me in as he buries his fingers in my tangle of hair. "Welcome to the dark side, Ever, I think you'll be quite happy here." He laughs, the sound of it enveloping me in a delicious frostbitten hug. "Not surprised you shrugged off that old wanker Damen. Figured you'd grow tired of him eventually. All of the *waiting*—the *angst*—the gawd-awful *soul searching*—not to mention the *do-gooding.*" He shakes his head and grimaces as though the thought alone pains him. "I don't know how you stood it for as long as you did. And for what, I might ask? Because I hate to break it to you, luv, but there are no future rewards up yonder when your future's right *here.*" He stamps his foot on the ground. "A bloody waste of time, it is. No use delaying gratification when the instant kind works best. There are pleasures to be had, Ever. Pleasures of a magnitude you can't even begin to understand. But, lucky for you, I'm the forgiving type. I'm more than willing to serve as your guide. So, tell me, where should we start, luv, your place or mine?"

His fingers trail along my cheek, my shoulder, working their way down to the loose neck of my dress. And even though the feel of it's icy, bracing, in the strongest sense of the word, I can't help but lean into it, can't help but close my eyes and immerse myself in the feel of it, urging him to scoop lower, explore further, prepared to go wherever he takes me—

"*Ever?* Is that *you*? Are you *fugging* kidding me?"

I open my eyes to find Haven standing behind us. Her eyes narrowed, blazing with anger as they dart between Roman and me. Not letting up in the slightest when he laughs and pushes me away, discarding me quickly and easily, as though it meant nothing to him.

"Told you she'd be back, luv." His gaze sails over my shaky, sweaty body, so overcome with unrequited yearning, it pains me to see him slide his arm around *her*. The two of them turning their backs on me and heading inside as he says, "You know Ever. She just can't stay away."

ELEVEN

I run.

Covering the blocks in a matter of seconds, appearing as a fast-moving blur to all whom I pass. But I don't care about that. Don't care what they think—what they see. I care about only one thing—ridding myself of this horrible invader, this mystical trespasser—so the old me can return.

Bursting through the door just as Jude's about to lock it, nearly knocking him over though he's quick to jump out of my way.

"I need help." I stand before him, gasping, wheezing, broken beyond repair. "I—I don't know where else to go."

He looks me over, eyes narrowed, brows knit with concern, leading me toward the back room where he pulls out a chair with his foot and motions for me to sit.

"*Easy,*" he coos. "Deep breaths. Seriously, Ever. Whatever it is, I'm sure it can be fixed."

I shake my head and lean toward him, gripping the arms of my chair, fighting to stay rooted, to not go back *there.* "But what if you're wrong?" I say, eyes wild, cheeks flushed, voice high-pitched and shaky. "What if it *can't* be worked out? What if I'm—what if I'm *broken* for good?"

He moves around his desk and drops onto his chair, swiveling back and forth as he slowly takes me in, his face still, placid, impossible to read. But something about the movement, that gentle, constant pivoting, instantly calms me. Allowing me to settle back in my seat, slow my breath, and focus on the way his dreadlocks spill over the colorful picture of Ganesh that's splashed across his tee.

"Look," I finally say, starting to feel better, almost human again. "I'm—I'm sorry for coming here like this. I was actually on my way over to give you *this*." I reach for my bag, rooting around for the small white package I then hand to him. Watching him peek at the contents as I say, "It's your prescription. I picked it up earlier and meant to leave it on your desk, but then I forgot all about it 'til now." He nods, silent for a moment, studying me carefully as he says, "Ever, what's this really about? Clearly, you're not here to talk about my meds." He pushes the pills aside with his cast, catching my look when he adds, "Trust me, I have no plans to take 'em. Pain pills and me—not a good mix. As I'm sure you've already witnessed."

And when he looks at me, I know he remembers. Everything. All of it. The full-on confession he made.

I press my lips together and lower my gaze, fiddling with the hem of my dress, knowing I'm just going through the motions when I say, "Well, you might want to take the antibiotics at least—you know, to ward off infection and all."

He leans back in his seat and places his feet on his desk, crossing his legs at the ankle as his amazing green eyes narrow on me. "What do you say we move past all this and get to the point—what's really going on with you?"

I take a deep breath, smoothing my dress over my knees before tentatively meeting his gaze. "I did come here to bring you the pills, really. But on the way over—something happened—and—" I look at him, knowing I need to just get to the point, spit it out already before he loses his patience with me. "I think I accidentally bound Roman to me."

He looks at me, trying hard not to balk, though he still kinda does.

"Or, actually, I bound myself to Roman. But not on purpose—it was an accident. I meant to do just the opposite, but then, when I tried to undo it, it just made things worse. And even though you have absolutely no reason to help me—believe it or not, I have nowhere to turn."

"Nowhere?" You sure about that?" He lifts his spliced brow.

Gathering my words, hoping they'll work to convince him, I heave an audible sigh when I say, "I know what you're thinking, but you may as well forget it. I can't tell Damen—he can never know what I've done. He doesn't work magick—doesn't really trust it for that matter—so it's not like he can do anything to help. I'll just be hurting and disappointing him for no good reason. But you—you're different. You know your way around a spell. And since I need help from someone who's familiar with this kind of thing—well, I thought you could show me how to set things right."

"Sounds like you're putting a lot of faith in me." He tosses his dreadlocks over his shoulder and rests his arms on his lap.

"Maybe." I shrug. "But then I truly believe that it's warranted. I mean, now that I've proved you're not evil—" I nod toward his arms, the sight of them sparking an idea, something

I just might broach at some point, something that just might be the perfect way to make it all up to him—but in the future, not now. First I need to get through this. Swallowing hard as I lower my gaze, horrified to have to admit this, to say the words out loud, but knowing it's the only way. "It's like I'm obsessed with Roman." I glance at him briefly, seeing him blanch slightly but grateful for his efforts to contain it. "I'm totally and completely fixated on him. He's all I think about. All I dream about. And no matter what I do, I can't seem to stop it."

He nods, head bobbing slightly, as though in deep contemplation. Like he's flipping through his mental spell-reversing book, searching for just the right cure. "This is a tough one, Ever." He takes a deep breath and levels his gaze right on mine. "It's—*complicated*."

I nod, hands clasped in my lap, already painfully aware of that.

"Binding spells—" He rubs his cast against his chin. "Well, they can't always be undone."

I lean forward, striving for calm, striving to speak past my agitated breath. "But—I thought *everything* can be undone—you just have to work the *right* spell at the *right* time—*right*?"

His shoulders rise and fall in a move so final it makes my stomach dip, his gaze on mine as he says, "Sorry, I'm just telling you what I've learned through my years of studying and practicing these things. But you've got *The Book,* you've got this supposed code that gets past the code—so, you tell me."

I sigh, leaning back in my seat, fingers picking at the hem of my dress. "*The Book*'s not much help. I mean, I pretty much did exactly what Romy and Rayne said—used most all the same elements—and—"

He looks at me. "The *exact* same elements?"

"Well, yeah." I shrug. "For the most part. I mean, in order to reverse a spell—you need to repeat the same steps as before—it says so right in the book and Romy and Rayne confirmed it."

He nods. Doesn't say a word, just nods. But his attempt at restraint rings loud and clear.

"So I can't imagine what made it go wrong. I mean, at first I thought I'd nailed it, but then it—it completely got away from me and started reversing itself all over again, repeating the same sequence of events as before."

"Ever, I know you repeated the *steps,* but did you also re-peat the same *tools*? The same herbs, crystals, and whatever else you might've used?"

"Some new, some old." I shrug, not quite getting his point.

"What's the main tool you used—the one that really got the spell rolling?"

"Well, after the bath, I—" I narrow my eyes and think, the answer coming instantly: "The athame." I look at him, both of us knowing that's *it*—the big wrong thing that I did. "I—I used it for a blood exchange, and—"

His eyes widen, his cheeks pale, and his aura begins to quiver in a way that's more than a little frightening. "And was this the same athame you used on *me*?" he asks, his con-cern ringing loud and clear.

I shake my head, seeing his face flood with relief. "No, that was just a quickly manifested replica. The real one's at home."

He nods, obviously glad to hear it but determined to move on. "Well, I hate to say it, but that's the one thing you wanted to make new. You need to offer the goddess some-thing new, pure, and unused. You can't serve her with the same tainted tools you used for the queen of the under-world."

Oh.

He looks at me, gaze saddened, eyes tugging down at the corners when he says, "I'd love to help you, really I would, but this kind of thing is a little over my head. Maybe you should consult with Romy and Rayne, they seem to know what they're doing."

"But do they?" I squint, unsure where I'm going with this, and really just thinking out loud when I say, "Because the thing is, I *did* listen to them. I did what they said. I mean, granted, they didn't like the athame, claimed I'd made it all wrong and wanted me to melt it down to a stub, but still, even when I refused, they just let it go. They never once said I couldn't use it again or that I had to use a whole new set of tools in order to reverse the spell. Somehow they failed to share that with me."

Our eyes meet, both of us wondering the same thing. *Why would they do that? Was it on purpose? Do they really dislike me that much?* With Jude dismissing the thought a lot quicker than I. But then, he doesn't know our history. A history so complicated and volatile, I can't rule it out.

"Listen, they're extremely close to Damen—they love him about as much as they hate me. Seriously." I nod, knowing it's not an exaggeration—it's completely and totally true. "And despite the fact they they're supposedly good witches, I wouldn't put it past them to do this, thinking they were teaching me a lesson, or heck, maybe even trying to keep Damen and me apart. I mean, who knows what they've got planned? But even if it wasn't intentional, even if they just simply didn't know any better, there's no way I can approach them. Because if they *did* do it on purpose, they'll tell Damen, and under no circumstances whatsoever can he find out about this—I can't hurt him that way. And if they *didn't*, well, then it's just one more piece of ammunition in their arsenal of things with which to ridicule me."

Jude leans toward me, his face determined when he says, "Ever, I get your dilemma, really I do. But don't you think you're coming off as just *a little bit* paranoid these days?"

I narrow my eyes and lean back in my chair, wondering if he's listened to a single word I've just said.

"I mean, first you accuse me of being a *rogue,* which, by the way, I still don't know what the heck that is other than it has something to do with Roman, who not only, well according to you anyway, runs his own tribe of *evildoers* but who you also just happen to both loathe and lust after due to some binding spell gone wrong. And while you can't be too sure, it's quite possible, or at least in your mind it is, that Romy and Rayne are out to get you, which is why they purposely left crucial pieces of information out of their instructions so that you could mess up in such a way that would keep you and Damen apart. And speaking of Damen, you're also convinced he'd never forgive you for this mess that you've made—and—" He shakes his head. "Do you see what I'm getting at?"

I frown, arms crossed, eyes narrowed to slits, refusing to acknowledge any of it—besides, it's not that simple, it goes much deeper than that.

"Ever, please, I want to help you, you should know that by now, but I'm also determined to do the right thing. You need to take this to Damen. I'm sure he'll understand and—"

"I've already explained," I say. "He doesn't trust magick

and he already warned me against using it. I can't bear for him to know I didn't listen, and just how low I've sunk."

Jude leans back and studies me closely, his voice a sigh when he says, "Ah, but you've no problem with me knowing, is that it?" He gives a half smile that never quite reaches his eyes.

I take a deep breath and look at him, determined to shoot as straight and openly as I can. "Trust me, this isn't comfortable for me either, but I've pretty much got nowhere else to go. But, hey, if you don't want to get involved, just say so and I'll . . ."

I grip my armrests, lifting myself out of my chair, preparing to leave. Stopped by the lure of those deep aqua green eyes coaxing me back into my seat, as he slides open a drawer, riffles through the contents, and says, "Looks like I'm already involved. Let's see what I can do."

TWELVE

"And here I thought I was destined to head off to Florence without a final good-bye from you!" Miles grasps me to him in what could only be described as a bear hug. Peering over my shoulder at Damen and eyeballing him carefully when he whispers, "Glad to see you're back together again."

I pull away and shoot him a dubious look. Remembering the last time I saw him, at the going-away party I threw for him last week, and how he urged me to move on from Damen and find happiness with Jude.

He reads my gaze as though reading my mind, his lips curving into a grin as he says, "So I want to see you happy— is that so bad?" He turns, giving Damen a little half wave, when he adds, "Heck, I want to see *everyone* happy—which is why you might want to steer clear of just about every room in this house except the one you're in now. And that includes the backyard."

Damen's arm tightens around me, pulling me into a protective embrace, his voice tinged with concern when he says,

"So there's someone on the guest list who might make us *unhappy*?"

I glance between them, already knowing the answer. I knew it the instant we got out of the car and walked up the drive to his door. The moment that strange, foreign pulse awakened inside me, alerting me to the one thing, the *only* thing I need to know:

Roman is here.

The rest is just details.

Miles screws his lips to the side and runs his fingers through his short dark hair. "Oh no, there was no guest list—just a random group of people who started stopping by around noon and haven't stopped yet. And just so you know, I know all about you and Haven, so—"

"Excuse me?" I study him closely, peering at his aura, its usual well-meaning yellow now tinged with a conflicted gray.

He looks at me, pursing his lips and shaking his head when he says, "Listen, I know all about it, she told me. And while I wish I could stick around and help you two work it out—"

"What did she say? What were her *exact words*?" I ask, my gaze fixed on Miles as Damen grips my waist tighter, both of us on high alert, watching as he shakes his head, and mimes a zipper being pulled across his mouth.

"Oh no, don't even go there. Seriously, Ever, don't even try. All I know is that you're no longer talking. As for the rest—I'm Switzerland. Totally neutral. I refuse to get involved. Because the truth is, I really *don't* wish I could stick around to fix it. I was just being nice. I can't wait to get to Florence and leave you guys here to work it out on your own. And you better work it out too, because I will *not* be forced to choose sides when I get back. I mean, you may have the advantage since you give me rides to school and all, but still, I've known Haven longer, and that's gotta count for something, right?" He closes his eyes and shakes his head, as though the whole mess is just too much to process.

"Miles, that's all well and good, but I'm afraid it's imperative we know exactly what it is Haven told you." Damen's voice is low, urgent, filled with intent, making it clear, or at least to me anyway, that if Miles doesn't fess up, he's just seconds away from breaking our vow to never spy on our friends' private thoughts and peer right inside his head to see for himself. "It won't get back to her if that's what you're worried about, but I'm afraid we must know."

Miles looks at him, heaving a dramatic sigh and rolling his eyes "*Et tu,* Damen?" he says, glancing between us, clearly unhappy with the peer pressure we're inflicting on him. "Fine, I'll tell you, but only because this time tomorrow I'm out of here—sailing through the clouds at thirty thousand feet, watching movies I've already seen and filling up on high-sodium food that's sure to bloat me. But just remember, no matter how ugly it gets, *you* asked for it." He looks at us, pausing dramatically, face gone all serious when he says, "She told me you guys are determined to keep her from Roman, because, and remember, these are *her* words *not* mine so don't shoot the messenger, but basically she thinks you're jealous. Well, not really you, Damen, but Ever for sure. She thinks Ever's jealous because, again, her words." He clears his throat, striving for just the right raspy-voiced, Haven inflection. "*I'm finally coming into my own and Ever can't stand the fact that she's no longer the special one.*" He rolls his eyes and shakes his head. And even though I feel bad that we made him repeat it, I'm also secretly thrilled that it isn't at all what I thought. She may hate me, but she's still managed to keep her immortality to herself—at least for now anyway.

Damen nods, coolly, calmly, but I can tell he's relieved too. And I just look at Miles, shrugging casually when I say, "Wow. I'm really sorry to hear that."

But the truth is, I've already moved on. That strange magick is stirring inside me, causing my heart to race, my palms to sweat, as that restless, twitchy feeling takes over again. And all I want to do is ditch these two as fast as I can so I can find *him*. Roman. I've got an uncontrollable hunger that needs to be fed, no matter the cost to me or my friends.

I swallow hard, taking slow measured breaths and struggling to steady myself. Clinging to the small glimmer of sanity that's managed to remain despite the battle that rages around it.

"So, there you have it. A good old-fashioned girl fight." Miles shrugs. "Too bad I'm not the type to appreciate that kind of thing—though you might."

He motions toward Damen, but Damen's quick to dispel it. "I assure you, I got over that type of thing a *long* time ago." He nods, a brief flash of sorrow crossing over his face, a memory of Drina and me that's here and gone before I can blink.

Miles nods, glancing between us when he adds, "Though she is right about one thing—"

Damen shifts ever so slightly, on high alert for whatever that might be, while I stand beside him, nervous, fidgety, only wishing *he'd* come to me.

"She really is looking pretty smokin' these days. I mean, I don't know if it's her new, post-apocalyptic, rock 'n' roll gypsy look she's got going, or what. But it's like she's finally finding herself, coming into her own like she said, you know?

And after being so lost for so long, it's got to be a pretty heady feeling to finally gain a little self-empowerment, so try to cut her some slack, okay? She'll come around. *Eventually.* But for now, I think we should just sit back and try not to take it personally. Or at least you guys should, because me— I'm headed for Florence—did I mention that?"

I nod, automatically, robotically, rearranging my face into what I hope comes off as a pleasant expression. Hoping everything about me appears pleasant, friendly, and completely agreeable, because inside, I'm stirring, burning, and there's no way in hell I'm gonna let her enjoy that ride if it involves bringing Roman along.

No.

Way.

But I don't say that. I don't say a word. I just shrug as though it hardly concerns me, as I continue to survey the room. Just biding my time until my favorite blue-eyed, blond-haired golden boy appears.

"So I guess what I'm trying to say is that no matter what happens between you guys, I'm *not* choosing sides, which also means you're all equally welcome here. But that doesn't mean I invited her entourage to stop by—Haven came up with that all on her own. Because honestly, don't tell her I said so, but Roman's kind of—" He frowns and stares off into space, searching for just the right word, before shaking his head and starting again. "Well—whatever—let's just say there's something kind of—*off* about him—something kind of—*strange*. I don't really know how to explain it, but it's kind of the same feeling I had with Drina."

His gaze switches between us, searching for confirmation that he really is onto something, but even though my attentions are elsewhere, Damen and I are united in this, standing side by side—a wall of nonchalance he cannot penetrate.

"Anyway." He shrugs. "He makes her happy, and that's all that matters. I mean, it's not like we can stop it, right?"

Oh, you have no idea. I narrow my gaze and press my lips together, struggling to keep it contained.

"I mean, seriously . . ."

Miles yammers on and on as I take the opportunity to peer into his head. Dipping in ever so slightly and taking a quick peek around, sensing his excitement for his trip, his anxiety at leaving Holt, and absolutely no knowledge whatsoever of rogues, immortals, or anything else of the sort.

". . . so basically you have eight weeks—two whole months to get it cleared up. And I'm counting on you, Ever, since we all know how stubborn Haven can be. I mean, I love her and all, but let's face it, she loves to be right more than anyone I know—and will fight to the absolute death to defend herself—even when she's dead wrong."

I nod, having already popped back out of his head and renewed my vow to never do it again. Watching as Damen reaches into his pocket and retrieves a piece of paper folded into a neat little square—a note he probably manifested just a second before.

"I made you that list we talked about." He nods, responding to Miles's blank look when he adds, "The list of places you should check out in *Firenze*—places you won't want to miss. It's a long one." He shrugs. "Should keep you busy for the next several weeks." His gaze meets Miles's, looking at him in a way that's calm, placid, devoid of any hints at ulterior motives, meant to convince. But I know better. Know without being told that he's bent on steering him away from the list Roman gave him a few weeks before—but what I don't know is *why*.

The last time I asked, he completely clammed up and refused to talk about it. All I know is that Roman is urging Miles to visit some out-of-the-way place that claims to host some rare antiquities and it's got Damen worried. Though I can't imagine why, since all of his paintings perished in a fire that he himself set over four hundred years ago—a fire that destroyed everything in his collection, including—for all intents and purposes—*him*.

Miles looks it over, eyes sweeping from top to bottom before folding it back up and shoving it into his shirt pocket. "Trust me, after seeing the grueling schedule they sent yesterday, I'll be lucky to find time to sleep. They're pretty serious about us spending every spare second improving our craft, you know, like an actual *acting camp*, and not quite the freewheeling Italian holiday I was expecting."

Damen nods, a flash of relief playing across his face so quickly you'd miss it if you blinked. But I didn't blink. I saw it. And if I wasn't so preoccupied with thoughts of Roman, I might pull him aside to ask why. But instead I just stand there, unable to ignore the fact that his usual tingle and heat is completely obliterated by the insistent pulse that now throbs in its place.

A pulse that's not the least bit deterred by the sight of Jude heading toward us.

He pauses, granting me a brief nod of acknowledgment before focusing on Damen. The two of them stiffening, straightening, squaring their shoulders, and expanding their chests in a way so primitive I'm reminded of what Jude said the other night—about the two of them being locked in a primal competition over me.

Two gorgeous, smart, gifted, talented guys, fighting over *me*. And all I can think about is the one in the next room. The one dating my friend. The one who's as evil as he is irresistible.

Damen motions toward Jude's bandaged arms, and says, "That's gotta hurt."

And the way he said it, the inflection in his voice, coupled with the look on his face, well, I can't help but wonder if he meant it in a *physical* way or an *emotional* one, since we all know I'm the one who made him that way.

Jude shrugs, a casual rise and fall of his shoulders that causes his dreadlocks to spill down his arms, gazing at me when he says, "Well, I've been better. But Ever's doing her best to make up for it."

Miles glances between us, nose and forehead all scrunched when he says, "Wait—are you saying *Ever* did that to you?"

I glance at Jude, having no idea how he might answer, and stopping just short of heaving an audible sigh of relief when he shakes his head and laughs.

"She's helping out in the store." He shrugs. "That's all I meant—nothing sinister—nothing nearly as embarrassing as getting smacked down by a girl."

And the second it's out, I laugh. Partly because everyone's so silent, caught up in a web of tension so thick you could chop it with an axe—and partly because I'm so highly wound, so twitchy and edgy, I can't think of what else to do. But unfortunately it happens to be one of those awful laughs. The loud, garish, horribly desperate kind that only manages to magnify just how truly awkward the moment really is.

Damen stands beside me, stoic, conflicted, determined to do what's right for us—for *me*—though not always sure what that is. And I feel so bad for causing this mess, for being such a terrible girlfriend, for longing for the one person who's made our lives nothing but difficult, that I shut my eyes briefly and send him a flood of telepathic red tulips in an attempt to make up for it. But instead of the flowers I intended, he receives a sputtering, drippy, malformed blotch of red on squiggly green stems. The lamest bouquet ever created.

He turns, squinting at me with concern as Jude takes the moment to say, "Listen, I'm gonna—*vamanos*. So, Miles—" His cast meets the center of Miles's palm, resulting in something between a slap and a shake. "And, Ever—" He turns toward me, his gaze lingering for just a few seconds too long, long enough to make me squirm, long enough for everyone to notice. And I can't help but wonder if he did it on purpose, so Damen will know I chose Jude over him in my time of need, or if he really is that bad a liar and is struggling to hide the secret we share. Switching his gaze to Damen as the two of them exchange a loaded look I can't read, turning away only when Miles ushers him out the front door. And that's all it takes to convince me to do the right thing. To stop pushing Damen away, come clean, and finally accept the help he's already offered to me.

I turn, grasping his arm as my eyes seek his, ready to spill the whole sordid tale, but my throat squeezes tight, halting my words and practically cutting off my air supply, turning what was meant to be a confession into a red-faced, sputtering, coughing fit.

And when Damen slides his arm around me and asks if I'm okay, it's all I can do not to push him away. But I don't, I summon all my strength to pull it together as best as I can. Bowing my head, closing my eyes, and waiting for the outburst to die down. Knowing I'm no longer in charge, of me, of anything. The monster is rising, now wide awake, and it's not about to let Damen come between Roman and me.

Miles closes the door behind Jude and turns to us and says, "Nope, nothing awkward about that." Glancing between us as he sighs and shakes his head.

I reach inside my bag, frantically fishing around until I find what I want. The small, sane part of me knowing I need to move this along, hand over the gift and make my way out of here before it's too late, before this strange magick takes over completely and forces me to do something I'll surely regret. Roman is getting closer. I can *feel* him drawing near. And I need to get out of here while I still can.

"We can't stay long, but I just wanted you to have this," I say, hoping he doesn't notice the tremor in my hands when I hand over the leather-bound journal I picked up at the store. Concentrating on taking slow deep breaths, determined to keep the beast at bay, watching as he runs his hand over the front before flipping through the rough-edged pages inside. Trying to rid my voice of its edginess when I say, "I mean, I know you'll probably blog your whole journey, but just in case you don't have Internet access, or you want to keep some stuff private, I thought you could write it down here."

Miles grins, looking at me when he says, "First a party and now a gift? You spoil me, Ever!"

And though I respond with a smile, the truth is, his words barely register. Everything is upstaged by the simple fact that Roman is here.

The second I see him, the invader takes over, effectively

smothering whatever small glimmer of me managed to hang on for this long, and instantly replacing it with an insistent thrum that grows increasingly bolder.

A thrum that won't stop until Roman and I join as one.

Damen's arm tightens around me, aware of the change in my energy, clearly on edge. Poised and ready for just about anything, as first Misa, then Marco and Rafe, say good-bye to Miles, as Haven, clad in a purple velvet dress that brings out the sheen of her perfect, pale skin, looks on. Her glinting eyes sweeping over me, as her heavily ringed fingers tap ominously against her hips. And if she still had an aura to view, there's no doubt I'd be gazing into a solid wall of the darkest, most blazing red.

But it's not like I need to read her energy to know how she's feeling or what she's thinking. She's exactly like me now—immortal—myopic—with only one goal in sight—Roman. Willing to do whatever it takes to stake her claim.

Her gaze rakes over me, working its way from my head to my toes. So sure of her powers, so overconfident in her fledgling abilities, I'm quickly dismissed with a casual shrug.

She leans in toward Miles, giving him a brief hug good-bye, quickly slipping out of the way when Roman grasps him in one of those brief, back-slapping man hugs, hand still gripping his shoulder when he says, "Now don't forget, just after you've crossed the Ponte Vecchio, head down the alley, take a left and then another, and it's the third door on the right. Big red door—can't miss it." Eyes gleaming in a billion points of light when he glances at Damen and sees the way the color just drained from his face. "It's worth the trip, mate, trust me on that." He turns toward Miles again. "Hell, ask Damen—wouldn't you say it's worth the trip? Surely you know the place?"

Damen gazes at Roman, jaw clenched, lids narrowed, striving for a calm, even tone when he says, "Can't say that I do."

But Roman just squints, head cocked to the side as he slips into a thick cockney brogue. "You sure 'bout that, mate? Coulda swore I sawr you in thar b'fore?"

"Doubtful," Damen says, the word hard, final, the challenge clearly displayed in his gaze.

But Roman just laughs, hands raised in surrender and turning toward me when he says, "Ever."

And that's all it takes. The mere mention of my name on his lips and I'm liquid.

Pure molten liquid.

Willing to follow wherever he leads.

I move toward him, lured by his steely blue gaze. Each small step bringing me closer to the images now unfolding in his head—the ones he's placed there for me. The exact kind of thing that would've disgusted me before—make me want to punch out his chakras and be done with all this. But not now.

Now I'm so breathless and heated I can't get there quickly enough.

Damen reaches toward me—both mentally and physically—trying to send me a message, trying to pull me back to him, but it's no use. His thoughts are mumbled, jumbled, making no sense at all. Just a long string of words I've no interest in.

Roman's the only thing that interests me now.

He's my sun, moon, and stars and I happily revolve all around him.

I take another step, my hands shaking, body aching, yearning for the chill of his touch on my skin. No longer caring who sees—what they'll think—only wanting to feed the hungry monster within me.

And just as I'm about to do it, about to take that final leap forward, he sweeps right past me and saunters outside to his car. Leaving me unsteady, uncertain, breathless, and confused—as Miles stands by, unsure what to do—and Damen looks on with concern.

Summoning every ounce of his will to hold it together, to keep things on track, at least while Miles is present, and going right back to where we left off when he says, "Roman's taste in art is pedestrian at best. Stick with my list and you can't go wrong." His face appearing composed, relaxed, but I know it's anything but. The energy that emanates off him tells a whole other story.

And I wish I could care in the way I'm supposed to—in the way that I eventually will once this pulse starts to fade and the impact of what I've just done comes reeling back at me. But that's a horrifying moment reserved for the future. Right now, all I can think about is *him*.

Where he's going.

If she's with him.

And what I can do to stop them.

Miles glances between us, wishing he could just board that jet and be done with all this. Nervously clearing his throat when he says, "So, now that that's over, you wanna join the rest of the party? The cast is up in the game room and we're about to perform the highlights of *Hairspray* pretty soon."

Damen starts to shake his head *no*, but I override him. Even though I want to do pretty much anything but take part in a show-tunes sing-along, if I've any hope of salvation, I need to stay here. Right here in this house where it's safe. If I go out-side, I'll go after *him,* and from that moment on, there'll be no turning back.

Besides, I need the distraction. I can't bear to see Damen's questioning gaze, the look of hurt on his face. I need some time to calm and center myself, so I can eventually explain the strange, awful truth of what's happening to me.

I grasp his hand tightly and lead him upstairs, hoping the energy veil that hovers between us will mask my clammy, cold skin, as I enter the game room with a smile and wave.

Remembering the secret Miles once told me about acting—that it's all about projecting—projecting—projecting—believing the lie so fervently the audience buys it too.

THIRTEEN

"**Damen—I—**" I try to tell him—try to force the words from my lips, but they won't come. My throat's gone all hot, tight, and crowded again. As though the beast knows my agenda and refuses to comply.

Damen looks at me, his growing concern clearly stamped on his face.

"Let's—let's go to Summerland," I croak, amazed I could even say that. "Back to Versailles." I nod, swiveling in my seat until I'm fully facing him, begging him with my eyes to go along with my plan.

"*Now?*" He brakes at a light and looks at me, his eyes narrowed, forehead scrunched—the telltale signs I'm being scrutinized.

I press my lips together and shrug, striving to appear relaxed, nonchalant, as though I'm really not all that attached to the outcome, when the truth is I've been twitchy and itchy from the moment we got to Miles's to the moment we left, and the only thing that will cure it, the only thing that will enable me to confide in Damen and ask for the help that I need is to get to Summerland ASAP. Here on the earth plane, I'm no longer in control of me.

"I thought you liked it there," I say, carefully avoiding his gaze. "I mean, after all, you're the one who created it."

He nods—nods in the way that you do when you're not just striving for patience but also trying to hide what you're thinking. And the truth is, I can't take it. I seriously can't stand it. I just want to go—*now*. Before this strange invader takes over completely.

"I *do* like it," he says, voice low, measured. "As you pointed out, I'm the one who made it. And while I'm glad you seem to really like it too—I'm also concerned."

I blow my hair out of my face and cross my arms before me, doing my best to broadcast my annoyance. I mean, it's not like I have a lot of time to waste here.

"Ever, I—"

He reaches toward me, but I quickly squirm out of his way. Yet another symptom of my awful addiction, and it's completely involuntary. The very reason I need to get out of this place.

He shakes his head and starts again, gaze deeply saddened when he says, "What's going on with you? You haven't been yourself for days. And just now, back at Miles's"—he glances over his shoulder as he quickly changes lanes—"well, I hate to say it, but the moment you saw Jude, well, let's just say there was a definite change in your energy, and then when Roman came into the room—" He swallows hard and clenches his jaw, taking a moment to pull it together before he says, "Ever, what's happened to you?"

I bow my head, aware of the sting at the back of my eyes as I try once again to tell him—but I can't—the magick won't let me. So instead, I turn to him and pick a fight, knowing the beast has no problem with that, and willing to do whatever it takes to convince him to follow me, to go away with me.

"This is *ridiculous!*" I say, instantly hating myself but left with no other choice. "Seriously. I can't believe you're saying this! In case you haven't noticed, my dream summer of lying on the beach with you doesn't seem like it's going to come to fruition anytime soon, so excuse me for wanting to grab the few moments I can to head off to Summerland!" I shake my head and look away, crossing my arms even tighter but mostly to hide the fact that they're shaking so badly I can barely control them. Knowing I'm being unfair, completely unreasonable, but if he'd just come with me, if I could just get him there, then I can explain everything.

Aware of the weight of his gaze on my face, the way he's taking in the newly dark circles just under my eyes, the fresh sprinkling of acne covering my chin, the way my clothes are starting to hang on me all droopy and loose, thanks to the weight that I've lost. Wondering what's brought this on, why I seem to be failing at just about everything. So genuinely concerned about me—it makes my heart ache.

And when he narrows his gaze even further, I know he's trying to reach me telepathically, to communicate in a way that's no longer an option—or at least not here anyways.

So I turn, turn toward the window, desperate to shield him from the horrible truth that I can no longer hear him. No longer have access to his thoughts, his energy, or even the tingle and heat his touch used to bring.

All of that's gone. Eradicated. The beast has taken it from me.

But only here. In Summerland I'll be rested, clear-skinned, just like the old me. And the two of us together will be everything we were ever meant to be.

"Just come with me," I plead, my voice hoarse and weak. "I can explain—but only there, not here. *Please?*"

He looks at me and sighs. Torn between wanting to please me and doing what he thinks best.

"No," he says in a way so unequivocal, so nonnegotiable, there's no mistaking what it means.

Not only is it a *no* to Summerland, it's a *no* to me. A *no* to the one and only thing that I need.

He shakes his head, face heavy with regret when he adds, "Ever, I'm sorry, really I am, but *no*. We're not going. I think it's better if we head home, back to my house, where we can sit down and have a nice long talk, get to the bottom of just what exactly is going on with you."

I sit beside him, hollow-eyed, zit-faced, twitchy and edgy, barely able to contain myself, barely holding it together as he makes a long verbal list of concerns. How I haven't been myself lately, how I don't even *look* like myself anymore, how much I've *changed* in every way, shape, and form—not one of these changes for the better.

But the truth is, the words sail right over me, like a vague and distant hum. I'm going to Summerland, with or without him, there's really no choice in the matter.

"Are you drinking your elixir? Do you need a new supply? Ever, *please,* talk to me—what's going on?"

I close my eyes and shake my head, blinking back the threat

of tears, unable to explain that I can't stop this runaway train. I'm no longer the conductor in charge of this thing.

He narrows his gaze, making one last attempt to reach me telepathically, but it's no use. I couldn't guess the message if I tried. My system is fried.

"You can't even hear me anymore, can you?"

He stops at a lighted crosswalk and reaches toward me again, but if nothing else I'm still light on my feet and quickly jump out of the car. My arms wrapped so tightly around me they're about to go numb. My fingers twitching, body thrumming, knowing if I don't get out of here quick, I'll have no choice but to go find him. *Roman.* No choice at all.

"Listen," I say, voice tremulous, completely unsteady, but knowing I need to get this settled either way, I'm down to the wire, I've no time to waste. "I'll explain when we get there—I swear. Just—it has to be there—*not* here. So—you coming or not?" I clench my jaw and grit my teeth, trying to keep them from chattering, keep my lips from trembling in a way he can't miss.

He swallows hard, brow slanted, eyes saddened, the word requiring a great deal of effort when he says, *"Not,"* so quietly I almost missed it. Then repeating it again when he adds, "I'd much rather stay here and get you some help."

I look at him, look at him for as long as I can stand, which, truth be told, isn't long at all. Wanting so badly to climb back into his nice warm car and hug him in the way that I used to, to feel his arms wrapped around me, to be soothed by his tingle and heat, and confess all my sins 'til they're washed away clean. But unfortunately that sentiment comes from the smallest part of me—the small glimmer of sanity that's quickly crushed by the part that prefers its fruit dirty, evil, and the more forbidden the better.

So, instead, I just nod, seeing his look of astonishment as I close my eyes and picture the portal—that glorious, shimmering portal. Stepping right through as I say, "Oh well, guess I'll go it alone then."

FOURTEEN

I land on my butt. Crash-land smack dab in front of the replica of that beautiful eighteenth-century palace where French royalty lived. But I don't go inside. Even though I begged to come to this very place, I can't bear to enter without Damen. It's *our* place. A place we share. A place where some of my fondest memories live. And there's no way I'll go there without him.

I get to my feet and brush myself off, glancing around as I try to get my bearings and determine my whereabouts. Knowing I could just imagine a destination and find myself magically there, but I'd rather walk, stroll at my leisure and take my sweet time. Enjoy the fact that I'm freed from the beast—even though it's probably just coiled up somewhere, just biding its time 'til I leave. But for now I'm determined to enjoy some relief.

I raise my hands before me, waving them through the shimmering mist, the hazy glow that originates from everywhere and nowhere. Soothed by the comfortably cool air that wafts over my skin, trusting I'll eventually end up some-where great—somewhere I really want to be. That's the beauty of Summerland—all roads lead to good.

Stopping to pause by the rainbow-colored stream that cuts through the vast fragrant field, I quickly manifest a small handheld mirror to check out my appearance. Relieved to see my eyes now returned to their normal bright blue, my hair back to a shining, lustrous shade of light golden blond, and my skin—my skin is virtually poreless and clear, while the circles that lived under my eyes are now gone. And I wish Damen could see me like this—looking like the old me—the me I used to be. Saddened to think his last memory is of that monstrous creation—the beast of my making. If he'd only agreed to come, I could've explained everything.

I wander through the field of shivering trees and pulsating flowers, the scent of those vibrant petals following me until I stumble upon the familiar paved road that leads into town and the Great Halls of Learning, where I decide to try my luck once again. And even though it was no help at all the last time I was there, it's a new day, a new, regenerated me, and I've got every reason to believe this time will be different.

I make my way past a collection of trendy boutiques, a movie theater, and a hair salon, crossing the street just in front of the art gallery, and passing a guy hawking candles, flowers, and small wooden toys, as I make my way through mobs of people all going about their business, an interesting mixture of the living and dead. Turning onto the empty alleyway that leads to the quiet boulevard that brings me to the steep swath of stairs I quickly scale. My gaze fixed on those impressive front doors, knowing there's still one more step that must be completed.

I stand before the Great Halls, taking in its elaborate carvings, imposing columns, and grand sloping roof—gazing upon a temple constructed purely of love, knowledge, and everything good. Anticipating the usual flicker of images, the Parthenon morphing into the Taj Mahal into the Lotus Temple into the great pyramids of Giza and so on—all the world's most beautiful and sacred places seamlessly blending, reshaping, and re-forming from one to the next—but it doesn't come. I don't see anything. Nothing but the impressive marble building that stands proud before me—the images required for entry, invisible to me.

I'm blacklisted.

Condemned.

Barred from entering the one and only place that can help me fix this mess that I'm in.

Even after I try to fake it, forcing myself to replay the images in the order I remember them, it won't budge. The Great Halls of Learning will not be fooled by the lowly likes of me.

I sink onto the steps and drop my head in my hands, hardly believing what I've become, just how low I've sunk. Wondering if this is what rock bottom feels like, surely being a Summerland reject is as bad as it gets.

"Scuse me!"

I scoot to the side and pull my legs in, wondering why Ms. Bossy Boots can't just move around me. I mean, seriously, I may be five eight, but it's not like I'm taking up all that much space.

My face still hidden by the palms of my hands, not wanting to be seen by some superior Summerland interloper who has access to all the greatest buildings, when:

"Wait—*Ever*?"

I freeze. I know that voice. Know it all too well.

"Ever—is that really *you*?"

I lift my head slowly, reluctant to meet Ava's gaze. The mere sight of her thick auburn hair and large brown eyes stirring something—something on the periphery that I can't quite grasp—can't quite make sense of. But it's not like it matters, because the truth is, she's pretty much the last person I wanted to see today, or any other day for that matter. But still, why here, why now, haven't I been punished enough?

"Trying to con your way in?" I ask, voice dripping with sarcasm as I harshly look her over. Realizing just after it's out that that's pretty much what I was just trying to do a few moments earlier, and horrified to realize that I've sunk so low I'm now equal with her.

She kneels down beside me, head tilted, regarding me closely when she says, "Are you okay?" Her gaze moving over me carefully, intently, almost as though she really does care.

But I know better. Ava only cares for one person—and that's Ava. As far as she's concerned, no one else is worth the bother. She proved that when she left Damen to die just after promising me she'd help him.

I look her over, surprised to see how she doesn't look so different than she did before she ran off with the elixir, but then again, she was starting from a pretty good place, so maybe she didn't require all that big a change.

"Am I *okay*?" I mimic, nailing her sugary-sweet, oh-so-concerned tone. Smirking when I add, "Well, I suppose I am. I suppose I'm just really and truly *okay*. All things considered anyway. Though I'm sure I'm not near as *okay* as you." I shrug. "But then again, who is?"

My eyes travel to her neck, in search of a telltale Ouroboros tattoo or some other sign of her new status as an immortal rogue. Surprised to see that not only is she free of all markings but also that her usual tangle of flashy, manifested jewelry has been pared down to a single, raw citrine hanging from a simple silver chain. Squinting as I struggle to recall what I've learned about that particular stone—something about it promoting abundance and joy and—oh yes, protecting all seven chakras—well, no wonder she's wearing it.

I press my lips together and heave an audible sigh, shooting her a look that leaves no room for doubt about just how I feel about her. "I mean, now that you've got the whole world at your feet—no one's doing better than *you,* right? So tell me, Ava, how does it *feel*? How does it *feel* to be the new, improved you? Was it worth *betraying* your friends for?"

She looks at me, eyes pulled down at the corners, concern clouding her face. "You've got it all wrong," she says. "It's not at all what you think!"

I rise to my feet, feeling shaky, off, but doing my best to hide it from her. Determined to leave her behind, unwilling to hear any more lies.

"I didn't take the elixir, Ever—I—"

I turn, eyes flashing with anger when I say, "You're *unbelievable*! Of course you took the elixir! Hel-*lo,* I came back. *See?*" I tug on my T-shirt and shake my head. "As it turns out, Ava, *nothing* went as we'd planned. No—correction, it may not have gone as *I* planned, but it certainly went as *you* planned. You left Damen alone, weak and defenseless, just as you'd planned all along. You left him just lying there, vulnerable, *dying,* right where Roman could get to him. And then, as if that wasn't enough, you paired up again that night with Haven, brewed a nice cup of belladonna tea for her to drink." I shake my head, wondering why I'm even bothering with this, bothering with her. She's taken enough from me already. I shouldn't give her any more.

I head down the stairs, legs heavy, leaden, as though they're reluctant to cooperate with the signals my brain clearly sends.

Struggling to place one foot before the other when she says, "I wish you wouldn't do that. I wish you'd give me a chance to explain."

But I just shrug it off and continue on my way, calling over my shoulder when I say, "Yeah, well, you can't always get what you want—you remember that song, right?"

She stands behind me, so quiet and still I can't help but glance over my shoulder to see what she's up to. My muscles tensed and poised just in case she's planning to attack, and surprised to find her with palms pressed together, bowing before me as her lips move in a whispered *"Namaste."*

Pausing briefly before turning toward the building, leaving me gaping, speechless, as those grand, imposing doors open before her and welcome her in.

FIFTEEN

"Hey."

I look up, surprised to see Jude standing before me, so engrossed in my work I didn't even hear him come in.

"How do you do that?" I squint, taking in his aura, now beaming a nice shade of blue.

"Do what?" He leans against the counter and looks me over.

"Always manage to sneak up on me like that?" My gaze rests on his black tee, curious to see who's being featured today. "What's that?" I motion toward it.

He closes his eyes and lifts his hands before him, attempting to draw his index fingers toward his thumbs but not getting very far before he gives up and chants, *"Ommmmmmm,"* the sound coming from deep within his diaphragm. Peeking at me when he adds, "It's the sound of existence—the sound of the universe."

I scrunch my nose, having no idea what he's getting at.

"The universe is made up of vibrating, pulsating energy, right?"

I nod. "So I've been told."

"Okay, so *Om* is thought to be the *sound* of that energy—that vast, cosmic energy. You've never heard that before? Don't you meditate?"

I shrug. I used to meditate. Used to cleanse my aura. Pretend roots were growing from the soles of my feet deep into the center of the earth and all sorts of feel-good nonsense like that. But not anymore. I mean, it's not like I have time to sit around observing my breath when my entire world is collapsing around me.

"You really should get back into it, you know. It really helps to balance and heal, not to mention how it—"

"And is it *healing* you?" I look pointedly at his arms, still debating whether or not to act on the idea I had the other night, adding up the pros and cons and still not coming any closer to a decision.

"Got a doctor appointment a bit later, so I guess we'll find out." He shrugs, eyes roving over me when he adds, "And speaking of—" Our gaze meets. "I was wondering if you could give me a lift. I could take the bus, but then I'll have to cut class a little short and I prefer not to do that, you know?"

"Class?" I look at him, drawing a blank.

"Yeah, you know, Psychic Development 101 with an emphasis on self-empowerment and Wicca—surely you remember?" He laughs.

I nod, rising from the stool, gladly giving it over to him. "How's that going, anyway?" I make my way around the counter so that he can take my place.

"Okay." He nods. "Your friend Honor seems to have a real knack for it."

I stop. Stop everything. He's got my full attention now. "Honor?"

He shrugs. "Yeah, you know. I thought you guys were friends?"

I shake my head, remembering what I observed on the last day of school, and the plans Honor has for a major Stacia coup. "We're classmates." I shrug, pressing against the wall and allowing him to pass. "Not really friends. Trust me, there's a difference."

He stops—stops when he should keep moving. Stops in a way that practically pins him against me. His eyes searching my face in a way that never fails to send an immediate flood of calm through my system—the first calm I've felt in— *days*. Not since before I left Summerland. After Summerland, all I could think about was Ava and how she managed to con her way in. And even though it only lasts a few seconds, even though he soon moves past me and onto the stool, the impact, the calming charge of his presence still lingers.

"She's either applying herself in a really big way or she's got a real knack for magick," he says, grabbing the box of receipts with two of his good fingers and awkwardly flipping through it. "Seems pretty single-minded though, so my guess is the former."

I squint, trying to recall what I know about Honor, but other than her position as Craig's girlfriend and Stacia's disgruntled BFF, it's not much.

I look at Jude, wondering if I should tell him that from what I saw that day when I peeked inside her head that Honor's intentions aren't all that—*honorable*. But it's not like Stacia's ever done me (or anyone else for that matter) any favors, so who am I to get involved?

"So, what time does class start?" I ask, deciding to stick to the practical as I make my way toward the back room.

"In an hour. Why?" He glances over his shoulder.

"I'll be in the back until you need me," I say, slinking into the office and shutting the door behind me. Retrieving *The Book* from its hiding place and slapping it onto the old wood desk. Taking a moment for a few deep, cleansing breaths before I hunch over it, tracing my fingers across the elaborate gold inscription on its front, debating whether or not I should do this.

The last time I visited this tome, things didn't go so well. And now that I know about Roman's connection to it—well, I'm no longer sure I can trust it. Because if he really is responsible for it ending up in my hands, then my reading it now would only make me (yet again!) a pawn in his plans. But then, if he does have influence over these pages, then maybe there's a clue buried somewhere, a clue as to how this game ends or how he plans to win.

Maybe, just like the akashic records in Summerland, it's all about asking the right kind of questions.

But while the akashic records permits only the worthy within its grand halls, *The Book of Shadows* only requires a code, followed by a coded question, preferably in rhyme.

So after softly chanting the rhyme Romy and Rayne taught me:

> *Within the world of magick—resides this very tome*
> *To which I am the chosen—returning to my home*
> *Within the realm of mystics—I shall now reside*
> *Allowed to glimpse upon this book—and see what lies inside.*

I sit there, feverishly trying to come up with a clever rhyming question to crack Roman's code—but my mind remains blank and *The Book* just sits there, its pages refusing to reveal anything new.

I sigh and lean back in my seat, swiveling from side to side as I take in the room, the various pictures and totems that line the walls, the myriad books piled onto the shelves, a room overflowing with so much potential, holding all the necessary ingredients for all manner of magical spells, and yet none of it inspires me, none of it offers any kind of help. And the truth is, there's no more time to waste. Summer is fading fast and I need to come up with a solution since there's no way I can keep avoiding Damen.

Damen.

I press my hands to my face, determined to keep the tears at bay. Forcing that salty sting back down my throat.

I haven't seen him since the day of Miles's party when I jumped out of his car and went to Summerland. Haven't answered his calls. Haven't answered the door. Have barely acknowledged the numerous bouquets of red tulips that now fill up my room. Knowing I don't deserve them—don't deserve him—until I can find a way to work this all out—find a way to ask for his help—or even find a way to ask Jude to ask him. But every time I start, the beast interferes—refusing to allow anything to come between Roman and me. And the truth is, I know I'm not just running out of time but running out of places to look. Jude's search has resulted in nothing, and everything I've tried so far has resulted in a complete and utter failure. And if last night is any indication, it's only getting worse.

I opened my eyes to a darkened room, the thick coastal

fog refusing even the vaguest sliver of moonlight to creep through. But still, I slipped out of bed and out of the house, my feet bare, clad only in a sheer cotton nightgown, with only one destination in mind. Drawn to Roman's house like a sleepwalker—like one of Dracula's overeager brides.

Moving quickly, effortlessly, through the quiet, empty streets, stopping just outside his window, as I crouched down low and peered through the gap in his blinds. Immediately sensing *her* presence, knowing she was in there—somewhere— enjoying the one thing that is meant to be mine.

My mind spinning, reeling, as my body ached with unsatisfied hunger and need. The beast raging inside me, urging me to stop thinking and get moving—just break down the door and eliminate her already. And I was just about to do it, just about to make a move, when she sensed me too. Storming toward the window with a gaze so hardened, so menacing, it was a brief slap of sanity—a reminder of who I am—who she is—and what we stand to lose if I allow the beast to win.

And before I had a chance to rethink it, I ran. All the way home and back to my bed, where I lay sweating, shaking, doing my best to quell the overwhelming need—to extinguish the dark flame inside me.

A flame that burns brighter, hotter, stronger each day.

A fire so insatiable it'll consume everything in its path— my small glimmer of sanity—my fragile connection to the future I want—and anything else that stands between Roman and me.

And just before I finally drifted off, I realized the worst part of all—by the time all that happens I'll be so far gone, I won't even realize my fall.

Jude enters the room and drops onto the seat—purposefully, meaningfully, clearly wanting to be seen.

"How'd it go?" I mumble, lifting my head from the desk where it's been resting for the last hour. My hands still shaking, legs still trembling, still fighting to suppress the overwhelming urge that's come to define me.

"I could ask you the same thing." He eyes me slowly. "Any progress?"

I shrug. Actually, I shrug *and* groan. Which, as far as I'm concerned, should be answer enough. Careful to keep my hands in my lap, out of his view, so he can't see them tremble.

"Still trying to crack the code?"

I glance at him briefly, then close my eyes and shake my head. I've given up on the book. As far as I'm concerned, it's only made things worse.

"I haven't been able to find anything either, but still. I'm happy to take another crack at it if you still want my help."

In a word—*yes*. I do want his help. I'll take all the help I can get. But with the beast now taking over, the words just won't come. My throat growing so hot and tight only silence will soothe it.

"Is it a rhyming thing?" he asks, refusing to let it go.

I shake my head, still unable to speak.

But he just shrugs, not the least bit daunted by my refusal to play. "I'm pretty good at chants if I do say so myself—pretty good at rapping too for that matter—wanna hear one?"

I close my eyes, wishing he'd move on.

"Wise decision." He smiles, oblivious to what I'm going

through. Pretending to wipe the imaginary sweat from his brow with his heavily bandaged hand, which only reminds me of that ride he asked me about.

I rise, expecting him to follow, but he just continues to sit there, staring at me in a way so intense, so insistent I can't help but croak, "What? What is it? Is Riley here?"

He shakes his head, swinging his dreadlocks off his shoulders and onto his back as those brilliant blue-green eyes pull down at the sides. "Haven't seen her in a while," he says, head tilted, gaze focused on mine. "I admit, I try from time to time, but I always come up empty." He shrugs. "I guess she just doesn't want to be reached right now."

I scrunch my brow, not sure I agree. Riley's sent me enough cryptic messages lately to make me highly doubt that, to make me feel like she *does* want to be reached.

"Do you think that maybe—" I pause, not wanting to sound ridiculous, but then deciding not to care. I've already looked plenty ridiculous in front of Jude, so what's one more time? "Do you think that maybe it's not that she doesn't want to come through but that she *can't* come through?" He looks at me, about to speak when I lift my finger and say, "And I don't mean *can't* as in not able or *can't find a way to manage it*, but more like, I don't know, like, maybe she's *not allowed* to come through? Maybe someone or something is stopping her?"

"Could be." He shrugs, his shoulders rising and falling so casually, so easily I'm not sure if he really does agree or if he's just humoring me. Wanting to spare my feelings from the cold, hard, unavoidable fact that my ghostly little sister has given up on me—that she's too busy with her afterlife activities to come out and play. "Has she shown up in any more dreams?" he adds, voice more than inquisitive, bordering on hopeful.

"No," I say, without a hint of hesitation, not wanting to think about that disturbing dream that I had where Damen was trapped behind glass and Riley stood off to the side, urging me to pay attention, to not look away.

"Wanna try to reach her now?" He looks at me, head cocked to the side.

But I just shake my head and sigh. I mean, sure I'd like to reach her—I'd like that very much. Who wouldn't want a visit from their adorably feisty, dead little sister? But when I think about the state that I'm in, there's no way I can do it. Even if she could help in some way, which I seriously doubt, but still, even if she could, I can't stand for her to see me like this. I don't want her to know what I've done. What I've become.

"I'm—I'm not really up for all that right now," I say, clearing my throat.

Jude leans back in his chair, foot propped on his knee, gaze unrelenting, never once straying from mine. "What exactly *are* you up for?" he asks, forehead scrunched as though he's truly concerned. "All you seem to do these days is work." He drops his foot on the floor and leans toward me, anchoring his bandaged arms on the desk when he adds, "Do you even realize it's summer out there? *Summer in Laguna Beach!* Half the population dreams of a sweet gig like that and you've barely taken notice. Believe me, if I weren't so banged up, I'd be out there surfing and enjoying every spare moment I could get. Not to mention, and correct me if I'm wrong, but isn't this your first summer here?"

I take a deep breath, remembering how last summer found me injured, hospitalized, newly orphaned, and burdened with psychic powers I couldn't bear, naively thinking that's as bad and weird as things could ever possibly get. Hardly able to believe it's already been a year since my entire life changed.

"I can handle the store. Hell, I can even get myself to the doctor, who cares if I'm late? But please, do yourself a favor and take a break. There's a whole world out there just waiting to be explored and with all the time you spend here indoors—well, it's not healthy."

I stand before him, a mess of shaking hands, trembling body, and ragged breath—a walking billboard for unhealthy living, desperately scoping the room for the first available exit.

"Ever? You okay?" He leans toward me.

I shake my head, unable to answer, unable to speak. Roman is out there. I can *feel* him drawing near. Having just left the store and wandering the village streets, headed right in my vicinity. And I know it's just a matter of time, maybe another minute, two at the most, and the old me will be gone, completely succumbed to the monster within.

I grip the edge of the desk, knuckles protruding, bony and white, fighting to steady myself, horrified at being seen like this, and needing to get away before it's too late—

Slipping around the desk so quickly I'm at Jude's side well before he can blink. My fingers clutching the graying white plaster that circles his arm, having no choice but to say, "If you want me to take you, we need to go now—it can't wait!"

He struggles to stand, a worried expression marring his face as he looks me over and says, "Ever, no offense, but I'm not sure I want to get in the car with you. You seem a little—*unhinged*—to say the least." He rubs his lips together and shakes his head, leveling those sea-green eyes right on mine in an attempt to connect, but it's no use. I'm lost, drowning, almost gone— "Seriously, I think you should step outside, get some fresh air, and take some deep breaths—*really,* you'll be amazed how much better you'll feel."

And as nice as that sounds, as well-meaning as he is, I know better. Outside is the last place I should be. That's where Roman is, drawing closer, closer by the second. Besides, that wasn't exactly what I meant when I said *we should go.* And even though I haven't really stopped to think it through, haven't really considered the full list of pros and cons since I first got the idea a few days ago, there's no time to waste, we're going, the two of us, because no matter what happens there, staying here will be worse.

With my heart crashing, my pulse thrumming, and Roman drawing insistently near—I grip Jude's cast tighter, hoping against hope I can still pull this off now that everything else has failed me.

Hoping I can still reach the one and only place where I'm still me.

Taking in his alarmed, perplexed gaze and knowing if I don't do this quick, it'll be too late for me.

Too late for all of us.

I'll be with Roman.

The dark magick will win.

Voice shaky and unsteady as I say, "I know this sounds crazy, but I need you to close your eyes and imagine a portal of shimmering gold light right before you. Concentrate with all your might, and don't ask any questions. Just trust me on this."

SIXTEEN

We stumble through the portal, the two of us, side by side, landing on that wonderfully buoyant grass before springing lightly to our feet. And the first thing I do is turn toward Jude, motioning to his arms when I say, "Look!"

He gazes down, eyes going wide as he glances between his bare arms and me, not quite comprehending.

"Surely during the course of your metaphysical studies you came across a mention of Summerland?" I smile, my face and shoulders lifting—*everything* lifting—freed from the monster within me—no matter how temporary.

He glances around, peering through the hazy, shimmering mist at the shivering trees, branches hanging heavy with ripe juicy fruit, the large colorful flowers with pulsating petals, and the quickly flowing rainbow-colored stream just beyond. "This is it?" he asks, face stamped with awe. "It really exists?"

I nod, any apprehension I had at bringing him here suddenly gone. Just because it was a bad idea to drag Ava along, doesn't mean the same thing will happen with Jude. They're totally different. *He's* different. Way more evolved than Ava could ever hope to be.

"Why did I bring you here?" I laugh, instantly reading the question he posed but hadn't yet voiced. Sending the answer telepathically when I think: *In order to heal you, of course!*

Careful to edit the other, more pressing reason, which is so that I could heal myself.

Thoughts are energy, I add, seeing the surprised look on his face. *You can sense them, hear them, even create with them. But if you'd rather we return to the hospital, then I'll be happy to make the portal again—*

He looks at me, about to speak when he changes his mind and thinks it instead. At first closing his eyes as though trying to concentrate, but soon realizing just how effortless and easy everything is, he looks right at me and allows the words to flow straight to my head:

I can't believe you waited this long to bring me here. I can't believe you let me suffer like that!

I laugh, nodding in agreement and knowing the best way to make up for it is to show him just what else is possible here.

"Close your eyes," I say, watching as he obeys without hesitation, his trust in me so complete, I can't help but flush. "Now think of anything you want—anything at all—and make sure you really do want it, because in an instant, it'll be yours—ready?

And I've barely had a chance to finish before I'm sitting on a pink sand beach, watching as he paddles out in an ocean comprised of the most beautiful blue water and surfing a series of the most perfect waves.

"Did you see those barrels?" he calls, board tucked under his arm as he makes his way in. "Amazing! You sure I'm not dreaming?"

I smile, remembering my first trip to Summerland and how enchanted I was. And no matter how many times I return, the magick of manifesting on such a grand scale never gets old. "It's no dream." I smile, seeing the way his dreads drip trails of salt water clear down his chest and into the low-slung waistband of his black and gray board shorts. Suddenly overcome by that calm languid feeling his proximity brings, and quickly averting my gaze when I say, "Trust me, it's much better than a dream." Thinking how lately, most of my dreams have become nightmares.

So, what's next? He drops his board on the sand and looks at me.

I shrug. *It's your moment, so it's really up to you. Whatever you want to try next is fine by me.* Trying to appear helpful, supportive, when the truth is, the longer he stays, the longer I have an excuse to avoid the earth plane where all of my troubles lay in wait.

He takes a deep breath and closes his eyes, making the board and the beach disappear in favor of the Indy 500 race-track. Navigating the course at near death-defying speeds as I sit high in the stands, egging him on. And just when I'm sure I can't take another monotonous lap, he switches the scene to a charming café in the Sydney harbor, with a first-class view of the bridge, the water, and the opera house beyond.

Raising his glass to mine as I say, "I didn't peg you as the Indy type."

He shrugs. "I'm not. But hey, you gotta try it while you can, right?"

I take a sip of my soda, grimacing at its sweet flavor, having grown to prefer the bitterness of the elixir. Watching as the view suddenly changes from the glistening Australian waters to one of windmills, tulips, and canals—a view that could mean only one thing.

"*Amsterdam?*" The word quivers in my throat, reminding me of our shared history, back when he was Bastiaan de Kool and I was his muse. And I can't help but wonder if he somehow senses it too. Like now that we're here, those long-ago memories are somehow restored, even though it's never worked that way for me.

He shrugs, surprised by my reaction when he says, "I've never been. I thought it would be cool. But if you'd rather I make something else—"

And before I can object, tell him to enjoy the fantasy for as long as he likes, I'm sitting in a gondola in Venice, dressed in an elaborate pink-and-cream-colored gown, a tangle of jewels at my neck. Lounging against a pile of red velvet cushions as I gaze upon the magnificent buildings lining our route, stealing the occasional glance at Jude, now dressed in the black pants, striped shirt, and straw hat of a traditional Venetian gondolier, watching as he steers us through the calm and still waters.

"Hey, you're pretty good at this." I laugh, determined to move past my Holland freakout a moment ago and onto where we are now. Closing my eyes to add just the slightest touch of a breeze—a breeze that sends his hat scattering straight into the water.

"This feels so natural," he says, instantly manifesting a new hat onto his head without missing a beat. "I must've been one of these guys in a past life—one who left some unfinished business behind." He stops rowing and leans on his oar. "I mean, if we truly are born to correct the mistakes of our past and move toward enlightenment, then maybe, once, a very long time ago, I was steering a beautiful fair maiden such as yourself and got so distracted by her beauty and charm I tipped this thing over and drowned."

"Who drowned?" I ask, voice edgy, far more serious than I intended.

"Me." He sighs dramatically, laughing as he adds, "What else is new? The maiden, as it turns out, was swiftly rescued by a tall, dark, and handsome young nobleman of great position and wealth, who, as these things so often go, just happened to possess a much bigger boat. And after quickly pulling her aboard, he warmed her up and dried her off, hell, he probably even resuscitated her with perfectly performed mouth-to-mouth, after which he showered her with not just his undivided attention but a succession of gifts, one more impressive than the next, until she finally stopped playing hard to get and agreed to marry him. And you know how it ends, right?"

I shake my head, throat hot and tight, unable to speak. Well aware that in his conscious mind, he's creating a harmless fairy tale, but unable to shake the feeling that this particular tale just might go a whole lot deeper than he thinks.

"Well, the two of them enjoyed a long, luxurious, and deliriously happy life—until they both died of old age and reincarnated so they can have the pleasure of finding each other and doing it all over again."

"And the gondolier? What happened to him—*you*?" I ask, unsure if I really want to hear. "I mean surely there's a reward for bringing two soul mates together?"

He shrugs, averting his gaze, back to rowing again. "The gondolier is destined to repeat the same pathetic scene over and over again, always pining after what is clearly meant for someone else. Same script, different time and place. Story of my life—or *lives* as the case may be."

And even though he laughs, it's not an invitation for me to join in. It's solitary, uninviting, too burdened with truth to leave any room for humor. His little story veering so unbelievably close to the truth of him and me, I can't even speak.

My gaze travels over him, wondering if I should tell him—about me—about us—but what good would it do? Maybe Damen was right when he said we're not meant to remember our past lives, that life is not meant to be an open-book test. We all have our own karma, our own obstacles to overcome, and apparently, like it or not, maybe I'm one of Jude's.

I clear my throat, deciding to put an end to all this and get to the third reason we came here. The one I hadn't really thought about until now. Hoping it'll benefit both of us, and praying I'm not making yet another colossal mistake when I say, "What do you say we ditch this place? There's something else I want you to see."

"Someplace better than this?" He yanks the oar out of the water and waves it around.

I nod, shutting my eyes briefly and quickly returning us to the vast fragrant field, where Jude's returned to his normal outfit of faded jeans, *Om* symbol tee, and the flip-flops he started in, and I ditch my elaborate, corseted gown in favor of cutoffs, a tank top, and sandals, before leading him along the stream, over to the road, down the alleyway, and onto the boulevard where the Great Halls of Learning can be found.

Turning to him as I say, "I have a confession to make."

He looks at me, spliced brow raised expectantly.

"I—I didn't bring you here just to cure you." He stops, looking at me in a way that makes me stop too. Taking a deep breath, knowing this is my chance, the only place I'll ever be able to say it, I square my shoulders, lift my chin, and say, "I actually need you to do something—something for me."

"O-*kay* . . ." He squints, his eyes kind, patient, waiting for me to get to it.

"You see—the thing is—" I twist my crystal horseshoe bracelet around and around, hardly able to look him in the eye. "Well, lately, that magick I told you about—the spell— it's gotten worse. It's like, everything's fine when I'm here, but back on the earth plane—I'm pretty much a wreck. It's like a disease. I'm consumed with thoughts of Roman, and in case you haven't noticed it's like my outer state is starting to reflect my inner state. I'm losing weight, losing sleep, and there's no getting around it—back home, on the earth plane, I look like crap. But every time I try to confide in Damen or ask him for help—heck, even when I try to ask you to ask him to help—it's like the spell takes over—the dark magick—or the beast as I've come to think of it—won't let me speak. It's like it doesn't want anything to come between Roman and me. But here in Summerland, it can't stop me. It's the only place where I'm my usual self again. And so, I thought that maybe by bringing you here, you could—"

"So why don't you just bring Damen to Summerland then? I don't get it." He cocks his head to the side and takes me in.

"Because he won't come." I sigh, gazing down at my feet. "He knows something's wrong, knows something's up with me, but he thinks it's because I'm addicted to this place or—or something like that. Anyway, he refuses to join me, and since

I'm unable to tell him the truth, he's standing firm, refuses to budge. And because of it, well, let's just say it's been way too long since I've even seen him." I swallow hard, wincing at the way my voice just cracked.

"And so—where do I come in?" He looks at me. "You want me to buzz back to the earth plane so I can tell Damen?"

"No," I say, shoulders lifting when I add, "Or at least not yet. First I'm going to take you somewhere, and if you're able to get inside—" I look at him, hoping against hope that he can. "Then I want you to seek help on my behalf—find a solution to my problem. And I know it sounds crazy, but trust me when I say that all you have to do is *desire* the answer and it'll come. I'd do it myself if I could—but I'm—I'm—no longer welcome in there."

He looks me over and nods, back to walking alongside me when he says, "So where is this place?" His expression transforming to one of awe as he follows the tip of my pointing finger all the way to that beautiful, grand old building, whispering, "So it *is* true!" His eyes lighting up as he takes the steep marble stairs in a handful of leaps.

Leaving me to stand there, jaw dropped to my knees, as both doors spring open and sweep him inside before I can blink.

The same two doors that slam closed on me.

I slump onto the steps, locked out again. Wondering just how long I'll be forced to wait it out 'til he's done doing—well, whatever it is he plans to do in there. Knowing it could be a very long time since, for a newbie especially, the Great Halls of Learning are just too good to resist.

I jump to my feet and brush myself off, refusing to sit outside like the loser I am, deciding to look around a little, maybe do some exploring. I'm always so single-minded when I come here, I rarely, if ever, take the time to just wander.

Knowing I can travel by whatever method I choose— subway, Vespa, heck, even astride a great painted elephant since there's really no limit to what you can do here—I choose to go on horseback instead. Re-creating a mount similar to one I first rode with Damen, back when he lured me here for the very first time, only this one's a mare.

I hop onto her back and settle into the saddle, running my hand over her silky, soft mane and down the side of her neck. Cooing softly into her ear as I give a gentle nudge in her gut and we set out on a leisurely walk with no real destination in mind. Remembering what the twins once told me about Summerland, that it's built of desires. That in order to *see* something, *do* something, *have* something, *experience* something, or *visit* something, you must first desire it.

I stop my mount briefly and shut my eyes, attempting to *desire* the answers I seek.

But, as it turns out, Summerland is smarter than that, so nothing really happens other than the fact that my horse grows bored and lets me know it by snorting, grunting, whisking her tail, and stomping the ground with her hooves. So I take a deep breath and try something else, thinking out of everything here, out of all the movie theaters, the galleries, the beauty salons, the great and wonderful buildings, what's the one thing I haven't yet seen that I should?

What's the one place I really need to know about?

And before I know it, my horse takes off at full gallop— mane flying, tail swishing, ears tucked back tightly, as I grip the reins and hang on for dear life. The scenery blurring and whirring right past me as I duck down low and squint against the gale. Covering a great distance of unfamiliar land in a matter of seconds, until my horse stops so suddenly, so unexpectedly, I vault right over her head and into the mud.

She whinnies loudly, rearing up on her hind legs before slamming back down on all fours, grunting and snorting and backing up slowly, as I struggle to my feet, slowly, carefully, not wanting to do anything sudden that might spook her even more.

More used to dealing with dogs than horses, I lower my voice, keeping it firm and steady as I point my finger and say, "Stay."

She looks at me, ears pinned back, clearly not liking my plan.

I swallow hard, swallow my fear, when I add, "Don't go. Stay right where you are."

Knowing she may not be much help if I was threatened in any real way, but still reluctant to be alone in this dank, creepy place.

I gaze down at my shorts, now covered with mud, and even after I close my eyes and try to replace them, try to clean myself up, I remain exactly the same. Instant manifestation doesn't work in these parts.

I take a deep breath and fight to steady myself, as eager to leave as my horse, but knowing I was sent here for a reason, that there's something I'm meant to see, I resolve to stay just a little bit longer. Squinting at the scenery before me, and noticing that instead of the usual, soft, golden radiance, the sky in these parts is all murky and gray. Instead of the shimmering mist that I'm used to, there's a steady downpour that leaves the ground so muddy and wet it seems it never lets up, but if the barren plants and trees are any indication, appearing so cracked and dry it's as though they haven't been watered for years, it's not exactly a nourishing rain.

I take a step forward, determined to decipher the message, learn why I'm here, but when my foot sinks so deep the mud swallows me up to my knees, I decide to let my horse take the lead. But no matter what I coo in her ear, what commands I give, she refuses to explore any further. She has one destination in mind and that's back to where we came from, so I finally give up and give her full rein.

Glancing over my shoulder as we leave and remembering what the twins once said:

"Summerland contains the possibility of all things."

And wondering if I somehow stumbled upon its other side.

SEVENTEEN

"What happened to you?"

I squint, having no idea what he's referring to until I follow his pointing finger all the way down to my mud-splattered legs and the flip-flops that used to be a cute, metallic gold but are now so crusted with dirt they're more like a bleach-tinged brown instead.

I frown, instantly swapping them out for a nice, new, clean version of the exact same thing, glad to know I'm back to the magical section of Summerland, which is far more preferable to the no-man's-land I visited earlier. Taking a moment to shrug on the soft lilac cardigan I also just manifested, wrapping it tightly around me as I say, "I got tired of waiting. I didn't know how long you'd be, so I went on a little—uh— field trip." I lift my shoulders like it was no big deal, like it was just your everyday, garden variety, late afternoon stroll— when the truth is with that weird, relentless rain, those barren trees, my horse's determination to get the heck out of there, it was anything but. But Jude already has enough to process without my adding a confusing new territory to the mix and I'm eager to find out what he's seen.

"But even more important than what happened to me is what happened to *you*?" I look him over from the top of his golden brown dreadlocks to the rubber soles of his flip-flops, noticing how on the outside he's pretty much the same as I left him, but inside, something has definitely changed. There's a shift in his energy, his demeanor. On the one hand, he seems lighter, brighter, brimming with confidence, yet he also seems distinctly edgy for someone who just visited one of the greatest wonders in all of the universe.

"Well—it was—*interesting*." He nods, his gaze meeting mine, but only for a moment before he quickly turns away.

And I can't believe he thinks he can get away with that. I mean, I think I deserve a little more after having brought him all the way here.

"Um, care to elaborate?" I arc my brow. "Exactly *how* was it interesting? What did you see, hear, learn? What did you do from the moment you entered to the moment you left? Did you get the answers I need?" Knowing I'm seconds away from peering into his mind to see for myself if he doesn't spill soon.

He takes a deep breath and turns, moving several paces away until he finally meets my gaze and says, "I'm not sure I really want to get into it just yet—it's a lot to process—I still need to make sense of it. It's all a bit—*complicated*—"

I squint, determined to see for myself. There are very few secrets in Summerland, especially for a newbie like him who doesn't have the first clue as to how it all works, but the second I run up against that solid brick wall, I know just where he's been.

The akashic records.

Remembering how Romy once said: *Not all thoughts can be read, only the ones you're permitted to see. Whatever you see in the akashic records is yours and yours to keep.*

I narrow my gaze, needing to know now more than ever, moving toward him, just about to push a bit further when I feel it—that swarm of warmth, of tingle and heat his mere presence brings. Turning to find Damen, making his way down those steep marble steps, until he stops—everything stops—and our eyes meet.

And I'm just about to call out to him—urge him to join me, knowing now's my chance to explain everything, when I see what he sees—me and Jude together, enjoying a nice trip to Summerland—Damen's and my special place. And before I can do anything, say anything—he's gone. Just blinked out of existence as though he was never really there.

Except he was.

His energy lingers. I can still feel him on my skin.

And one glance at Jude is all it takes to confirm it. Seeing the way his eyes go wide, the way his lips part—the way he reaches toward me, wanting to comfort, but I pull away quickly. Sickened by what Damen must think—how we must've appeared to his eyes.

"You should go," I say, my back turned toward him, my voice crisp and tight. "Just close your eyes, make the portal, and go. *Please.*"

"Ever—" he says, reaching for me again, but I'm already gone, moving on to some other place.

EIGHTEEN

I walk. Walk until I've no idea how far I've gone. Walk until I'm sure Damen can no longer see me. Determined to outwalk my problems but not getting very far, finally understanding that old adage on the coffee mug my eighth-grade English teacher used to have: WHEREVER YOU GO—THERE YOU ARE.

You can't outwalk your problems. Can never run fast enough to evade them completely. This is my journey, and there's just no escaping it.

And even though Summerland provides such sweet, glorious release—its effect is only temporary at best. No matter how long I manage to stay here, I'm pretty sure things will do a one-eighty the second I return to the earth plane.

I wander farther, trying to decide between stopping by the theater to catch an old movie, or maybe even heading over to Paris to take a nice relaxing stroll along the River Seine, or even a quick hike through the ruins of Machu Picchu, or a run through the Roman Coliseum, when I come across a smattering of cottages that brings me to a halt.

The outside is plain, modest, consisting of wood shingles, small windows, and pointy, triangular roofs—but even though there's seemingly nothing special about any of them, there's one in particular that beckons to me, glowing in a way that lures me down the narrow dirt path until I'm standing just outside the door. Having no idea why I'm here but still debating whether or not I should try to go in.

"Ain't seen 'em round these parts fer weeks."

I turn to find an old man poised at the edge of the path, dressed conservatively in white shirt, black sweater, and black pants, a few wispy gray hairs brushed sideways over his shiny bald scalp, leaning on an elaborately carved cane that seems to testify more to his love of its craftsmanship than any real physical need.

I squint, unsure what to say. I don't even know why I'm here, much less whom he's referring to.

"Them two girls—the dark-haired ones. Twins they were. Could barely tell 'em apart meself—though the missus had 'em down. The nice one—she liked chocolate, and lots of it." He chuckles, smiling at the memory. "And the other one—the quiet, stubborn one—she preferred popcorn, couldn't get enough of it. But only the stove-popped kind, none of that instant manifested stuff." He nods, looking at me, really taking me in, not the least bit shocked by my modern dress in these parts. "The missus she indulged 'em, she did. Felt sorry for 'em, worried about 'em a good bit too, I'd say. Then, after all that, after all these years, they just up and leave with nary a word." He shakes his head again, but this time he doesn't laugh or smile, just gives me a bewildered look, as though hoping I can help him make sense of it.

I swallow hard, my gaze darting between the front door

and him, pulse quickening, heart racing, knowing without asking, knowing deep down inside that this is where they stayed—this is where Romy and Rayne lived for the last three hundred and some-odd years.

But still needing a verbal confirmation, just to make sure, I say, "Did—did you say the *twins?*" My mind reeling, as I take in the plain familiar cottage, an exact replica of the one I saw in the vision the day I first found them squatting at Ava's when I grabbed Romy's arm and watched their entire life story unfold—all of it racing toward me in a jumble of pictures—this house—their aunt—the Salem Witch Trials she was determined to shield them from—and it all led to *this.*

"Romy and Rayne." He nods, looking me over with cheeks so red, a nose so bulbous, and eyes so kind he seems almost manifested, fake, a lifelike replica of the quintessential jolly old Englishman on his way home from the pub. But since he doesn't waver or fade in and out, since he remains right there before me with that same friendly grin on his face, I know he's for real. Maybe living, maybe dead—can't be too sure about that, but definitely, positively, the real deal. "Them's the ones you's looking for, yes?"

I nod, even though I'm not sure. *Was I looking for them? Is that why I'm here?* I glance at him, wincing when he gives me a look so odd I can't help but let out a nervous giggle. Clearing my throat and attempting to pull it together when I add, "I'm just sorry to hear they're not around, I was hoping I could catch them."

He nods, nods as though he completely understands and sympathizes with my predicament. Leaning with both hands on his cane as he says, "The missus and me grew quite fond of 'em, seeing as we all arrived around the same time. What we can't decide is if they finally decided to cross the bridge and be done with it, or if they's made the trip back. What do you think?"

I press my lips together and shrug, not wanting to let on that I already know the answer to that one, and relieved when he doesn't press further, just nods and shrugs too.

"Missus swears they crossed the bridge, said the little 'uns got tired of waiting for whomever's they's waiting for. But I say different. Rayne might've gone, but she'd never convince that sister of hers, that Romy—she's a stubborn one all right."

I squint, sure I misunderstood, shaking my head as I say, "Wait—you mean *Rayne's* the stubborn one, right? Romy's the kinder, gentler one."

I nod, expecting him to nod too, but he just gives me that same odd look and digs his cane deeper into the dirt. "Meant what I said, I did. Well, good day to you, miss."

I stand there, watching him walk away, head up, spine straight, cane swinging happily, hardly believing he's chosen to leave it like that and wondering if my question somehow offended him.

I mean, he *is* kind of old, and the twins *do* look exactly alike, or at least they did when they lived here and wore those private-school uniforms every day, and I can only imagine how they dressed before Riley got ahold of them. But something about the way he said it, so sure, so confident, I can't help but wonder if I've got it all wrong. Or if that mean, bratty, resentful side of Rayne is reserved just for me.

Hoping he can hear me before he gets too far away, I call, "Sir—um, excuse me—but do you think it's okay if I go in and take a look? I promise I won't disturb anything."

He turns, waving his cane jauntily as he says, "Help yourself. Ain't nothin' 'ere that can't be replaced."

He turns, continuing on his way as I push the door inward and step inside, my foot meeting a simple, red, braided rug that softens the creak of my weight on the old wooden floor. Pausing long enough for my eyes to adjust to the dim light as I peer into a large square room dotted with a few uncomfortable-looking, straight-backed chairs, a medium-sized table, and a large wooden rocker beside a stone hearth full of ashes from a fire that was recently burned. Knowing I've just walked into an exact replica of the world Romy and Rayne both fled in 1692 only to re-create it right here—minus the hypocrisy, lies, and unabashed cruelty of course.

I make my way through the room, gazing up at the heavy wood beams lining the ceiling as my fingers trail along the plain, rough walls, the tables piled high with leather-bound books, along with an assortment of candles and oil lamps used to provide reading light. Unable to shake this sneaky, guilty feeling that I'm prying into something, peering into a private life I'm not sure I should see.

But, at the same time, I know it's no accident that I'm here, I was meant to find this, of that I've no doubt. Because if nothing else, I know enough about Summerland to know that events are not at all random. Somewhere in these walls is something I'm meant to see. And as I wander into a small, plain bedroom I immediately recognize it as a replica of the bedroom of the aunt who raised them—the one who urged them to hide out here in Summerland in order to spare them from the Salem Witch Trials—the ultimate source of her own gruesome demise. The bed is narrow, uncomfortable-looking, offset by a small, square table holding a large leather-bound book and some dried flowers and herbs resting on top. And other than another braided rug and a tall, slim wardrobe in the corner, its door cracked just enough to glimpse the brown cotton dress hanging inside, the rest of the room is left bare.

And I can't help but wonder if Romy and Rayne ever manifested her into existence like I once did with Damen. Can't help but wonder just how long they fought to hold on to their life as they knew it before finally giving up, and settling for this—an imitation of what was.

I close the door behind me and head for the short ladder that leads to the loft, ducking my head against the dramatically sloped ceiling and wincing as the wood groans loudly under my feet. Quickly moving to an area where the ceiling rises higher, I straighten up and take in the narrow twin beds, and the small wooden table between them holding a pile of books and a well-used oil lamp—pretty much the same setup as their aunt's—except for the walls that are littered with new millennium, pop-culture references that could only be the result of Riley's influence. Every square inch of space covered with a collage of Riley's favorites, who, knowing Riley, the twins had no choice but to pledge their allegiance to.

My eyes dart around the room, surrounded by the happy, shiny faces of former Disney stars turned teenaged tycoons, a lineup of *American Idols,* and just about anyone else who once graced the cover of *Teen Beat* magazine. And when I see the piece of notebook paper tacked to the door, I can't help but laugh, knowing this class schedule, this roster of their manifested boarding school events, could come from no one other than my ghostly little sister.

1st period—Fashion for Beginners: Do's & Don'ts & Mustn't Evers

2nd period—Hair 101: Basic styling techniques, a prerequisite to Hair 102

Break—10 minutes: To be used for gossip & grooming

3rd period—Celebrity Basics: Who's hot, who's not, and who's not at all what they want you to think

4th period—Popularity: A comprehensive course on how to get it & keep it without losing yourself in the process

Lunch—30 minutes: To be used for gossiping, grooming, and eating if you must

5th period—Kiss & Makeup: Everything you ever wanted to know about lip gloss but were afraid to ask

6th period—Kissing 101: What's ick, what's sick, and what makes him tick

A full roster of Riley's usual obsessions, the last of which I'm sure she never got a chance to experiment with.

And just as I'm about to leave, sure there's nothing more to see, I spot a beautiful, round jeweled frame, perched up high on the armoire, and I rise up on my toes to get it. Knowing it can't belong to Romy and Rayne since photography wasn't even invented until long after they left Salem, and gasping audibly when I take it all in, my eyes sweeping over a picture of *us*.

Me, Riley, and our sweet yellow Lab, Buttercup.

The mere sight of it eliciting a memory so clear, so palpable, it slams like a punch in the gut. Forcing me down to my knees and onto the floor, paying little notice of the rough wood scratching my skin, paying no mind to the tears that stream down my cheeks and onto the glass, leaving it streaky, blurry, but I'm no longer looking at the picture, I'm watching the event in my head. Replaying the moment when Riley and I leaned all over each other, smiling and laughing, and hamming it up as Buttercup barked excitedly and ran circles around us.

All of it just moments before the accident.

The very last photo ever taken of us.

A photo I'd forgotten about since Riley died long before she ever got a chance to download it.

I gaze around the room, my vision blurred by tears, my voice tentative, squeaky, as I call, "*Riley?* Riley—are you—*watching this?*" Wondering if she's here, if she set this whole thing up, if she's off in a corner somewhere, observing me.

Using the hem of my sweater to wipe first my face, then the glass, knowing that even though she fails to respond, even though I can no longer access her, this is her doing. She re-created this picture. Wanted me to have yet another reminder of what we once shared and who I once was, just one year before.

And even though I'm tempted to try to take it back to Laguna, I leave it right where I found it instead. It's a Summerland thing. It'll never survive the return trip home. Besides, for some strange reason, I like knowing it's here.

I make my way down the ladder and back through the great room, sure I've seen all I was meant to and preparing to leave. Almost at the front door when I notice a painting I missed on my way in. Its frame simple, black, crudely crafted from a few strips of painted wood. But it's the subject that grabs my interest, a finely honed portrait of an attractive yet somewhat plain woman—or at least by today's standards anyway. Her skin is pale, her lips are thin, and her dark brown hair is scraped severely off her face, pulled back into what was probably a tightly coiled bun. But no matter how serious the pose, no matter how stern the expression, there's something much lighter shining in her eyes, as though she's merely playing the part of a proper, subdued woman of her time, posing this way for propriety's sake, while inside lurked a fire few people would've guessed at.

And the longer I stare into those eyes—the more sure I am. Even though I try to talk myself out of it, convince myself it's not possible, not in the most remote way—that subliminal hint that's been edging at me, persisting off and on for the last several weeks, has now manifested before me, in a way so clear, so startling, it can't be ignored.

My whispered gasp, echoing through the room but heard only by me, as I flee out the door and back to the earth plane.

Eager to get away from the face looming before me—away from a past that has just, remarkably, come full circle again.

NINETEEN

I don't even think about it. Don't even stop to think twice. I just make the portal, land back in the earth plane, and head for Damen's.

But then, just as I'm pulling up to his gate, I think better.

The twins will be there.

The twins are *always* there.

And this is definitely something that shouldn't be discussed in their presence.

But since the gates are already in motion and Sheila is happily waving me in, I drive right through and head for the park instead. Parking my car at the curb and heading straight for the swings, I settle onto the small bucket seat and propel myself forward with such force, I actually wonder if I'll loop all the way around before coming back down. But I don't, I just sway back and forth, enjoying the rush of wind on my cheeks as I fly ever higher, and the slight dip in my belly when I come crashing back down. Closing my eyes and calling Damen to me—using whatever powers I still have before the monster can awaken and begin its favorite pastime of sabotaging me. Adding up the seconds, and not even getting to ten before he's standing before me.

The air has changed, ignited by his presence, his gaze sending a delicious warm tingle over my skin. And when I open my eyes to meet his—it's like the first time we met in the parking lot at school—mesmerizing, magical, a moment of complete and total surrender. The sun at his back, enveloping him in a blaze of bold orange, golds, and reds so brilliant, it's as though they're emanating from him. And I hold on to the moment, hold it for as long as I can. All too aware that it's just a matter of time before it dulls and I become numb to him again.

He takes the swing alongside me, gliding high into the sky and instantly matching my pace. The two of us swooping to such deliriously, wonderful heights, only to plummet right back down again—an analogy of our relationship for the last four hundred years.

But when he gazes at me with an expectant look on his face, I know I'm about to disappoint him. I'm not here for the reason he thinks.

I take a deep breath, speaking past the lump in my throat when I say, "Listen." I turn toward him. "I know things are kind of—*strained*—" I pause, knowing that hardly describes it but continuing anyway. "But, well, after you left, I came across something so extraordinary, I rushed here to tell you. And if we can just push all this other stuff aside, at least for now, I think you're gonna want to hear this."

He cocks his head and drinks me in, his gaze so deep, dark, and intense it halts the words right in my throat.

Forcing me to gaze down at the ground, marking a series

of small circles into the dirt with my toe, pushing the words from my lips when I say, "I know this'll probably sound crazy, so crazy you probably won't even believe it at first—but I'm telling you—no matter how far-fetched it may seem, it's totally and completely real, I saw it for myself." I pause, sneaking a peek and seeing him nod in that encouraging yet patient way that he has. Then I clear my throat and start again, wondering why I'm so nervous when he's probably the only person I know who would truly understand. "So, you know how you always say the eyes are the window to the soul and the mirror to the past and all that? And how you can recognize someone from your past lives simply by looking into their eyes?"

He nods, unhurried, noncommittal, as though he's got all the time in the world to see where this leads.

"Anyway, my point is—" I take a deep breath, hoping he won't think I'm any crazier than he already does when I blurt, *"Ava-is-Romy-and-Rayne's-aunt!"* The words rushing out of me so quickly it sounds like one very long word, as he just continues to sit there, looking as cool and calm as can be.

"Remember when I told you how I had that vision where I watched their life unfold and I saw their aunt? Well, as crazy as it sounds, that aunt is now *Ava*. She died during the Salem Witch Trials and came back in this life as Ava." I shrug, not really sure how you follow up a statement like that.

His lips curve ever so slightly as his gaze lightens, pushing his swing slowly back and forth when he says, "I know."

I squint, unsure if I heard him correctly.

He moves, veering so close our knees nearly touch, looking at me when he says, "Ava told me."

I jump out of my swing so hard and fast the chains slam

together and spin in on themselves—winding all the way up before dropping back down, circling around and around in a fury of movement that makes a horrible, dull, clanking sound. My knees wobbly, unsteady, as I narrow my gaze and slowly take him in—wondering how this guy who claims to love me for all of my lives could possibly befriend her, endanger the twins, and betray me like that.

But he just looks at me without the slightest trace of concern. "Ever, please." He shakes his head. "It's not what you think."

I press my lips together and avert my gaze, wondering where I've heard that before. Oh right, Ava. It's pretty much her favorite, most oft-repeated phrase and I can't believe he fell for it.

"She saw it on a visit to the akashic records. And today, when I was unable to find a way to help you, I confirmed it. She's been getting her place ready, trying to find the right time to tell them, and, well, even though I believed her, I wasn't really sure what would truly be best for them. And so, today, when I asked for a little guidance, what the best course for them would be, the story was revealed. In fact, they're with her right now."

"So, that's it then." I look at him. "Ava's no longer evil, she's reunited with the twins, and we get our lives back." I try to laugh, but it doesn't come out quite the way I intended.

"Do we? Get our lives back?" He cocks his head to the side and looks at me.

I sigh, knowing I've no choice but to try to explain it, it's the least I can do.

I drop onto my swing, fingers twisting and looping around the thick metal chains as I look at him and say, "Today—in

Summerland—despite how it looked, it wasn't *at all* what it seemed. And I was going to explain it—explain *everything* that's been happening—but when you disappeared so fast I—" I press my lips together and look away.

"So, why not explain it now?" Damen says, eyeing me closely. "I'm right here. You have my full attention." His voice so stiff and formal, my entire heart breaks. Just crumbles into a million jagged pieces as he sits there beside me, so handsome, so strong, so well-intentioned—wanting only to do the right thing, no matter what it costs him.

And I want so badly to just reach out and hug him tightly to me, find a way to explain it away. But I can't, the words are held hostage by the monster within, so instead I just shrug and hear myself say, "It—it was totally and completely inno-cent. Seriously. I did it for *us*—despite how it looked."

Damen looks at me with so much patience and love—I can't help but feel guilty. "So tell me, did you get what you set out for?" he asks, the question so loaded I can only guess at the real intention behind it.

I pause, trying not to wince under his dark, probing gaze, palms slick with sweat when I say, "You know how bad I've been feeling for attacking him and all—and so, I thought that if I took him to Summerland, then maybe he could be healed and—"

"*And*—?" he prompts, voice laced with the patience of six hundred years, and I can't help but wonder if he ever gets tired of it—of being so tolerant, so long-suffering—especially when it comes to dealing with me.

"*And*—" I try to say it, try to tell him what's happening to me, but I can't. The beast is awake, the dark magick's taking hold, and I'm barely hanging on as it is. I shake my head, nervously picking at the faux tortoiseshell buttons lining the front of my sweater, as I say, "And—*nothing*. Seriously, that's it. I just hoped it would heal him, and apparently it did."

Damen considers me, his face composed, relaxed, as though he completely understands. And the thing is, *he does* understand. He understands way beyond my own fumbling words. He understands all too well.

"So, since we were already there, I figured I'd show him around, and the second he saw the Hall, well, he rushed inside—and the rest—as they say—is *history*." My gaze meets his, the irony of the word lost on neither of us.

"And did you join him—in the Hall?" His eyes narrow to slits, looking at me as though he already knows—knows that I'm no longer welcome there—but wants to hear me say it. Wants the full confession as to just how dark and twisted I've become.

I take a deep breath and casually push my hair off my face. "No, I just—" I pause, wondering if I should tell him about my trail ride to no-man's-land, but quickly deciding against it—wondering if maybe what I witnessed was more a reflection of me—my inner state—than an actual place. "I, uh, I just hung around and waited." I shrug. "I mean, I got a little bored and definitely thought about leaving and all, but I also wanted to make sure he could find his way home, so I—um—I hung out." I nod, a little too forcefully, in a way that's not even close to being convincing.

The two of us exchanging a long, painful look, both of us aware that I'm lying—that I just gave what is quite possibly one of my worst performances ever. And for some strange, unknown reason, he grants me a shrug so final, so dismissive, I can't help but feel disappointed. That small, sane, glimmer of me wishing he'd find a way to coax it out of me, so we could be done with all this. But he just continues to look at me, until I turn away and say, "Nice to know you'll still visit Summerland on your own, even though you refuse to go there with me." Knowing he doesn't deserve that, but still, there it is.

He grabs hold of my swing and pulls me to him, jaw clenched, fingers squeezing the chain, words coming from between gritted teeth when he says, "Ever, I didn't go there for me—I went there for *you*."

I swallow hard, and as much as I want to look away, I can't, my gaze is locked on his.

"I tried to find a way to reach you—to help you. You've been so distant—not at all like yourself, and it's been days since we've spent any real time together. It's pretty clear you're doing your best to avoid me, you never want to be with me anymore, at least not here on the earth plane."

"That's not true!" The words come out too high-pitched and shaky to ever be believed, but I forge ahead anyway. "I mean, apparently you haven't noticed, but I've been working *a lot* lately. So far my summer's been spent shelving books, working the register, and giving psychic readings under the code name of Avalon. So, yeah, maybe I want to spend my spare time indulging myself in a little escape—is that so bad?" I press my lips together and look him right in the eye, knowing most of that was true and wondering if he'll call me on the parts that aren't.

But he just shakes his head, refusing to be swayed. "And now that Jude's better—now that you've healed him with a trip to Summerland—I can't help but wonder what excuse you'll find next."

I suck in my breath and avert my gaze, surprised to hear him answer like that, and the truth is, I have no idea how to respond, no idea what comes next. Kicking a small pebble with the toe of my shoe, unable to confide, too tired and beaten to come up with anything else.

"You know, you used to be as bright and shining here on the earth plane as you were today in Summerland." I swallow hard and bow my head, hardly believing my ears when he goes on to say, "I know about the magick, Ever." His voice low, almost a whisper, though the words reverberate like a scream. "I know you're in way over your head. And I wish you'd let me help you."

I stiffen. My whole body stiffens as my heart crashes violently against my chest.

"I know the signs—the jitteriness, the lying, the weight loss, the—*diminished appearance*. You're an addict, Ever. Addicted to the dark side of magick. Jude never should've gotten you into this." He shakes his head, his gaze never once leaving me. "But the sooner you admit it, the sooner I can help make you better."

"It's not—" I struggle to speak, but the words won't come. The monster's in control, dead set on blowing us apart. "Isn't that why you went to the Great Halls of Learning? So you could help me?" I look at him, seeing the way his expression changes to one of hurt surprise. But it's not enough to stop the beast, nope, not even close. This train is just now pulling out of the station and still has a long way to go. "So tell me, what *did* you see? What did the almighty akashic records share with *you*?"

"Nothing," he says, voice tired, full of defeat. "I didn't learn a thing. Apparently when the problem is of the person's own making, access is forbidden where others are concerned. I'm banned from interfering in any way, shape, or form." He shrugs. "It's all part of the journey I guess. Still, one thing is clear, Ever. Last Thursday night, Roman mentioned a spell—and ever since Jude gave you that book nothing's been the same—with you—between us—everything's changed." He looks at me, waiting for confirmation, but it won't come, can't come. "You two share a long and complicated history—and it's quite clear he's not over you yet. And I can't help but feel that he's getting in the way—that *magick* is getting in the way, and, Ever, it'll destroy you if you're not careful—I've seen it happen before."

My eyes search his face, knowing he's trying to send me an image, a message of some sort, but that strange foreign pulse is at full thrum—the dark flame burning bright—weakening my powers to where I can no longer grasp Damen's thoughts, his energy, his tingle and heat—can't grasp anything at all.

He moves toward me, gripping my shoulders long before I can blink, gazing into my eyes with determination and purpose, fully resolved to deal with this once and for all.

But as much as I want to, I can't let him in, can't let him see me like this. The revulsion he'll see in my eyes isn't coming from me, it's the beast, but he won't know the difference.

And even though it kills me to do it, even though it only proves that he's right, that I really am dangerously and recklessly out of control, I still just shake my head and walk away, all the way to the curb where my car's parked.

Calling over my shoulder to say, "Sorry, Damen, but you're wrong. Dead wrong. I'm just overworked and overtired, just like I keep telling you. And if you ever feel like cutting me some slack—well, you know where to find me."

TWENTY

I don't even make it out of the gate before my car is gone, and my butt slams against the pavement so hard and fast it's a moment before I realize it vanished right out from under me. I gaze around in a daze, trying to determine how that could've happened, when a speeding Mercedes comes barreling toward me, nearly running me over as its driver honks, flips me the bird, and yells a slew of obscenities my way.

Scrambling to the side, I shut my eyes tightly, determined to manifest a new car, something more powerful and quicker this time. Imagining a flaming red Lamborghini, and seeing it so clearly before me, I'm shocked to open my eyes and find its not there. And after taking a deep breath and trying again, first aiming for a Porsche, then a Miata like the one I have at home, it still doesn't work so I try for a silver Prius like the one Munoz drives, followed by a Smart Car—but nothing comes. Nothing at all. And I'm so desperate for wheels by this point, I'll happily settle for a scooter, but when I can't even manifest that, I half jokingly try for a pair of Rollerblades instead. Discovering just how bad it's gotten for me when all I end up with is a pair of white leather boots with two strips of metal where the wheels should be. And that's when I decide to run instead. Happy to know that if nothing else, I still have my own strength and speed.

My feet pounding the asphalt, heels slamming easily, effortlessly, as I make my way along the curving, swooping hills of Coast Highway, fully intent on heading straight home only to run right past the turn and head elsewhere instead. Somewhere better. Somewhere that has everything I need—everything I could ever desire. So single-minded in my vision, so determined to reach my destination no matter the cost, I move faster, quicker, and in no time at all, I'm there.

Right outside Roman's door.

My body shaking with longing, anticipation, as the dark flame inside me burns so brightly it threatens to incinerate my insides. Closing my eyes and *sensing* him, *feeling* him.

Roman's inside.

And all I have to do is push the door open and he's mine.

In one fluid movement, I'm in. The door slamming so hard against the wall, the entire house reverberates from the force, as I slink down the hall, quickly, silently, finding Roman in his den, lounging on the couch, arms spread wide, face expectant, as though he's been waiting for me.

"Ever." He nods, not the least bit surprised, not missing a beat. "You really have an issue with doors, don't you? Is that another one I'll have to replace?"

I move toward him without hesitation, his name a purr on my lips as my body anticipates the chill of his gaze.

He nods, slowly, steadily, as though listening to a rhythm heard only by him. Allowing his Ouroboros tattoo to flash in and out of view, his voice low and measured, when he says, "Nice of you to drop by darlin', but truth be told, I liked you better the last time you came over. You know, when you stood outside my window in that fetching see-through nightie of yours?" His lips lift at the corner as he slips a cigarette between them, sparks the tip, and takes a long, thoughtful drag. Carefully blowing a succession of perfectly timed smoke rings my way when he adds, "As it stands now—well, you're hardly at your finest. In fact, you're looking rather—*peckish,* aren't you?"

I rub my lips together, moistening them with my tongue as I attempt to comb my fingers through my sad snarl of hair. What used to be a glossy thick mane I was inordinately proud of is now reduced to a dull, ratted nest of split ends. I should've done more, should've made some sort of effort, worn some perfume, dabbed on a little concealer, taken the time to manifest some new clothes that actually fit my newly shrunken form. Cringing under the weight of his glare, the way it rakes over my emaciated body, clearly far from impressed with what I have to offer.

"Seriously, darlin', if you're gonna come crashin' your way in 'ere like that, then you need to look a little more presentable. I'm not Damen, luv. I won't go shaggin' just any ol' thing. I've got me standards, you know?"

I close my eyes, willing to do whatever it takes to please him, to *be* with him, and knowing I've succeeded when I see the glazed look that comes over his face.

"*Drina!*" He whispers, cigarette tumbling from his lips and burning a hole in the carpet as his eyes drink me in. Seeing creamy pale skin, pink rosy lips, and a blaze of coppery red hair that falls over my shoulders, as I kneel down before him, extinguish the cigarette between my long, tapered fingers, and place my hands on his knees.

"My God—it—it can't be—*is it really*—?" He shakes his head and rubs his eyes, gazing into ones the color of emeralds and wanting so badly to believe.

I close my eyes, enjoying the feel of him, the chill of him, sliding my hands ever higher, up over his knees, all the way to his thighs, so close to getting what I want, moving higher still, and then—

Haven is behind me. Her eyes blazing, hands curled into fists, and I can't help but wonder just how long she's been watching, since I didn't even hear her come in, didn't even *sense* her for that matter. But then, Haven's of no real consequence here. She's merely the annoying barrier that's got a bad habit of getting in my way. One I can easily obliterate.

"What the fug do you think you're doing, Ever?" She moves toward me, her harsh, narrowed gaze raking over me, meant to intimidate, but it won't work, can't work, she just doesn't know it yet.

"Ever?" Roman squints, his eyes darting between us, unable to see what she sees. "What're you talking about, luv, this isn't Ever—it's—"

But that's all it takes, the mere suggestion of her words and he's able to see *me*, see right through the façade I created.

"*Bloody hell!*" He shouts, pushing me away so hard I fly across the room, over a table, and into a chair, before I land next to where Haven is standing. "What kind of crap move you trying to pull, anyway?" He scowls, furious at having been played like that.

I swallow hard, my eyes never once leaving his, as Haven moves toward me in a swirl of black leather and lace, her frosty cold breath slamming my cheek as the bite of her nails cuts into my wrist. "Don't you have somewhere else to be?" she says, the words ground out from behind tightly clenched teeth. "Seriously, Ever, does Damen know you're here?"

Damen.

The name stirring something—something down deep. Something that causes my hand to clutch at my amulet as I take a tiny step back.

Her gaze scathing, face creased with fury, when she says, "You really can't stand it, can you? Can't stand for me to have something you don't." She shakes her head. "Warning me against Roman, trying to scare me away so you could have him all to yourself. Well, I've got news for you, Ever—I'm changed. Changed in ways you can't even begin to imagine." And though I try to yank my hand away, try to step back and break free, her grip's too strong, too determined, and if her eyes are any indication, she's far from through with me. "You've no business here. You shouldn't have come. I don't want you here, Roman doesn't want you here—can't you see what a joke you've become?" She focuses on my acne-splattered chin, my newly sunken chest—the exact opposite of her porcelain-skinned perfection and well-defined curves. "Why don't you just turn around and go back to wherever you came from, okay? I live by *my own* rules now, and this is how it goes: *You* don't get the heck out, *you* try to overstay your visit and do something crazy, and *you're* the one who's gonna get *hurt.*" Her fingers snake around my wrist 'til they're flush with her thumb, her eyes never once straying from mine. "You look like crap. A snaggle-haired, zit-faced wreck." She shakes her head in a shiny whirl of black wavy strands and platinum-tinged bangs. "What happened, Ever? Damen change his mind about wanting to spend the rest of eternity with you and cut off your elixir supply?"

I open my mouth, wanting to speak, but no words will come. So I switch my gaze to Roman, begging, pleading for him to step in and help me, but he just waves it away, his eyes signaling he's finished with me. Now that he knows I'm not Drina, I'm on my own.

Left with no other choice, I raise my wrist, the one she's gripping so hard it's gone white and numb, and flip her around so suddenly, so unexpectedly, her back's flush to my chest before she can fight it.

My lips tipped toward her ear when I say, "Sorry, but I just won't tolerate that kind of talk." Feeling her struggle against me, trying to break free, but it's no use, no one beats the monster, no one but—

My gaze wanders to the gilt-framed mirror hanging before us, struck by our image—Haven's hate-filled gaze a perfect match for my own—with my own face so angry, so distorted so—*monstrous*—I hardly recognize it. Finally able to see what they've seen all along, the complete degradation of what I've become.

My fingers loosen, just enough to allow her to break free. Spinning on me in a cloud of fury, fist held high, a map of all seven chakras held firmly in mind.

But before she can complete the swing, I'm gone. The excruciatingly loud crack of her back hitting the wall lingering behind as I push her off and flee for the street.

Assuring myself she'll be fine, just fine, immortals always heal.

But no longer sure if I will.

TWENTY-ONE

When I reach the store, I expect to find Jude, but instead the door is locked and the sign flipped to CLOSED. And after trying and failing to unlock it with my mind, I fumble through my bag, searching for the key with fingers so shaky, I end up dropping it twice before I finally get in. Whizzing past the bookshelves and CD racks so quickly, I forget about the fixture of angel figurines to my right and slam it so hard they crash to the ground in a pile of broken pieces and heavy shards of glass. But I don't stop to fix it. Don't even give it a second look. I just keep going, making my way into the back room and over to the desk where I pull out the chair and completely collapse.

Slumped over the desk, my forehead pressed to the wood, as I fight to steady my pulse and slow my breath. Horrified by my actions, by how low I've sunk. The scene from ten minutes ago repeating again and again in my head.

I stay like that for a while, until my skin starts to cool and my mind starts to clear, and when I finally lift my head and take a good look around, I notice the calendar's been torn off the wall and propped up before me. Today's date circled in red along with a question mark, my name underlined right beside it, and the words, *Maybe this'll work?* written in Jude's messy scrawl.

And just like *that,* I get it. The solution I've been waiting for is now, thanks to Jude, right within my reach. And it's so unbelievably obvious I can't believe I didn't think of it before. Gaping at Jude's sloppy circle, and the smaller, printed circle within it illustrating the moon and its phases. And the fact that this one is completely colored in signals that today, the moon is going dark.

Hecate is rising again.

And suddenly, I know exactly what to do.

Instead of waiting for the moon to go light and asking the goddess to cancel the queen like the twins had me do (which, by the way, probably only served to piss off the queen which is why it failed so miserably), I should've waited for today, for the moon to go dark again, so I could head right back to the source—pick up right where I started—with Hecate, ruler of the underworld—and forge an alliance with her.

I reach into the drawer, bypassing *The Book of Shadows,* and rummaging around for some of the supplies that I'll need. Making a mental promise to make it up to Jude later, as I cram an assortment of crystals, herbs, and candles into my bag before slinging it over my shoulder and heading for the beach—the only place I can think of that'll provide not only the privacy I seek but the body of water required for the ritual bath that I need.

And in no time at all I'm standing at the edge of the cliff, toes curled around the rock as I gaze out at an ocean so dark it blends with the sky. Recalling the same sort of night just one month before, when I came here with Damen, so sure I couldn't possibly sink any lower than turning my best friend into an immortal, completely clueless to the fact that I was about to take it even further.

I make my way down the trail, anxious to begin. Carefully picking my way around jutting rocks and jagged turns, heart crashing hard against my chest as my body goes clammy with sweat, aware of *that feeling* rising inside me and knowing I need to get started before it takes over again. Feet carving deep into the sand as I make my way toward the cave, trusting it'll be empty, just like we left it, knowing it's just like Damen said: *People rarely see what's in front of them.* And they certainly never see this.

I drop my bag to the ground and reach for a long taper and small box of matches, the swish and sizzle of the match striking the case the only accompaniment to the gently pounding waves. Securing the burning candle into the sand, I go about the business of arranging the rest of my tools on a blanket. Taking a moment to get it all organized before shedding my clothes and heading outside.

I wrap my arms tightly around me, bracing against the wind that pricks at my skin, and attempting to warm it away. Determined to ignore the protruding stack of ribs that poke at my fingers, the way my hip bones jut out in front of me, telling myself it's all over now, the cure is near, no one, not even the monster, can stop me from recovering.

Rushing toward the foamy, white spray, my teeth gnashing against its bitter, frigid bite, I dive under a series of waves, eyes shut tight against the stinging saltiness, ears filled with that loud, roaring hum. Shifting onto my back as soon as the onslaught is over and the ocean has calmed. My hair spread out all around me, my body weightless, unburdened, I bring my knees to my chest and gaze up at a sky so dark, so stark, so vast and mysterious, I can't even fathom it. Grasping the amulet Damen placed at my neck, and calling upon the collection of crystals to aid and protect, to keep the monster at bay long enough to do what needs to be done. Placing my fate in Hecate's hands, entrusting that, just like the yin and the yang, every dark has its light.

I submerge myself again and again, until I'm cleansed and renewed and ready to begin, wading toward the shore, my body wet, dripping, covered in goose bumps I barely take notice of. The chill now abated by the warm assurance, the complete certainty, that I'm just seconds away from slaying the beast and saving myself.

The cave walls flicker from the light of the candle, causing a succession of dark and light shadows. And after cleansing my athame, waving it three times through the flame, I kneel in the center of the magick circle I've made. Incense in one hand, athame in the other, re-creating a ritual similar to the one that went before, only this time I add:

> *I call upon Hecate, the queen of the underworld, magick,*
> *and the darkest of moons*
> *Please unweave this spell, loosen this bind, and extinguish*
> *this dark flame that looms*
> *Oh, great patron of witches, beloved mother, maiden, and crone*
> *This is my mote, my will, my might*
> *So let it be done!*

Gasping in awe as a howl of wind swirls through the space and an applause of thunder cracks overhead. The force of it causing a vibration so potent it knocks the stack of chairs to the ground as the earth begins to shift and move. A rhythmic, seismic shaking and trembling, a pulse originating from somewhere down deep—growing stronger, more violent, its circumference increasing—causing layers of rock to break free from the walls and crumble around me.

Everything collapsing, disintegrating, until there's nothing left but the ground I kneel on, a mountain of debris, and an expanse of night sky.

The earth still settling, still moving around me as I rise and give thanks. Picking my way through the smoke and ruin, as I run my hands through my thick, glossy hair and manifest a clean set of clothes so quickly and easily, I've no doubt my will has been done.

TWENTY-TWO

"Are we there yet?"

My fingers pick at the soft, silky blindfold Damen used to cover my eyes. A silly formality since we both know I don't have to *look* to *see,* but still, he's so intent on keeping the secret, he chooses to cover every single one of his bases, whether or not it's actually necessary.

He laughs, the sound so melodic it makes my heart swell. Grasping my hand, his fingers entwined around mine, as the *almost* feel of his palm emits the warmest, most delicious tingle and heat—a sensation I'll never take for granted again, especially after knowing what it's like to lose it completely.

"Ready?" he asks, moving behind me and untying the knot at the back of my head, dropping the blindfold and taking a moment to smooth down my hair, before spinning me around and adding, *"Happy Birthday!"*

I smile—smile before I've even had a chance to open my eyes. Already convinced that whatever it is, it's sure to be good.

And the second I see it, I gasp, my jaw dropped, hand clutching my neck, gazing upon a scene so wondrous it hardly seems possible—even for Summerland.

"When did you do this?" I ask, struggling to take it all in. Gazing upon an exquisite utopia, a seemingly endless field of blazing red tulips with an exquisite pavilion placed right in its center. "Surely you didn't create this all now?"

He shrugs, eyes grazing over my face in a way that makes my whole body grow hot. "I've had this planned for a while, and while the pavilion is not entirely of my making, I did alter it a good bit, the tulips are an added touch I created for you." He looks at me, pulling me to him when he says, "All I wanted was for you to get well so we could enjoy it together—just the two of us, you know?"

I nod, his loving, grateful gaze causing my cheeks to flush as an inexplicable shyness suddenly takes over. "Just *us*?" I tilt my head and take him in. "You mean we don't have to hurry back for my surprise party?"

Damen laughs, nodding as he leads me deep into a field of the most vibrant, blazing red. "They're still setting up—I promised we'd stop by a little later, but for now, what do you think?"

I blink, blink several times in quick succession since I don't want to cry. Not here. Not now. Not in this magnificent field meant to represent our undying love. Swallowing hard and speaking past the lump in my throat when I say, "I think—I think you're the most amazing person in the entire world—and I think that I'm so incredibly lucky to know you—to *love* you—and I think—I think I have no idea what I'd ever do without you—and I think that I'm so incredibly grateful that you didn't give up on me."

"I'd never give up on you," he says, face gone suddenly serious as his eyes search mine.

"Well, you must've been tempted." I turn, remembering how dark things got, how far gone I was, and bidding a silent thanks to Hecate for fulfilling my wish and giving me back everything that matters most in my world.

"Not even for a second," he says, hand at my chin, turning me toward him again. "Not even once."

"You were right, you know—about the magick?" I bite down on my lip and gaze at him shyly.

But he just nods, it's not like I didn't just admit to anything he didn't already guess at.

"I—I did a spell—a binding spell—and, well, it sort of had the opposite effect of what I was hoping. I accidentally bound myself to Roman." I swallow hard, seeing him continue to gaze at me with a face so expressionless, it's impossible to read. "And—at first I didn't tell you because—well—because I was too ashamed. It's like—like I was *obsessed* with him, and—" I shake my head, grimacing when I remember the things I said and did. "Anyway, the only place I was healthy was right here in Summerland. That's why I was begging you to come. Partly so I could feel whole again, and partly because the monster— the *magick*—wouldn't let me confide on the earth plane, every time I tried it shut down the words and wouldn't allow them to come—and all this is to say—"

He places his hand on my cheek and looks at me. "Ever," he whispers, "it's okay."

"I'm sorry," I mumble, feeling his arms circling around my back as he presses me to him. "So very, very sorry."

"And so it's over now? You've fixed it?" He pulls away and tilts his head, taking me in.

"Yeah." I nod, wiping my eyes with the back of my hand. "It's all good now—I'm better—and my obsession with Roman is over. I—I just thought you should know. I hated keeping it from you."

He leans toward me and presses his lips to my forehead, looking at me when he says, "And now, *mademoiselle,* would you like to begin?" Waving his arm in a wide arc and bowing down low.

I smile, my hand clasped in his as he whisks me across the field and inside that gorgeous pavilion, a building so beautiful, so exquisitely wrought, I can't help but gasp yet again.

"What is this place?" I ask, taking in the polished white marble floors, the domed ceilings covered in the most jaw-dropping frescoes featuring luminous, pink-cheeked cherubs frolicking among other celestial beings.

He smiles, motioning me onto a creamy white couch so plush, so soft and cushy, it's like a giant marshmallow cloud. "It's your birthday present. And, as oddly coincidental as it may be, it's your anniversary present as well."

I squint, my mind running backward, pilfering through a long list of memories, and coming up empty. It's not yet been a year since we first got together—or at least this time around anyway, so I really have no clue as to just what "anniversary" he's referring to.

"August eighth." He nods, seeing the confused look on my face. "August eighth, sixteen oh eight, to be exact, was the day we first met."

"Seriously?" I gasp, it's all I can manage, I'm so shocked by the news.

"Seriously." He smiles, leaning back against the cloud of cushions and pulling me close. "But you don't have to take my word for it, you know. Here, see for yourself." He picks up a remote from the large table before us and points it toward the large circular screen that surrounds the entire far wall of the room. "In fact, you're not limited to just *seeing* it, you can even *experience* it if you wish, it's really up to you."

I squint, having no idea what he's getting at, no idea what's happening here.

"I've been working on this forever and I think it's finally ready. Think of my little invention as a sort of *interactive theater*. One where you can either sit back and enjoy the show or jump right in and participate—it's your choice. But first there are a few things you must know. One, you can't change the outcome, the script is predetermined, and two"—he leans toward me, his finger trailing over my cheek—"here in Summerland all endings are happy. Anything even the slightest bit tragic or disturbing has been carefully omitted, so no worries. You may even enjoy a surprise or two. I know I did."

"Are they *real* surprises or ones manufactured by you?" I snuggle against him.

But he's quick to shake his head. "Real. Totally and completely real. My memories, as you know, go *way* back, so far back that sometimes, well, they get a bit fuzzy. So I decided to do a bit of research over in the Great Halls of Learning, a sort of *refresher course* if you will, and as it just so happens, I was reminded of a few things I'd forgotten."

"Such as . . . ?" I glance at him briefly, before pressing my lips to that wonderful spot where his shoulder meets his neck, instantly soothed by the *almost* feel of his skin and his warm musky scent.

"Such as *this*," he whispers, shifting me so I'm facing the screen and not him. The two of us snuggling into each other as he squeezes a button on the remote and we watch as the screen comes to life, filling with images so large, so multi-dimensional, it's as though we're right in it.

And the moment I see that busy city square with its cobblestone streets and crowds of people all hurrying around each other much as they do today, as though they all have somewhere important to be, I know just where we are. There may be horses and carriages instead of cars, there may be overly formal attire compared to our modern, casual wear, but with the abundance of vendors loudly hawking their wares, the similarities are astonishing—I'm looking at a seventeenth-century mini-mall.

I peer at Damen, the question posed in my eyes, seeing him smile in answer as he helps me to stand. Leading me toward the screen so quickly I can't help but stop, convinced my nose is going to smack right into it, when he leans toward me and whispers, *"Believe."*

So I do.

I take that big leap of faith and keep going, right into the hard crystal screen that instantly softens and yields and welcomes us in. And not just as oddly dressed extras, but in period-appropriate attire, the two of us cast in the leading roles.

I gaze down at my hands, surprised to find them so rough and calloused though immediately recognizing them from my Parisian life, when I was Evaline, a lowly servant facing a life of mind-numbing manual labor until Damen came along.

I run them over the front of my dress, noting the itch of the fabric, the modest, severe cut resulting in a fit that's not the least bit flattering. But still, it's clean and well pressed, so I try to take a small bit of pride in that. And even though my blond hair is braided and twisted and scraped off my face, an unruly tendril or two still manage to find their escape.

The vendor snaps at me in French, and even though I'm aware I'm only playing a part, that this isn't the language I speak, somehow I'm able to not just understand but also to reply. Recognizing me as one of his most discerning customers, he hands me a ripe, red tomato he claims as his best, watching as I turn it over and over in the palm of my hand, inspecting its color, its firmness of touch, nodding my consent and juggling for the change in my pouch when someone bumps against me so abruptly, the fruit slips from my grip and falls to the ground.

I gaze at my feet, heart sinking when I see the clumpy, red, splattered mess. Knowing it'll come at great cost to me, that the kitchen staff will never agree to cover it, I spin on my heel, a word of reproach pressing forth from my lips, when I see that it's *him*.

He of the dark glossy hair, deep glinting gaze, gorgeously tailored clothes, and the finest carriage to ever grace these parts aside from the queen's. The one they call Damen— Damen Auguste. The one I seem to run into an awful lot these days.

I lift my skirts and kneel toward the ground, hoping to salvage whatever I can and not getting very far before I'm stopped by his hand on my arm, a touch that sends a swarm of tingle and heat right through to my bones.

"*Pardon,*" he murmurs, bowing before me and seeing that the vendor is reimbursed for the loss.

And even though I'm intrigued, even though my heart's beating wildly, hammering hard against my chest, even though that odd sense of tingle and heat persistently lingers, I turn away, and move on. Sure that he's just playing with me, painfully aware that he's well out of my league. Only to have him catch up to me and say, "Evaline—stop!"

I turn, my eyes meeting his, knowing we'll continue this cat and mouse game, if for nothing else but propriety's sake. But also knowing that eventually, if he keeps it up, if he doesn't grow bored or lose interest, I'll gladly surrender, of that there's no doubt.

He smiles, placing his hand on my arm as he thinks: *This is how we started—and this is how we continued for some time. Shall we fast-forward to the good parts?*

I nod, and the next thing I know, I'm standing before a great, gilded mirror, gazing at the image reflected before me. Noting how my plain ugly dress has been swapped for one of a fabric so rich, so soft and silky, it practically glides right over my body. Its low neckline the perfect showcase for my pale décolletage and generous smattering of jewels so shiny and brilliant, I hardly see anything else.

He stands behind me, catching my eye as he smiles his approval, and I can't help but wonder how I got here, how a poor, orphaned servant like me ended up in a place so grand, with a man so gorgeous, so—*magical*—he's almost too good to be true.

He offers his hand and leads me to an extravagantly dressed table for two. The sort of table I'm more used to servicing than sitting at. But now, with Damen at my side, and his servants dismissed for the night, I watch as he raises a finely cut crystal carafe so slowly, so tentatively, with a hand gone so suddenly shaky it's clear there's an internal battle waging within him.

He meets my gaze, his face a conflicted maze. Frowning

slightly as he places the carafe back on the table and chooses the bottle of red wine instead.

I gasp, my eyes wide, lips parted, though no words will come—the full realization of this one simple act suddenly dawning on me. *You almost did it! You came so close. Why did you stop?* Knowing that if he'd gone through with it, served me the elixir right from the start—everything would've been different.

Every. Single. Thing.

Drina never could've killed me—Roman never could've tricked me—and Damen and I would've lived happily ever after and after and after—pretty much the opposite of the way we live now.

His eyes search mine, gaze probing and deep, shaking his head as he thinks: *I was so unsure—didn't know how you'd accept it—if you'd accept it—didn't think it was my place to force it on you. But that's not why I brought you here, my only intent was to show you that your Parisian life, hard as it was, wasn't all misery. We had our share of magical moments—moments like this—and we would've had more—if it weren't for—*

He leaves that part hanging. We both know where it ends. But before I can even raise my glass to his, the dinner is over, and he's walking me home. Leading me around to the back, stopping just shy of the servants' entrance, where he encircles his arms around my waist and pulls me close, kissing me so passionately, so deeply, I never want it to end. The feel of his lips upon mine so soft and insistent, so warm and inviting, stirring something down deep—something so familiar—something so—*real*—

I pull away, eyes wide, gazing into his, as my fingers explore my soft, swollen lips, the place on my cheeks left raw and tender from where his stubble has grazed them. No energy field hovering between us, no protective veil of any kind. Nothing but the glorious feel of his skin on mine.

He smiles, fingers moving over my cheeks, down my neck, along my collarbone, and quickly replacing his fingers with his lips. *It's real,* he thinks. *No shield is necessary. There is no danger here.*

I look at him, my mind racing with the possibilities. *Is it—is it really possible that we can be together—now—here?* Hoping against hope that it is.

But he takes a deep breath and joins his fingers with mine, touching me in a way we haven't experienced for *months* when he thinks: *I'm afraid this is merely a theater of the past. You can edit the script, but you're not allowed to change it, ad-lib it, or add experiences that never occurred.*

I nod, saddened by the news but eager to begin again, pulling him back to me and pressing my lips against his, determined to be happy with whatever is allowed, for however long it can last.

And so we kiss at the servants' door—he in his fine-woven black waistcoat and I in my plain servant's wear.

We kiss in the stables—he in full English hunting attire and I in my tight riding breeches, sharply tailored red jacket, and shiny black boots.

We kiss by the waterside—he in the plain white shirt and black slacks of the day and I in grossly unflattering Puritan wear.

We kiss in a field of tulips so red, they're a nearly perfect match for my blaze of thick, wavy hair. He in a filmy white shirt and loose trousers, I in a blush-colored slip of silk, strategically knotted and tied. Taking the occasional break so he can continue to paint me, adding a stroke here, a dab there, only to throw down his brush, pull me back to him, and kiss me again.

All of my lives so different, and yet somehow playing out almost exactly the same—the two of us finding each other and falling quickly, only to have Damen, determined to not act rashly, to gain my full trust before feeding me the elixir, hesitate for so long it gave Drina enough time to catch on and eliminate me.

And that's why you wasted no time when you found me after the accident, I think. Cradled in the warmth of his arms, my cheek pressed tightly to his chest, *seeing* the moment from *his* perspective—how he'd found me when I was ten (thanks to a little help from Romy and Rayne and Summerland)—and how he spent the next several years biding his time until enough years had passed and he moved to Eugene, Oregon. Having just enrolled in my high school when the accident happened and destroyed all his plans.

I watch him at the scene—see how he hesitates—nervously fretting—begging for guidance. Panicking when the silver cord that attaches the body to the soul became so tense, so stretched, it snapped yet again, instantly forming his decision to press the bottle to my lips and force me to drink, forced me back to life, to become immortal like him.

Any regrets? He gazes at me, urging me to be honest, no matter what.

But I just shake my head. Smiling as I pull him back to me, back to that blazing red field of that long-ago day.

TWENTY-THREE

"You ready?"

Damen's fingers graze over my lips, the *almost* feel of them infusing me with the memory of a kiss so real, so tangible, I'm tempted to drag him right back to Summerland and start up all over again.

Only I can't. We can't. We already committed to this. And though it can never compare to the birthday celebration Damen just gave me, everyone's waiting and there's no turning back.

I take a deep breath and gaze at the house just before us. Its façade simple, attractive, in that cozy, welcoming way, despite that fact that it's hosted some of the very worst scenes of my not-so-long-ago past.

"Let's go back to Paris," I murmur, only half joking. "You don't even have to edit out the nasty parts. Seriously. I'd much rather put on the crunchy brown dress and scrub the *latrines*—or whatever they called them back then—than face *this*."

"*Latrines?*" He looks at me and shakes his head, the sweet tinkle of his laugh flowing over me as his dark eyes glint. "Sorry, Ever, but there were no *latrines* back then. No *restrooms,* or *bathrooms,* or *water closets* even. That was the time of *chamber pots.* A sort of, well, ceramic pot, kept under one's bed. And trust me, that is one memory you do *not* want to relive."

I grimace, unable to imagine how completely gross that must've been to use such a device, much less to have to empty it. Visibly wincing when I say, "See? If I could only explain to Munoz that the real reason I'm just not that into his class is because history tends to lose its appeal for those who were actually forced to *live* it."

Damen laughs, head thrown back in a way that makes his neck so inviting, so enticing, it's all I can do not to press my lips hard against it. "Trust me, we've *all* lived it. Most of us just don't get the chance to remember it, much less *relive* it." He looks at me, his face gone serious when he says, "So, are you ready? I know it's awkward, and I know you're still a long way from ever trusting her again, but they're waiting, so at the very least, let's just stop in and allow them the pleasure of shouting *Happy Birthday,* okay?"

He looks at me, gaze warm, open, and I know if I said no, showed the slightest bit of resistance, he'd go with it. But I won't. Because the truth is, he's right. I have to face her again eventually. Not to mention how I'd really like her to look me in the eye as she tries to convince me of her highly unlikely story.

I nod slowly, reluctantly, moving toward the door when he says, "Now remember—*act surprised.*" Rapping his knuckles once, twice, then merging his brows when no one bothers to answer it in a well-rehearsed chorus of "*Surprise!*"

He pushes the door open, leading me past the entry, down the hall, and into the sunny yellow kitchen beyond, only to find Ava, dressed in a brown strapless dress and gold sandals, casually helping herself to a drink that's suspiciously red.

"*Sangria,*" she says, shaking her head and laughing when she adds, "Really, Ever, just how long will it take for you to trust me again?"

I press my lips together and shrug, doubting I'll ever be able to trust her again, despite what Damen's told me. I need to hear it from her, then I'll decide.

"Everyone's out back." She nods, looking at me when she adds, "So tell me, were you surprised?"

"Only by the lack of surprise." I grant her a half smile, that's the best I can manage, and she's lucky to even get that. And that has far less to do with how I may feel about her personally, and more to do with the fact that she's gladly taken over the care and feeding of the twins, allowing Damen and me our privacy again.

"So it *did* work!" She laughs, ushering Damen and me out back where everyone's gathered. "We figured the only way to throw you off the scent was to do the opposite of what you expect."

I step onto the patio, seeing Romy and Rayne lying on the grass, stringing necklaces from a large, gleaming bowl of crystals and beads, then draping them around the stone statue of Buddha, while Jude lounges alongside them, eyes closed, face tilted toward the sun, his arms back to new, courtesy of Summerland. And despite the surge of warmth, love, and security that tingles right through me as Damen leans into my shoulder and squeezes my hand, I can't help but feel saddened when I gaze upon my supposed group of friends.

A woman I don't like, much less trust; twins who openly resent me—one more than the other, but *still*; and an apparent love interest from the past who just so happens to be the long-time, bitter rival of my soul mate. And the only thing that makes me feel the slightest bit better is Miles, and the fact that if he wasn't in Florence, he'd surely be here with me.

But not Haven.

After I became myself again and tried to explain it to her, she was still too irate to do anything but scream at me. And so I pretty much had no choice but to give her a little time to cool off—I just hope she'll come around eventually and see what Roman is *really* about.

And standing here like this, with my sad little birthday party playing out before me—well, it only drives home the fact that I've lost her—her trust—her friendship—and I've no idea if I can ever get it back. I mean, just when we have more in common than ever before—just when I can finally share the secrets I've been hiding the whole time I've known her—I mess everything up so badly she ditches me for my immortal enemy.

I sigh under my breath, sure I can't possibly feel any worse, when Honor squeezes through the French doors and heads straight for Jude. Dropping down beside him and arranging her dress so comfortably and casually I can't help but gape. Can't hide my openmouthed, gawking confusion when she turns to me and twists her wrist back and forth in an awkward little wave.

I nod, barely, imperceptibly, unable to speak past the lump in my throat, unable to make sense of this scene.

Are they dating? Or just hanging out because of their shared interest in magick? Did he truly not get it when I explained that

we're merely classmates not *friends, and the huge gaping differ-*
ence that divides the two?

And as my eyes sweep over them, all of them, I can't believe this is it. That this is what it's come to. Almost a year in
this town, trying to forge some kind of life, and my only real
lasting relationship is with Damen, which, truth be told, I've
managed to push beyond all reasonable limits.

Ava clears her throat and offers us a drink, in what I'm
sure is an attempt at a feigned bit of normalcy for Honor and
Jude's sake, since they're pretty much the only ones here
who don't know the real truth about Damen and me—or at
least not to the full extent anyway.

But I just shake my head and wave it away, convincing myself that it's better like this, really and truly the only way. The
fewer connections I make, the fewer good-byes I'll have to
say. But even though I know for a fact that it's true, it doesn't
do much to fill up that big empty space lurking inside me.

I squeeze Damen's hand, telepathically assuring him not
to worry, to just stay put and I'll be back soon. Then I make
my way inside, at first thinking I'll make for the bathroom,
splash some cold water over my face and try to get some of
that good feeling back, but when I see the door to Ava's
"sacred space" I duck in there instead. Startled to see the
purple walls and indigo door transformed into a pastel haven
of preppy décor—a room that's got to be Romy's since Rayne
would never go for such a look.

I perch on the edge of her bed, fingers smoothing the soft
green duvet as I gaze at the floor just before me, remembering the day when everything changed. The day I said
good-bye to Damen, the day I was foolish enough to trust
him to Ava's care. So convinced I was doing the right thing—

the *only* thing—little did I know how that one small choice would have such huge repercussions that would pretty much impact the rest of my life—the rest of *eternity*.

I take a deep breath and rest my head in my hands, telling myself to get up, get back out there, make an attempt at small talk, then find an excuse to leave. Rubbing my eyes and running my fingers through my hair and over my clothes, just about to do exactly that when Ava comes in and says, "Oh good, I've been hoping for a moment alone with you."

I press my lips together, fighting the overwhelming urge to rush toward her and punch out all her chakras, if for no other reason than to see, once and for all, just whose side she's really on. But I don't. I don't do a thing. Instead, I stay right where I am and wait for her to begin.

"You know, you're right about me." She nods, leaning against Romy's dresser, legs crossed at the ankles, though her arms remain open and loose. "I did run off with the elixir. And I did leave Damen exposed and defenseless. There's just no getting around it."

I gaze at her, my heart beating frantically, even though I already knew it, even though Damen explained it to me, it's a whole other experience to hear her actually admit it.

"But before you rush to conclusions, I'm afraid there's a little more to it than that. Despite what you may think, I was never in cahoots with Roman. I wasn't partnered with him, friendly with him, or working with him in any way, shape, or form. He came by for a reading once, yes, way back when I first started. And, to be honest, his energy was so off—so disconcerting—I gave him a silent blessing and sent him on his way. But the reason I did what I did—the reason I failed to look after Damen, well, it's complicated—"

"I'll bet." I lift my brow and shake my head. I've no intention of cutting her any slack or letting her dance around it with some overly complex explanation.

She nods, determined to take it in stride. True to her usual self, she's unfazed by my outburst. "At first, I admit, I got a little caught up in all the possibilities of Summerland, of all the glorious gifts that it offered. You have to understand I've been out on my own for so long, supporting myself and working hard for everything that I have with no help from anyone, and more often than not, just barely scraping by—"

"Are you seriously expecting me to feel sorry for you? Because if so—save it. Seriously. It won't work." I shake my head and roll my eyes.

"Just trying to give you a little background." She shrugs, clasping her hands before her and flexing her fingers. "It's not a bid for sympathy, believe me. If nothing else, I think I've learned an important lesson in taking responsibility for my own life. I'm just trying to explain my initial reaction to Summerland, how enthralled I was by the ability to just manifest any material thing I could want. And I know I went a little overboard, and I know how much it annoyed you. But, after a while, I realized I could build myself a mansion full of treasures in Summerland, but it wouldn't make me any happier—either there or on the earth plane. And that's when I decided to go a little deeper, try to improve myself in ways I'd never truly attempted before. Sure, I had my sacred space and my meditations, but once I set my sights on gaining access to the Great Halls of Learning, well, that's when I was forced to walk all that talk I'd been spouting for years. And so—I gave up everything else and concentrated solely on that, and it wasn't long before I was in, and I never looked back."

I look at her, my eyes narrowed to slits, and all I can think is: *Well, bravo for you, Ava, bravo for you.*

"I know what you are, Ever. Damen too. And while I don't necessarily agree with it, it's not my place to interfere."

"Is that why you tried to have him killed? Is that how you deal with things you don't *approve* of? Sounds like interfering to me." I glare at her, digging my toe into the carpet as deep as it'll go.

She shakes her head, her voice calm, gaze fixed on mine. "I didn't know any of this when I left Damen that day. Back then, I truly believed that everything would be reversed— just as you believed too. You'd go back in time, Damen would go back as well, and while I wasn't sure of just what the elixir was, I had my suspicions, had every intention of drinking it too—but then, for some reason, just when I was about to—I stopped. I just couldn't go through with it. I guess the enormity of it got to me—the enormity of living *forever*." She looks at me. "That's pretty serious stuff—don't you think?"

I shrug. Shrug *and* roll my eyes. So far she hasn't said a thing to change my mind about her, and I'm still not convinced she didn't drink it, for that matter.

"So, in the end, I tossed it, made the portal to Summerland, and started searching for answers—for *peace*."

"And did you find any?" I ask, the tone in my voice making it clear that I don't really care either way.

"Yes." She smiles. "My peace is in knowing that we've all got our own journey—our own destiny to fulfill. And now, I finally know mine." I look at her, seeing the way her face lights up when she adds, "I'm here to use my gifts to help those who need it, to live without fear, to trust that I'll always have enough to get by, and to finish raising the twins in a way I failed to manage before." She gives me a look, a look like she wants to reach out and hug me, but luckily she settles for running her hand through her hair and staying right where she is. "I'm sorry about what happened, Ever. I never thought it would end up like this. And while I may not approve of what you and Damen are, it's really not my place to judge. You've got your own journey to walk."

"Yeah? And what's that?" I ask, my eyes meeting hers, surprised by the amount of yearning in my voice, hoping she might have some sort of clue as to just what it is that I'm here for. Because so far, I have no idea.

But Ava just shrugs, her kind brown eyes sparkling on mine when she says, "Oh, no." She smiles and shakes her head. "I'm afraid that's for you to discover all on your own. But believe me, Ever, I've no doubt it's going to be big."

TWENTY-FOUR

By the time I get home, it's late. And even though Damen offers to help me carry my gifts up the stairs and into my room, even though part of me is tempted to let him do exactly that, I just give him a quick kiss on the cheek and head in on my own. Wanting only to dive into the welcoming cocoon of my bed, so I can have the final hour of my birthday to myself.

I pick my way up the stairs, carefully, quietly, not wanting to alert Sabine whose light is peeking out from under her door. Having just dropped the bundle of presents onto my desk, when she pads down the hall and comes in.

"Happy Birthday." She smiles, wrapped in a robe so creamy and plush it looks like a cloud of whipped cream. Squinting at the clock on my nightstand when she says, "It *is* still your birthday, right?"

"Seventeen." I nod. "And not a day older." Watching as she makes her way in and perches on the edge of my bed, eyeballing the pile of gifts—a couple of metaphysical books from Ava that I pretty much "read" the moment I touched them, an amethyst geode from Jude, a T-shirt that says NEVER SUMMON ANYTHING YOU CAN'T BANISH from Rayne (ha-ha), and another one with a colorful spiral symbol from Romy that probably came from the same Wiccan store, along with an iTunes gift card from Honor who handed it to me as she mumbled, "Um, because you seem to really like music with the way you're always, you know, all plugged in and all." Oh, and vase after vase of brilliant red tulips that Damen must've manifested the moment he drove away.

"That's quite a bounty you got there," she says as I take it all in, trying to see it in the same way she sees it, more as a celebration of my existence and less a reminder of those who are missing.

I drop onto my desk chair and kick off my sandals, sensing she's here for a purpose and hoping she'll hurry up and get to it.

"I won't keep you long—it's late and you're probably tired," she says, accurately reading my mood.

And even though I start to protest, out of politeness if nothing else, I don't get very far before I stop. Because as nice as it is to visit with her, as seldom as I get to see her alone these days, I really do wish we could push this little visit to tomorrow. I'm just not up for one of her long, meandering talks.

But, of course, that particular mood she doesn't sense, she just looks me over with her narrowed gaze when she says, "So, how's everything—your job—Damen? I hardly ever see you these days."

I nod, assuring her it's all *good*, careful to put a little oomph into the word, hoping it'll serve to convince her.

She nods, gaze lightening in relief when she adds, "Well, you look good. You got so thin there for a while that I—" She shakes her head, a trace of just how worried she was clouding her gaze and making me feel about *this* big. "But you seem to be filling out again. Your skin's all cleared up too—which is good—" She presses down on her lips, as though carefully weighing what she's about to say next, before plunging ahead. "You know, Ever, when I said I wanted you to work this summer, I didn't exactly mean it quite in the way that you took it. I was referring more to a part-time gig, something to keep you occupied for a few hours each day, but the way you've been going at it—" She stops and shakes her head. "Well, I'm pretty sure you're putting in more hours than I am. And now with just a handful of weeks until school starts again—well, I think you should consider giving notice, so you can enjoy a little time on the beach, spend some time with your friends."

"What friends?" I shrug, feeling that sting at the back of each eye as my stomach takes a little dip. But still, I said it. Admitted a truth so painful, she can't help but shift and gaze at the floor. Taking a moment to compose herself before lifting her eyes to meet mine and motioning toward the pile of birthday booty when she says, "Well, excuse me for saying so, but I think the evidence proves otherwise."

I close my eyes and shake my head, furiously dabbing at my cheeks as I quickly turn away, thinking of the one friend who wasn't there today, who probably won't be there ever again, thanks to the monster and me.

"Hey—you okay?" She reaches toward me, wanting only to comfort, but pulling away just as quickly, remembering how finicky I am about being touched.

I take a deep breath and nod, knowing how much she worries, and wishing I hadn't dragged her into this. Because the truth is, I *am* okay. Like she said, my clothes no longer hang on me, my skin is clear, my relationship is back on track, and that horrible beast, that strange foreign pulse that once ruled me, hasn't been seen or heard from since that night on the beach. And even though there will always be that huge gaping hole my family's absence has left, even though I'll have to say good-bye to Sabine someday soon, Damen will always be there. If he's proved nothing else this past year, it's clear that he's fully committed to me—*to us*. No matter how bad things get, he's not the least bit put off. And in the end, that's all I can ask. Everything else, well, it just is what it is.

I look at Sabine and nod, firmer this time, like I truly do mean it. I made up my mind months ago, pledged my allegiance to immortality and now there's no looking back—just a long forward march into infinity.

"Just a small case of the birthday blues, I guess." Looking at her when I add, "Surely you're familiar with the pain of growing older?" Smiling in a way that starts at my lips but creeps all the way up to my eyes—a smile that encourages her to smile too.

"You have my sympathies." She laughs. "Though you'll have them even more when it's your turn to be forty." She rises from the bed and makes for the door, hands buried deep in the pockets of her robe when she says, "Oh, I almost forgot, I left a few things on your dresser over there." She nods in that general direction. "The one from me—well, I think you'll be surprised when you see it. I know I was when I found it, but I was also hoping you could carve out some time from your busy schedule so that we could have lunch and go shopping."

I nod. "I'd like that," I tell her, realizing just after I said it that I really, really would. It's been a while since we've enjoyed some good, girly fun.

"Oh, and the other one—the card"—she shrugs—"it came today. I found it shoved under the door when I got home. I have no idea who it's from, though it's clearly addressed to you."

I glance at the dresser, taking in a rectangular package beside a large pink envelope that almost seems to—*glow*—only in a foreboding, ominous way.

"Anyway, I just wanted to wish you a happy birthday." She peeks at the clock. "You've only got a few minutes left, so be sure to enjoy it!"

The second the door closes behind her I make for the dresser and grab the box. Its contents revealed the instant I touch it.

I tear off the paper as fast as I can, dropping the shredded bits to the floor and lifting the lid to reveal a slim, purple leather photo album containing all the photos Riley took on that fateful trip to the lake—including the one I saw in Summerland. And as I flip through them, I can't help but wonder if she somehow arranged this—if she can *see* this—*see* me? But I don't call out to her again, that never leads anywhere anymore. I just wipe my face of tears and whisper a quiet *Thanks*. Placing it on my nightstand, knowing I'll want to keep it someplace close where I can look at it again and again. Then I reach for the envelope with my name inscribed on its front in an overly formal scrawl—sucking in my breath as it shimmers and glows in my hand, and knowing from the way my whole body chills it's from *him*.

Tipping my nail under the flap, determined to get this

over with fast, I glance at its pink, glittery cover before flipping it open and skimming the usual, preprinted message before my gaze drops to the lower left corner, where Roman's written a note in his loopy, cursive scrawl, reads:

> *It's time to claim that which you most desire*
> *Today on your birthday I'll grant a cease-fire*
> *Be at my house before midnight tonight*
> *A second too late and this offer expires*
> *Hope to see you soon!*
> *Roman*
> *xoxo*

TWENTY-FIVE

By the time I get to Roman's I have only minutes to spare. Two to be exact, and I'm hoping his clock is reflecting that too. But this time, instead of charging the door like I usually do, I rap my knuckles against it and wait. Because if we truly are calling a truce like he says, then a show of manners can't hurt.

I wait, adding up the seconds as I glance at my watch, the soft sound of his approaching feet signaling that my moment has come—the result of magick done right.

The door swings open and he stands there before me, all sparkly blue eyes, glistening white teeth, and suntanned skin. A black silky robe kind of thing, what was once called a smoking jacket, hanging loose off his shoulders, exposing an ample expanse of bare chest, abs that are remarkably defined, and a pair of old faded jeans that hang low on his hips.

And that's all it takes. One passing glance at the bounty before me and my body begins to tremble, my knees start to sag, and my pulse quickens in a way so horrible, so dreadfully familiar, a new understanding slowly creeps over me:

The monster isn't slain! Isn't banished at all! It merely retreated, hunkered down somewhere deep, biding its time, and rebuilding its strength until it could rise up again . . .

I swallow hard, forcing a nod as though everything's fine. Aware of his gaze sweeping over me, not missing a thing, knowing I need to get through this no matter what, there's no way I can fail when everything I need is so well within my reach.

He motions me in, head cocked to the side. "Glad to see you're on time," he says, studying me carefully.

I turn, not even halfway down the hall before I stop and reconsider. Seeing the look of amusement that crosses his face as the color drains from mine. "Just in time for what, exactly? What's this about?" I narrow my gaze, pressing up against the wall as he slinks past and urges me to follow.

"Why it's about your birthday, of course!" He laughs, glancing over his shoulder and shaking his head. "That Damen's such a sentimental wanker—I'm sure he did his best to make your day *special*. Though, I daresay not nearly as *special* as I'm about to make it."

I stand my ground, refusing to budge. But despite the fact that my hands and legs are so shaky it feels as though the sockets are coming loose, my voice stays controlled, measured, giving nothing away. "Fulfilling your promise and giving me what I want will make it special enough. No need to offer me a seat I won't take, and a drink I'll refuse. Why don't we just fast-forward from here and get to it, okay?"

He looks at me, eyes creasing with laughter as a smile tugs at his lips. "Wow, that Damen's one lucky bloke." He shakes his head and rakes his fingers through his golden tousle of curls. "None of that time-wasting foreplay for you. Seems our little Ever here would rather skip right past the appetizers and get to the main course—and, luv, I can't applaud you loudly enough for that."

I force my face to remain blank, impassive, despite how much his words may disturb me. Painfully aware of this dark flame burning hotter inside me, now fanned by his presence.

"And while you may not desire a drink or a seat, as it just so happens I do. And since I'm the host of this little soiree, I'm afraid you'll just have to humor me."

He swoops toward the den in a swirl of black silk, sidling behind the bar and filling a heavy crystal goblet with a generous splash of red. Wiggling the glass before me, encouraging the opalescent liquid to spark and shine as it runs up and down the sides, reminding me of what Haven once said about it being more potent than Damen's and wondering if it's true. If it gives them some sort of advantage—if it would work that way for me too or end up making me as crazy and dangerous as them.

I rub my lips together and struggle to steady myself. My fingers growing fidgety, twitchy, knowing it's not much longer before I lose it completely.

"So sorry about your little problem with Haven." Roman nods, raising his glass and taking a long, steady sip. "But people change, you know? Not all friendships are built to last."

"I haven't given up." I shrug, the words ringing with far more assurance than I feel. "I'm sure we'll be able to work it out," I add, that strange foreign pulse throbbing within me when he tilts his head to the side and allows his Ouroboros tattoo to flash in and out of view.

"You sure about that, luv?" He looks at me, fingers idly

circling the stem of his glass as his gaze moves over me in that slow, leisurely, intimate way that he has. Choosing to linger on the deep V of my dress when he says, "I mean, no offense darlin', but I beg to differ. It's been my experience that when two determined *birds* want the same thing—well, someone's bound to get hurt—or *worse*—as you well know."

I move toward him—not the monster but me (though the monster certainly doesn't object), gaze fixed on his when I say, "But Haven and I don't want the same thing. She wants *you* and I want something entirely different."

He peers at me from over the rim of his glass, the goblet obscuring everything but his steely blue gaze. "Oh, yeah, and what's that, luv?"

"You already know." I shrug, moving my hand from my hip and clasping it behind my back so he can't see the way it trembles and shakes. "Isn't that why you summoned me here?"

He nods, setting his drink on the gold-beaded coaster. "Still, I'd love to hear you say it. Love to hear the words spoken out loud—from your lips to my ears."

I take a deep breath, take in his heavy-lidded gaze, wide inviting lips, and broad expanse of chest, my gaze lured down to his abs, and lower still, when I say, "The antidote." Pushing the words past my lips, wondering if he has any idea of the battle waging inside me. "I want *the antidote*," I repeat, firmer this time. Adding, "As you well know."

And before I can stop it, he's standing beside me. Face composed, hands relaxed, hanging loose at his sides. The chill of his skin emanating over me in a wave of cool, sweet relief when he says, "I want you to know that I brought you here with the purest intentions. After seeing the way you've suffered over these past few months, I'm fully prepared to call it off and give you what you want. And even though it's been a good bit of fun, or at least it has for me anyway." He shrugs. "Much like you, Ever, I'm ready to move on. Back to London, that is. This town's too laid back for my tastes, I require a bit more action than this."

"You're leaving?" I blurt, the words coming so quickly I'm not sure who's responsible for voicing them.

"Does that upset you?" He smiles, gaze searching my face.

"Hardly." I scowl, rolling my eyes and averting my gaze, hoping to distract him from the tremor in my voice.

"I'll try not to take that personally." He smiles, Ouroboros tattoo flashing in and out of view, its beady eyes seeking mine as its tongue slithers about. "But before I go, I thought I'd tie up a few loose ends, and seeing as it's your birthday and all, I thought I'd start with you. Give you the gift you want most. The *one thing* you want more than anything else in the world, that no other person, living or dead, could ever give you—" He trails his finger down my arm, lightly, quickly, the memory of it lingering long after he's turned away and moved on.

I stare at his retreating back, knowing I can't afford this, can't afford to slip up. Reminding myself of the magical feel of Damen's lips just a few hours before, and how very close I am to reclaiming that—but only if I can keep myself in check.

Roman turns, finger beckoning for me to follow and *tsking* at my resistance when he says, "Trust me, luv, I've no plans to trick you or drag you off to my chambers." He shakes his head and laughs. "There'll be plenty of time for that later, if that's what you choose. But for now, I've got something a little more technical planned. And speaking of, have you ever taken a lie detector test?"

I narrow my gaze, having no idea what he's getting at but sure it's a trap. Eyes on his back as he leads me down the hall, through the kitchen, and out the back door, all the way past the hot tub perched off the side of the porch, and over to a room, like a converted detached garage that, upon entering, seems equal parts antiquities storehouse and mad-scientist lab.

"I hate to say it, luv, and believe me, I mean absolutely no offense, but you have been known to lie on occasion—mostly on the occasions when it benefits *you*. And since I'm a man of integrity, since I promised to give you the one thing you *truly want more than anything else in the world,* I feel it's only right that we're both completely clear on just what that is. There's clearly something odd going on between you and me. Do I really need to remind you of how you threw yourself at me the last time you were here?"

"It's not—" I start, not getting very far before he holds up his hand.

"Please." He smirks. "Spare me the excuses, luv. I have a much more direct way of getting the answers I seek."

I press my lips into a frown, having seen enough TV crime shows to recognize the contraption he's leading me toward. Fully expecting me to strap myself in and consent to a polygraph test I've no doubt he's rigged.

"Forget it," I say, spinning on my heel, ready to leave. "You're just gonna have to take me at my word, or the deal's off."

Having just reached the door when he says, "Well, there *is* something else we can try."

I stop.

"And trust me, there's no way to *rig* this one, especially for people like us. And as it just so happens, it fits right in with all of that metaphysical *everything is energy and joined as one* crap you're so enamored of."

I sigh loudly, audibly, tapping my foot against the floor, hoping to release some of this energy building inside me, as well as clue him in to just how impatient I'm getting.

But Roman's not about to be hurried, or rushed, or operate on any sort of schedule other than his own. His fingers absently picking at a loose thread on his jacket as he looks me over and says, "You see, Ever, the thing is, it's been scientifically proven that the truth is always, *always* stronger than a lie. That if you were to measure the two side by side—pit one against the other, so to speak—the truth would always be the victor. What do you think?"

I roll my eyes, the act alone signaling what I think of that and just about everything else that's taken place up to this point.

But Roman's unmoved, determined to play it his way when he says, "And as it just so happens, there's a very easy way in which to test this—one that cannot be rigged and requires nothing more than your own physiology. Care to try?"

Uh, not really! I start to say, *want* to say, but the monster is rising and won't let me speak, which only encourages Roman to continue.

"Now, would you or would you not say that we're both of equal strength? That among our kind there are no real physical differences in terms of strength and speed between men and women?"

I shrug, never having really thought about it either way and not really interested in starting now.

"So, with that in mind, I'd like to demonstrate something

I think you'll find quite interesting. And, on a side note, I assure you I'm not trying to play you, it's not a game, and no one gets hurt. I'm sincere about giving you the *thing you want most,* and this is the best way I can think of to determine what that is. I'll even go first, so you can see I have no tricks up my sleeve—so to speak."

He stands before me, arm raised to his side, parallel to the concrete floor. Nodding as he says, "Now go ahead, place your two fingers on my arm and give it a little push downward as I resist and push up. Nothing funny here, I promise. You'll see."

My eyes meet his, seeing the challenge in his gaze and knowing I have no choice but to go forward and meet it, since he alone holds the key. I have to play the game, his rules, his way.

I stare at his arm hovering before me, tanned, strong, begging to be touched. And even though I know I can't do it, can't contain it, still, I clench my teeth and try. Pressing my fingers against it, the chill of his skin emanating through the soft, silky fabric of his sleeve, causing the dark flame inside me to spark and blaze.

Roman's voice a soft, thick whisper in my ear when he says, "*Feel* that?"

I look at him, aware of nothing more than the insistent pulse now thrumming inside me as my body fills with heat. Heat that seeks nothing more than his cool, sweet relief.

"Okay, so now I want you to ask me a question, a simple yes or no question, one that you already know the answer to. Giving me a moment to concentrate on the answer and state it both mentally and verbally as you try to push my arm down with two fingers."

I glance between my watch and him, knee jiggling like crazy, knowing I don't have much longer.

But he just nods, arm raised, encouraging gaze on mine. "The truth strengthens, lies weaken—now's your chance to test that theory on me, so we can then test it on you. It's the only way to prove what you really do want, Ever. So, go ahead, ask me a question, whatever you want. I'll even lower my shield so you can read my thoughts and see I'm not cheating."

He looks at me, the weight of his gaze causing my pulse to quicken and my heart to crash until I can't—*I can't*—

"Ask me a question, Ever." He peers at me closely. "Ask me anything you want. The sooner we finish with me, the sooner we can get on to you and determine just what it is you desire most."

I stand beside him, struggling to steel myself, to center myself, but it's no use, I can't do it, can't play this game anymore.

"Would you rather we skip ahead?" he asks, gaze moving over me, slowly, deeply. "Would you prefer I test *you* instead?"

He waits, giving me a moment to collect myself, to take a deep breath and bid a silent plea to Hecate, asking her for the strength to get through this, to get what I came for. But when I look at Roman again, I realize Hecate has left me, I'm all on my own.

"It *is* the antidote you want, right?" he asks, turning toward me, so close I can feel his breath on my cheek, his lips just inches from mine. "That *is* the one true thing you desire above all else?"

Yes! I shout, the word coming from somewhere down deep as my mind repeats it with such force I'm sure he can hear it.

Only he can't hear it.

Because it was never voiced.

It's just an empty sound that bounces around in my head until it finally dies out.

And the second his eyes meet mine—*I'm gone*.

The flame roaring through me, setting my body ablaze, as my fingers, hungry for the feel of his flesh, grasp and claw at that smooth expanse of golden tanned chest.

"Careful, luv." He grips my wrists and pulls me tightly to him, eyes narrowed, lips moist and wet. "I've never been one for the scratch marks, no matter how fast they may fade." Holding me away from him as his gaze trails down my body—hungry, predatory, and I the banquet before him. "Also, we'll have none of this nonsense." He laughs, loosening the amulet from my neck and tossing it clear to the other side of the room where it rolls and bounces and clinks against the ground.

But I don't care about that, don't care about anything but the feel of his fingers snaking their way down my back, the way he buries his face in my hair and presses his nose to my neck, inhaling strongly, deeply, filling himself with my scent. His gaze burning into mine as he lifts me into his arms and lowers me onto the couch. Ridding himself of his jacket and unfastening his jeans as I run my hands over his skin and pull him down to me, eager for the feel of his kiss, his lips upon mine.

Gasping when he pushes me away, removes my hands from his neck, and says, "Take it easy, luv. You're the one who doesn't like all that foreplay, remember? There's plenty of time for that later, but first, let's get this thing done. After all, you've been waiting for—what? Four hundred years, is it?"

I pull him back to me, hungry for more—more of his skin—more of the taste of him—my body pushing, arching, desperate to meet his, my lips swollen, greedy for all he can give. Wanting him to want me in the way I want him, and willing to do whatever it takes to get him to kiss me—then suddenly remembering just what that is . . .

He wedges his knee between mine, losing his jeans and squaring his hips, positioning himself as he says, "This'll only hurt a minute, luv, and then—"

And then he looks at me and everything stops—his eyes glazed with longing, lips parted in wonder, as *that look*—the look I've been longing for, yearning for, suddenly takes over.

The look that tells me he wants me—*needs* me—as much as I want and need him.

I pull him down to me, desperate to finally feel the press of his lips when he bends toward me, voice a whisper of hushed reverence when he says, *"Drina—"*

I pull back, squinting, confused, looking into his eyes and seeing what he sees—flaming red hair, porcelain skin, emerald green eyes—a reflection that doesn't belong to—*me.*

"Drina . . ." he mumbles, "Drina, I . . ."

And while my body's still responding, encouraging his touch, his gentle caress of my skin, my heart's shrinking back, refusing to play. Something is wrong—something's gone very—*very*—*wrong*—something that clings to the outer edges, just starting to form and take shape, when he tugs at my dress and it slips right away.

And when I gaze at him, see that glazed look in his eyes, I know it's almost here. My birthday gift—the thing I wanted most—is about to be mine.

Vaguely aware that from this moment on, nothing will ever be the same.

Nothing.

Never. Ever. Again.

He moves my legs apart as I brace for that brief flash of pain. Turning my head to face the mirror on the far wall, only to be met by an image of a girl with flaming red hair, luminescent pale skin, emerald green eyes, and a smile so feral I recognize it immediately.

The same image he sees when he looks at me.

Only it's not really me. *Not me at all!*

"Ready, luv?" Roman gazes down at me, anticipation marked on his face.

And while my head nods in assent and my body lifts to meet his, it's not really me who's responding. The monster may rule my body, but it's got nothing to do with my heart or my soul.

Like Roman said earlier: *In the end, the truth always wins.*

And lucky for me, my soul knows the score.

I close my eyes and focus on my heart chakra, *seeing* that spinning green wheel of energy emanating right from the center of my chest, encouraging it to grow outward, expand, getting bigger and bigger until—

Roman mumbles my name, only it's not really my name, it's *her* name, voice thick with anticipation, eager to begin, having no idea what I'm up to, that, for a moment anyway, I've managed to win.

I bring my knee up and jam it straight into him. My ears ringing with the sound of his agonized scream, as his hands clutch between his legs and his eyes roll back in his head. I slip out from under him, moving hurriedly, quickly, knowing it's just a matter of seconds before he's healed and back at full strength again.

"Where are you hiding it?" I ask, frantically tugging on

my clothes and slamming my amulet back down around my neck, knowing without looking that he sees me as the blond-haired, blue-eyed *me* again. "Where is it?" I demand, glancing around the small, well-ordered lab.

He ducks his head, carefully inspecting himself, as he mutters, "*Damn it,* Ever—"

But I've no time for that. "Tell me where it is!" I shout, struggling to focus on my heart chakra as I clutch the amulet tightly to my chest.

"Are you crazy?" He shrugs on his jeans and scowls. "You pull a crap move like that and expect me to help you?" He shakes his head. "Forget it. You could've had that antidote, you could've walked away with it ten minutes ago, but you made your choice, Ever. Fair and square as we both know. I was fully prepared to hand it over, and *no,* it's *not* here, so don't bother ransacking the place in search of it. Seriously, just how *daft* do you think I am?" He pulls on his smoking jacket and yanks it closed across his chest, as though to keep from tempting me again. But despite the monster still clamoring inside, I'm no longer interested. The beast may be alive and well, but my heart and soul are now leading. "I was fully prepared to lead you to it, but you chose otherwise. And just because you had a last minute change of *heart*—" He lifts his brow in a way that tells me he knows the source of my strength. "That doesn't change a thing. You chose *me,* Ever. *I'm* what you wanted most. But now, after the stunt you just pulled, you'll get neither." He shakes his head. "No second chances after a crap move like that."

I stand before him, the dark flame raging within, urging me toward those ocean blue eyes, golden tousle of hair, moist waiting lips, trim, slinky hips . . .

"No," I mumble, taking a step back. "*I* don't want you. *I've* never wanted you. It's not *me*—it's—it's *something else.* This isn't my fault, I'm not in control!"

I press my lips together, knowing there's only one way out of here, but that I shouldn't do it in front of him, shouldn't raise his suspicions like that. But still, it's not like I can trust my legs to carry me anywhere but to his bed.

I clutch the amulet to my chest as I concentrate on the shimmering, golden veil. Envisioning the portal to Summerland and seeing it spring open before me, just about to step through when he says, "Foolish Ever, don't you realize there's no longer any difference between you and your—*monster*? You *are* the monster. It's your dark side, your shadow self, and you've now joined as one."

TWENTY-SIX

I land in that vast fragrant field. Reluctantly, guiltily, knowing I shouldn't have done it. Shouldn't have come here like this. Shouldn't have let Roman watch me disappear. But what choice did I have?

My resolve was running thin, chipped away by the monster within, and just a few seconds more in his presence would've surely been the end. The end of me. The end of all I hold dear.

Because the thing is—Roman is right. Totally and completely right. The only reason I lost, the only reason I failed to get what I want, is because the monster *is* me, there's no difference between us. It makes all the moves, calls all the shots, while I'm just along for the ride, with no idea how to pull the brakes or get off. I'm all out of options. I've no idea where to turn. All I know is:

The reversal spell failed, as did the bid to Hecate.

And Damen, well, Damen can't save me.

Can't ever learn about the repulsive thing I almost just did.

Can't spend the next hundred years saving me from myself.

I've sunk so deep, fallen so far, there's no getting up. No getting my life back on track. No way I can head back to the earth plane and risk all of that.

So I wander, with absolutely no destination in mind and no idea what I'll do once I get there. I wander along the rainbow-colored stream, feet moving idly, unhurried, just ambling along, barely paying any notice when the stream ends and the ground beneath my feet becomes a mushy, soggy, wet path.

Barely noticing when the air cools by several degrees, and that light golden shimmer grows thicker, denser, hard to see through.

And maybe that explains my shock when I see it. When I realize I've unknowingly reached the place where the mist is always at its thickest, where it's easy to get turned around to the point of no return. Taking in its familiar sloping outline, the frayed and worn ropes, the slatted, splintering wood, its shape wavering in and out of focus, obscured by the fog, but still, even so, there's no denying what it is.

No mistaking the bridge that crosses to the *other side*.

The Bridge of Souls.

I kneel down beside it, knees sinking into the damp, mist-laden earth, wondering if it's some kind of sign, if I was led here on purpose, if I'm meant to finally cross it.

What if the opportunity I previously denied is now being offered again? A no-questions-asked, special deal for repeat customers like me.

I reach for the handrail, an old frayed rope that looks as though it could snap at any second, seeing the way the fog grows increasingly thicker toward the middle, becoming so dense, its final destination is a white, shrouded mystery. Reminding myself that this is the very same bridge I urged Riley to cross, the same one that my parents and Buttercup took to the other side. And if they were able to cross it and come out okay, then really, how bad could it be?

I mean, what if I just got up, brushed myself off, took a deep breath, and crossed it?

What if all it takes to solve all my problems, rid myself of the monster, extinguish this flame, and see my family again is just one small step, followed by another?

A handful of steps toward their warm, welcoming arms.

A handful of steps away from Roman, Haven, the twins, Ava, and the horrible mess that I've made.

A handful of steps toward the peace that I seek.

I mean, seriously, what could it hurt? Surely I'll find my family all waiting for me—just like you see on all those afterlife shows on TV?

I grasp the rope tighter and push myself to my feet, my legs shaky, unstable, as I lean forward ever so slightly and strain to get a better view. Wondering just how far I'd have to go before I'd reach the point of no return. Remembering how Riley claimed to make it about halfway, before she turned right back around and went looking for me, only to get so confused by the mist, she couldn't find it again—or at least not for a while anyway.

But even if I did decide to keep going, make my way clear across to the *other side,* would the final destination be the same for me as it was for them? Or would it be more like a freight train suddenly switching its tracks, leading me toward the eternal abyss of the Shadowland instead of the sweet ever after?

I take a deep breath and shift, lifting my foot off the wet soggy ground, just about to make a move when I'm suddenly overcome by a soothing wave of calm—a peaceful rush that can only mean one thing—that only one person can yield in me. A calm so opposite Damen's tingle and heat, I'm not the least bit surprised when I turn to find Jude beside me.

"You know where that leads, right?" He motions toward the gently swaying bridge, struggling to keep his voice crisp, clear, but the nervous tremor reveals all.

"I know where it leads for other people." I shrug, glancing between him and the bridge. "Though I've no idea where it'll take me."

He squints, head tilted as he studies me slowly, carefully, proceeding with caution when he says, "It leads to the other side. For *everyone*. No separate lines. No segregation of any kind. Leave that sort of judgment for the earth plane, not here."

I shrug, unconvinced. He doesn't know what I know. Hasn't seen what I've seen. So how could he possibly know anything about what does or doesn't apply to me?

"Even so." He nods, sensing my thoughts loud and clear. "I'm just not sure you should even be considering that yet. Life is short enough already, you know? Even on the days when it seems really, really long. By the time it's all over, it's really just a flash, a blip in eternity, trust me on that."

"Maybe for you, but not for me," I say, meeting his gaze in a way so open and honest it's clear I'm inviting him in. Ready to spill, confide the whole sordid tale, lay it all out on the table, everything I've held back all along—all he has to do is ask and the full confession is his. "For me, it's hardly what you'd call a blip."

He rubs his chin and merges his brow, clearly trying to make sense of my words.

And that's all it takes. His *desire* to understand, and it all comes tumbling out. Everything. All of it. A complete and total spillage of words, coming so fast and furious they're all mumbled and jumbled together. Stretching all the way back to that very first day at the site of the accident, when Damen first fed me the elixir and turned me into what I am now, to the truth about Roman, who he really is, and how he ensured that Damen and I can never be together, about Ava and the twins and the strange past that connects them, how I turned Haven into a freak like me, about the chakras and how targeting our weaknesses is the only way to obliterate us, and, of course, I tell him about the Shadowland, the eternal abyss where all immortals go—the only thing that's keeping me on this side of the bridge. The words spewing so quickly I can't stop them. Don't even try to stop them. So relieved to unburden myself, egged on by his efforts to stay calm, to not totally freak, to just let me continue saying my piece.

And when I get to the part about Roman, about my horrible attraction to him, how the insistent dark flame continues to burn within me, and the degrading moment I just barely escaped, he looks at me and says, "Ever, please, slow down. I can barely keep it all straight."

I nod, my heart racing, cheeks flushing, my arms wrapped tightly around me. My hair clinging in long, stringy, wet clumps to my cheeks, my shoulders, my back, weighted down by heavy, round dewdrops that continue to fall without ceasing. Watching as a virtual chorus line of new arrivals eagerly make their way to the other side, the bridge drooping and swaying as they march straight ahead, each of their eyes emitting the most miraculous, glorious light.

"Listen, can we—go someplace else?" He nods toward the line of people so long, I wonder if some sort of catastrophe has just taken place. "I'm a little creeped out by all this."

"*You're* the one who decided to come here." I shrug, feeling inexplicably defensive, not to mention plagued by confessor's remorse. I mean, here I just exposed my story, in all its hushed, secretive entirety, just laid it all out there in the open for him to see, and all he can say is *slow down* and *let's split this scene*? I shake my head and roll my eyes. That is hardly the feedback I was looking for. "I mean, seriously. It's not like I invited you to join me, you just showed up."

He looks at me, undeterred by my mood swing, his lips lifting at the corners when he says, "Well, not exactly . . ."

I peer at him, wondering what that means.

"I heard your distress call and came to investigate. I was looking for *you*, not—not *this*."

I narrow my gaze, just about to refute it when I remember my first meeting with the twins, a meeting that unfolded in much the same way.

"I wasn't going to cross," I say, cheeks heating in embarrassment. "I mean, maybe I considered it, but only for a second and not *seriously*, well, not *really*. I was merely *curious*—that's all. Besides, I happen to know a few people who live over there and, well, sometimes I miss them—"

"And so you thought you'd pay them a quick visit?" His tone is light, but the words weigh heavy, heavier than he thinks.

I shake my head and gaze down at my mud-covered feet.

"So—what then? What is it that stopped you, Ever? Was it me?"

I take a deep breath, one, followed by another, needing a moment before I lift my gaze to meet his. "I—I wasn't going to do it. I mean, yeah, I was a little tempted and all, but I would've stopped—with or without you showing up." I shrug, my eyes searching his. "Partly because it's not right to leave so much undone, so many mistakes for everyone else to clean up, and partly because knowing what I know about an immortal's soul and where it ends up, well, no matter how much I may think I deserve nothing less, I'm not about to race toward that end. I've seen the *other side,* or at least the one meant for me. And I'm sorry to say it, but it's hardly the place where my family went. I'm afraid if I want to see them again, I'll have a lot more luck going through you than I ever will crossing that bridge, not to mention—"

He looks at me, waiting.

I sigh and kick at the ground, determined to confess the most important reason of all, no matter how bad it makes him feel, and looking him in the eye and squaring my shoulders when I say, "Not to mention the fact that I could never do that to Damen." My eyes meet Jude's before I quickly look away. "I could never abandon him like that—not after—" I pause, trying to swallow past the lump in my throat. "Not after all that he's done for *me.*" I rub my arms for warmth, though I'm not really cold. Just awkward. Awkward and uncomfortable, for sure.

But Jude just nods, assuring me it will all be okay. His hand pressed to the small of my back as he quietly leads me away from the bridge, from the long line of souls happily leaping to the other side, and all the way back to the earth plane.

TWENTY-SEVEN

"So here's what you do." He lets the engine idle as he turns toward me. "First, you go inside and come clean." He lifts his finger to silence me the second I start to butt in. "You just sit yourself down and tell the whole dirty tale—leave nothing out. Because despite your previous experiences with her, from all that I've seen, and all that I've learned, you're in good hands. Really. She's smarter than you think, and she's been doing this sort of thing for many lifetimes now. Not to mention, she's pretty much the only one I can think of who'll actually be of any real, unbiased help."

"How do you know about her former lifetimes?" I ask, a sudden chill blanketing my skin. "I mean, other than the stuff I already told you?"

He looks at me, holding the moment for so long, I'm just about to break it when he says, "I've been to the Great Halls of Learning. I pretty much know everything now."

I nod, swallowing hard, trying not to freak. Because even though I just let him in on what basically amounts to the mother lode of confessionals, still, it's not like I told him *everything*.

But he just shrugs, not missing a beat. "And then, when you're done in there, you need to go to Damen's. I don't care what you tell him, that's your deal. But you've really put him through the ringer lately, and no matter how I may feel about him . . ." He stops and shakes his head. "Well, just do it, okay? You're not better yet—you proved that tonight, and you need him on your side to help get you through it. It's the right thing to do. And take some time off work while you're at it. Seriously, I can handle it. Besides, Honor's offered to fill in, so maybe I'll give her the chance."

I nod, impressed by how noble he's being, taking the high road and urging me toward his rival for the last several centuries. Gripping the door handle, sure that we're finished and about to climb out, when he places his hand on my leg, leans toward me and says, "There's more."

I turn, seeing how serious he's gone as his long, cool fingers squeeze at my knee.

"While I promise not to interfere in your relationship with Damen, I'm not about to back down either. Four hundred years of losing out on the girl of my dreams isn't sitting very well with me these days."

"You—you know about that?" I gasp, my hand flying to my throat as my voice fades.

"You mean the Parisian stable boy, the British earl, the New England parishioner, and the artist otherwise known as Bastiaan De Kool?" His eyes meet mine, two aqua pools burning with the desire of hundreds of years. "Yeah." He nods. "I know all about it. And *more*." I shake my head, having no idea what to say, where I can possibly go from here, his fingers moving from my knee to my cheek when he says, "Don't tell me you don't feel it too—I know that you do. I can see it in your gaze, in the way you respond to my touch. Hell, I even saw the way you reacted when you saw me with Honor earlier—*today*—?" He peeks at his wrist, but since he's not wearing a watch, he just shrugs and waves it away. "Anyway, I'm not into Honor, not like you think. It's strictly a student-teacher thing—a friendship, nothing more." He tilts his head as his fingers, the silky soft tips of his fingers, gently glide over my cheek, so soothing, so enticing, I couldn't turn away if I wanted. "I have no interest in anyone else. It's been you all along. And while you may not feel the same now, I want you to know that we have no restrictions, nothing to keep us apart. Nothing but *you*, that is. You're the one who decides in the end." He pulls away, the memory of his touch still lingering, as his gaze burns into mine. "But whatever you decide, there's no denying *this*"—he reaches toward me again—"*is there?*"

And when he looks at me, his head tilted in a way that allows a generous spray of dreadlocks to fall across his face and over his shoulder, when he lifts that single spliced brow ever so slightly, when his smile encourages those dimples to come out and play, when he looks at me *like that*—it's like a challenge I cannot meet.

Yes, I feel something when we touch. *Yes,* he's undeniably sexy and cute and someone I can count on. *Yes,* on more than one occasion I've found myself just the slightest bit tempted by him. But even after it's added all up, it still doesn't equal what I feel for Damen. Never has. Never will. Damen's the one for me. And if I accomplish nothing else on this crazy, insane day, I've at least got to be straight with Jude, no matter how much it may hurt. . . .

"Jude—" I start, but he presses his finger to my lips, stopping the word from going any further.

"Go inside, Ever." He nods, pushing my hair off my face and tucking it back behind my ear, fingers lingering a few seconds too long, reluctant to leave. "Make amends, reverse your spell, find an antidote to the antidote, do whatever it is that you need to do. Because no matter how you feel about me, no matter what choice you make, at the end of the day, I just want you to be happy. But I also want you to know that I haven't given up—and that I don't plan on doing so anytime soon. I'm already four hundred years into this, so I may as well go the distance. And while the last few centuries may not have resulted in a very fair fight, at least now, with the aid of Summerland, I'm a little more equally equipped. I may not be immortal, probably wouldn't ever choose that path for myself, but hey, it's like they say, knowledge is power, right? And now, thanks to you and the Great Halls of Learning, I've got that in spades."

I take a deep breath and push out of the car and into her house without even pausing to knock. And even though I failed to call or warn her that I was on my way, even though the hands on the clock point to a time that's well past the usual visiting hours, I'm not the least bit surprised to find Ava in her kitchen, brewing a fresh pot of tea, and smiling when she says, "Hey, Ever, I've been waiting for you. I'm so glad you made it."

TWENTY-EIGHT

She pushes the plate of cookies toward me, out of habit, without thinking. Shaking her head and laughing softly under her breath as she tries to yank them away, but not getting very far before I reach out and snatch one out from under the bottom. Creamy beige in color, round, bendy, and decorated with thick squares of sugar all along the top, breaking a piece off the side and placing it onto my tongue, remembering how it used to be my most favorite kind, and wishing I could enjoy sweets, any food really, in the same way I used to.

"You don't have to eat them on my account," she says, lifting her cup to her lips and blowing on her tea once, twice, before taking a sip. "Trust me, the twins like them plenty enough for both of us, so I won't be offended if you're no longer interested."

I shrug, wanting to tell her how sometimes, when I miss being normal, I go through the motions of eating and drinking and buying things at the store instead of manifesting them, just to prove I still can. But it doesn't usually last all that long, and lately it only comes around when it's late and I'm tired, and more than a little lost, as I am now. Other times, I can't imagine ever wanting to return to that brand of ordinary.

But, instead, I just look at her and say, "So how are the twins?" Breaking off another bite of cookie, remembering how it used to taste, sweet, rich, delicious, not all cardboardy bland like this and knowing it's me that's changed, not the recipe.

"You know, it's funny." She sets down her cup and leans toward me, fingers playing at her woven green placemat as though ironing it with her hands. "We've all settled in so well and so quickly, it's like no time has passed. Who would've thought?" She gives a half smile and shakes her head at the wonder of it. "I know reincarnation is primarily about karma and unfinished business of our past, but I never dreamed it would end up quite so—*literal*—for me."

"And their magick—is it coming back?"

She takes a breath, slow and deep, fingers reaching for her cup again, anchoring firmly around the handle but stopping just short of lifting it when she says, "No. Not yet. But maybe that's not such a bad thing." She shrugs.

I look at her, confused by what that could possibly mean.

"Well, it hasn't seemed to work out so well for you now, has it?"

I drop my hands to my lap, clasping, twisting, pulling at my fingers, the hunched-over, nervous sight of me alone pretty much all the answer she needs.

"And while I used to practice magick too—well, obviously." She drops her tongue out the side and raises her hand in a way meant to signify a noose, then bursting into laughter and wagging her finger at me when I gape. "Oh lighten up." She smiles, a quick flash of teeth. "No use crying about a past I can't change. Each step leads us to the next, and as it stands, the next step is right here." She gives the table a flat-palmed slap. "Because of my past life experiences, because you helped me to access the Summerland, where I eventually got to the Great Halls of Learning, I'm much more able to understand the things I could only guess at before."

"Yeah, like what?" I squint, slipping right back into my old, belligerent ways, not even giving her a chance to speak her piece without a rude interruption from me.

But Ava, true to her usual ways, chooses to ignore it, continuing on as though I didn't even say it. "I've learned that magick, like manifesting, is really just the simple manipulation of energy. But where manifesting is usually reserved for manipulating matter, magick, in the wrong hands anyway—" She pauses to look at me, her gaze screaming *your hands!* or at least that's how it seems to me. "Well, if not practiced correctly, without proper intent, it tends to manipulate *people,* and *that's* where the trouble begins."

"Wish the twins would've warned me of that," I mumble, hardly believing I'm blaming them, but still, there it is.

"Maybe they failed to mention it, but I'm sure Damen didn't?" She looks at me, clearly not buying it from the arch of her brow and tilt of her chin. "Ever, if you came here for help, which, considering the time and the circumstances, I'm assuming you did, then please allow me to do that—*help.* There's no need for excuses, I'm not here to judge you in any way, shape, or form. You made a mistake, you're not the first, and you certainly won't be the last. And while I'm sure you feel that your particular mistake is extraordinarily big, insurmountable even, contrary to what you might think, these types of things can always be undone, and oftentimes aren't nearly as lethal as we think—or, should I say, as we *allow* them to be."

"Oh, so now I'm allowing it?" I start, the argument coming so readily, so easy, but my heart isn't in it, and I quickly flash my palm and wave it away. Sighing as I add, "You know, for someone who needs help as often as I do, you'd think I'd be a little better at accepting it." I roll my eyes and shake my head, the gesture directed at me, not her.

She shrugs, removing an oatmeal cookie from the stack and plopping a raisin into her mouth. "It's never easy for the stubborn." She smiles, her gaze meeting mine. "But I think we're past all that now, right?" Seeing my nod of consent, and forging ahead when she adds, "The thing is, Ever, with both magick and manifesting, it's the *intent* that matters most—the result that you're focusing on. Your intention is the most important tool you have at your disposal. You're familiar with the Law of Attraction, right?" She looks at me, running her hand over her silky sleeve. "That we attract that which we focus on? Well, it's no different here. When you focus on what you fear—you get more of what you fear. When you focus on what you don't want—you get more of what you don't want. When you focus on attempting to control others—you attract more of being controlled. Your attention to them brings more *of* them, and more *like* them, into your life. Imposing your will upon others in order to persuade them to do something they're normally unwilling to do—well, not only does it *not* work but it also has a way of boomeranging right back at you. Resulting in karma, as every action does, only this isn't the kind that works in your favor, unless you're up for learning a few very important lessons, that is . . ."

But even though she continues to talk, my mind is still

stuck on that part about karma, about it boomeranging back. Remembering how the twins said something similar, something like: *It's wrong to use magick for selfish, nefarious reasons. There's karma to pay, and it'll come back times three.*

I swallow hard and reach for my tea, her words glancing over me when she says, "Ever, you must understand that all of this time you've been resisting in the very worst way. Resisting against me, when I tried to help you, resisting against Damen when he grew concerned for you, resisting against Roman and the horrible things he's done to you—" She lifts her hand, seeing how I'm about to refute that last one and silencing me with one raised finger when she says, "And the thing about resistance, the irony of it is, you end up spending so much time and energy focusing on the things you're resisting, the things you *don't* want, that you end up attracting exactly those things."

I look at her, not sure that I follow. Am I not supposed to resist against Roman? I mean, hel-*lo*, look what just happened, or what almost just happened, when I almost allowed myself to give in.

She squares her shoulders, placing her hands on either side of her cup when she meets my gaze and begins again. "Everything is energy, right?"

So I've heard.

"So if your thoughts are energy, and energy attracts, then all of your thoughts about all of the things you fear the most— well, you're actually *making* them happen. You're manifesting them into existence simply by obsessing over them. Or, more simply put, and, as it happens, very apropos for you, as the alchemists said: *'As above, so below, as within, so without.'*"

"That's *simply put*?" I shake my head and swirl my tea

around and around. She may as well be speaking in tongues for all I understood.

She smiles, her eyes patient, kind. "What it means is that what's inside us will also be found outside of us. That our inner states of consciousness, the thoughts that we focus on, will always be reflected in our outer lives. There's no escaping it, Ever, it just is. But what you failed to realize is that the magick isn't *out there*—it's not in the hands of the goddess or the queen—it's *in here*." She thumps her fist against her chest, gazing at me as her whole face lifts. "The only reason Roman has any power over you is because you gave it to him—you handed it right over! *Yes*, I know he tricked you, and *yes*, I know how he's keeping you from ever truly being with Damen, and *yes*, that must be unimaginably horrible, but if you'll just stop resisting what already *is*, if you just stop focusing on Roman and the rotten things that he's done, you'll be able to break this awful bond you've built with him. And soon, after a decent amount of meditation and cleansing, he won't be able to bother you anymore—not even close."

"But he'll still have the antidote—he'll still—" I start, but it's no use, Ava's on a roll and she's not finished yet.

"You're right. He will still have the antidote, and he'll probably be reluctant to give it to you. But that is a situation you cannot change. And your obsessing over it, and weaving all manner of spells, won't change it either. In fact, it'll only make it worse. By doing that, you've made him the focus of your universe, the exact result you didn't want, and trust me, Roman is well aware of this. He works hard to steal your focus, it's what every narcissist wants. So, if you truly want to resolve this and get your life back on track, then just *stop*. *Stop* focusing your energy on the things you don't want. *Stop* putting your energy into Roman. Just refuse to even go there and see where that leads." She leans toward me, tucking her wavy, auburn hair back behind her ear. "My guess is, once he sees you happily adapting to your situation, living your life and enjoying yourselves *despite* your limitations, he'll grow bored of the game and give in. But like this, the way you're handling it now, you may as well be hand-feeding prime rib to a tiger, you're only satisfying his most primal need. The beast is inside you, Ever, because *you* put it there. But trust me, you can rid yourself of it just as easily."

"How?" I shrug, understanding everything she just said, I mean, once she explained it, it all made perfect sense. And yet I can still feel that horrible, insistent pulse thrumming just under the surface, and it's kind of hard to believe it's just a simple matter of changing my focus. "When I tried to reverse it, it just made it worse. Then, when I appealed to Hecate for help, it seemed to work for a little while, but then, just now, when I saw Roman again—" The color rises to my cheeks as my whole body heats, horrified to remember what almost became of me. "Well, let's just say I discovered it hadn't gone anywhere, it was alive and kicking and ready to party. And while I get what you're saying, at least I think I do, I can't see how simply changing my thoughts is ever going to help. I mean, Hecate's in charge, not me, and I've no idea how to get her to step down."

But Ava just looks at me, her voice lowered when she says, "But that's where you're wrong. Hecate's not in charge, *you* are. You've been in charge all along. And though I hate to say it, because I know how uncomfortable it always makes people to hear it, the monster isn't some foreign being that's found its way in you, it isn't a demonic possession or anything like that—it's *you*. The monster is the dark side of *you*."

I tilt back in my seat and shake my head. "Great, that's just *great*. So you're saying my attraction to Roman is for real? Nice, Ava, thanks for that." I sigh, loudly, audibly, and grant her a nice, dramatic eye roll to go with it.

"Told you it never goes over so well." She shrugs, proving she's pretty much immune to my insolent reactions by this point. "But you must admit that, superficially speaking anyway, he *is* stunning, quite gorgeous really—" She smiles, practically begging me to agree. But when it goes unmet, she just shrugs again and says, "But that's not what I meant. You know about the yin yang symbol, right?"

I nod. "The outer circle represents everything, while the black and white parts represent the two energies that cause everything to happen." I shrug. "Oh, and they each contain a small seed of each other . . ." I squirm in my seat, suddenly sensing where this is headed and not sure if I'm ready to tag along.

"Exactly." She nods. "And believe me, people are no different. For example, let's say you have a girl, she's made a few mistakes"—her eyes meet mine—"and she's so down on herself, feeling so undeserving of all the love and support that's being offered, so sure she has to go it alone, make amends on her terms, her way, and ultimately becoming so obsessed with her tormentor, she ends up cutting off all those around her, so she has more time to concentrate on the one person she despises the most, channeling all of her attention on him, until, well, obviously I'm referring to you and you know how it ends . . . my point is, each of us has a shadow of darkness, every single one of us, *no exceptions*. But when you focus so heavily on the dark side, well, we're back to the Law of Attraction again— *like attracts like*—hence your *monstrous* attraction to Roman."

"*A shadow of darkness?*" I look at her, having heard something similar, just a few hours before. "You mean like—a *shadow self*?"

"So now you're quoting Jung?" She laughs.

I squint, having no idea who that is.

"Dr. Carl Jung." She laughs. "He wrote all about the shadow self, basically saying it's the part of us that is unconscious and repressed, the parts we work hard to deny. Where'd you hear it?"

"Roman." I close my eyes and shake my head. "He's always ten steps ahead of me, and he basically said the same thing you did, that the monster was me. It was pretty much his final taunt before I fled the scene."

She nods, holding up her finger and closing her eyes. "Let me see if I can—"

And the next thing I know she's balancing an old leather book in her hands.

"How'd you . . . ?" I look at her, eyes wide, jaw dropped.

But she just smiles. "Everything you can do in Summerland you can do here too, you know? Aren't you the one who told me that? But it wasn't instant manifestation like you think, it was merely telekinesis—I summoned it from my bookshelf in the other room."

"Yeah, but still . . ." I gape at the book, amazed by how quickly she was able to retrieve it. Amazed by how she's mastered so many things, and yet she still chooses to live like *this*—nice, comfortable, but still pretty simple by the usual, opulent, coastal Orange County standards. Narrowing my gaze as I look her over again, seeing how she's stuck with the chunk of raw citrine on the simple silver chain over the elaborate gold and jewels she always wore in Summerland, despite the fact that she can now have whatever she wants. And I can't help but wonder if she really has changed. If maybe she's not that same old Ava I once knew.

She shifts in her seat, setting the book down before her and skipping to just the right page, her finger tracing the line as she reads, "Everyone carries a shadow, and the less it is embodied in the individual's conscious life, the blacker and denser it is . . . The psychological rule says that when an inner situation is not made conscious, it happens outside as fate . . . forms an unconscious snag, thwarting our most well-meant intentions . . . and so on." She snaps it shut and looks at me when she adds, "Or so says Dr. Carl G. Jung, and who are we to refute him?" She smiles. "Ever, whether or not we reach our full potential and fulfill our true destinies is up to us. It's completely of our own making. Remember what I said earlier—*as within, so without*? What we think about, what we concentrate on, will always, *always,* be reflected on the outside. So I ask you, what do *you* want to concentrate on? Who do you want to become from this point forward? How do you want your destiny to unfold? You've got a path, a purpose, and though I've no idea what that is, I've got this uncanny feeling it's something powerful and big. And though you've wandered a bit off course, if you'll let me, I can lead you back to the trail, all you have to do is say the word."

I gaze down at my teacup, the broken pieces of cookie, knowing that everything I've done so far, every ingloriously ill-advised move, has led me back here. Back to Ava's kitchen. The last place I ever thought I'd return to.

Tracing my finger around and around the rim of the saucer, weighing my choices, which are admittedly few, and lifting my gaze to meet hers as I smile and say, "Word."

TWENTY-NINE

Before I can knock, Damen is there. But then, he's always been there. And I mean that both literally and figuratively. He's been there the last four hundred years just as he's there now, feet bare, robe hanging open, hair tousled in an insanely appealing way, peering at me from a heavily lidded, sleepy gaze.

"Hey," he says, his voice thick, rough, new to the day.

"Hey yourself." I smile, moving right past him and starting for his stairs, grasping his hand in mine as I pull him along. "You really weren't kidding about always being able to sense me when I'm near, were you?"

He tightens his fingers around mine, using the ones on his free hand to push through his glossy tangle of hair, trying to tame it, make sense of it, but I just smile and urge him to keep it that way. It's so rare I see him like that, drowsy, scruffy, a little disheveled, and I have to say, I kind of like it.

"So what gives?" He follows me into his special room, scratching his chin as he watches me fawn over his collection of very old things.

"Well, for starters, I'm better." I turn my back on the very serious Picasso version of him in favor of the much cuter, way sexier, real version of him. My gaze meeting his when I add, "I mean, I may not be totally and completely *there* yet, but I'm definitely headed in the right direction. If I stick with the program, it shouldn't take long."

"Program?" He leans against the old velvet settee as his gaze sails over me, studying me so closely, I can't help but run my hands over my dress, quickly, self-consciously, thinking I should've at least taken the time to manifest something less rumpled, something new and cute, before rushing over like I did.

But I was so pumped from my talk with Ava, and the series of healing and cleansing meditations she put me through, well, I couldn't wait. Couldn't wait to tell him—to be with him again.

"Ava's got me on a sort of—cleansing fast." I laugh. "Only it's the mental kind, not the green tea and twigs kind. She says it'll make me—well—" I shrug. "Better, whole again, new and improved."

"But—I thought you were better yesterday? Or at least that's what you told me in Summerland." He cocks his head.

I nod, determined to focus on my earlier trip with him, and not the one that followed that horrible scene with Roman when I ran into Jude. "Yeah, but—now I feel even better—stronger—just like my old self." I look at him, knowing I have to admit this next part, it's part of the cleansing ritual—coming clean, making amends, not so different from your typical twelve-step program, but then, I wasn't so different from any other addict struggling with a horrible addiction.

"Ava says I was addicted to negativity." I swallow hard and

look at him, forcing myself to keep his gaze. "It wasn't just the magick or Roman. According to her, I was addicted to thinking about my fears, about all the bad things in my life, like— you know, like my bad decisions, and our inability to really be together, and, well, stuff like that. And that by doing that, by focusing on all that, I actually ended up attracting—um, all kinds of darkness and sadness and—well—*Roman,* which resulted in me cutting off the people I love most. Like *you,* for instance."

I swallow hard and move toward him, part of my brain shouting: *Tell him! Tell him what really led you to this conclusion. What happened with Roman—just how dark and twisted you got!*

While the other part, the part I choose to listen to, says: *You've said plenty enough already—time to move on! The last thing he wants are the disgusting details.*

He moves toward me, reaches for my hands and pulls me close to him, answering the question in my gaze when he says, "I forgive you, Ever. I'll always forgive you. I know your admitting to all this wasn't easy, but I really do appreciate it."

I swallow hard, knowing that now is my chance, my very last chance, that it's far better he hear it from me than from Roman. But just as I'm about to, he runs his hand down my back and the thought melts away, until all I can focus on is the feel of him, the warmth of his breath on my cheek, the soft *almost* feel of his lips at my ear, the amazing sensation of tingle and heat that courses all the way from my head to my toes. His lips finding mine, pushing, pressing, as that ever-present shield hovers between us. But I'm done with resenting it, done with paying it any notice at all. I'm determined to celebrate things just as they are.

"Wanna go make out in Summerland?" he whispers, only

half joking. "You can be the muse and I can be the artist, and—"

"And you can kiss me so much you never actually finish that painting?" I pull away and laugh, but he just pulls me back to him.

"But—I've already painted you." He smiles. "The only painting of mine that truly matters." Then seeing my quizzical look, he adds, "You know, the one that's somewhere in the Getty as we speak?"

"Ah yes." I laugh, remembering that magical night, when he painted a version of me so beautiful, so angelic, I was sure I didn't deserve it. But I'm done thinking like that. If what Ava says is right, if like attracts like and water really does seek its own level and all that, then I'd much rather reach for Damen's level than Roman's, and here's where I start. "It's probably in some underground lab, in some high-security, windowless basement, where hundreds of art historians are gathered for the sole purpose of studying it, trying to determine who painted it, and where it could've possibly come from."

"You think?" He gazes into the distance, obviously enjoying the idea.

"So," I murmur, pressing my lips to his jaw, as my fingers play at the silky collar of his robe. "When do we get to celebrate *your* birthday? And how will I ever possibly top the present you gave me?"

He turns his head and sighs, the kind of sigh that comes from somewhere down deep, and I don't mean physically, but emotionally. It's a sigh filled with sadness and regret. It's the sound of melancholy.

"Ever, you don't need to concern yourself with my birth-day. I haven't celebrated a birthday of mine since—"

Since his tenth. Of course! That horrible day that started off so good and ended with him being forced to watch his parents get murdered. How could I forget?

"Damen, I'm—"

I start to apologize, but he waves it away, turning his back and heading for the Velázquez painting of him astride the rearing, white stallion with the thick, curly mane. Fiddling with the corner of the oversized, ornate, gilt frame as though it desperately needs adjusting even though it's clear that it doesn't.

"No need to apologize," he says, still unwilling to look at me. "Really. I guess marking the years doesn't feel quite so important after you've lived through so many of them."

"Will it be that way for me?" I ask, having a hard time not caring about a birthday, or even worse, forgetting which day it falls on.

"I won't let it be that way for you." He turns, face lighting up as he takes me in. "Every day will be a celebration—from here on out. I promise you that."

But even though he's sincere, even though he means just exactly that, I still look at him and shake my head. Because the truth is, as committed as I am to clearing my energy and only focusing on the good, positive things that I want, life is still life. It's still tough, complicated, and more than a little messy, with lessons to be learned, mistakes to be made, triumphs and disappointments to be had, and not every day is meant to be a party. And I think I finally realize, finally accept that that's perfectly okay. I mean, from what I saw, even Summerland has its dark side, its own version of a shadow self, a small dark corner in the midst of all that light—or at least that's how it appeared to me.

I look at him, knowing I need to tell him, wondering why I haven't mentioned it yet, when my phone rings, and we look at each other and shout, "Guess!" A game we sometimes play to see whose psychic powers are stronger, faster, and we're only allowed one second to answer.

"Sabine!" I nod, logically assuming she woke up, found my bed empty, and is now calmly going about discovering whether I've been abducted or left of my own free will.

But less than a fraction of a second later Damen says, "Miles." But his voice isn't at all playful, and his gaze goes dark and worried.

I pull my phone from my bag, and sure enough, there's that photo I took of Miles in full-on Tracy Turnblad drag, striking a pose and beaming at me.

"Hey, Miles," I say, met by an earful of buzz, hum, and static, the usual transatlantic phone call soundtrack.

"Did I wake you?" he asks, his voice sounding small, distant. "Cuz if I did, well, be glad you're not me. My body clock's been screwed up for days. I sleep when I should be eating, and eat when I should be— Well, strike that, since it's Italy and the food is *amazing,* I pretty much eat all of the time. Seriously. I don't know how these people do it and continue to look so smokin'. It's not fair. A couple days of the old *dolce vita* and I'm a pudgy, bloated mess—and yet, I'm *lovin'* it. I'm so serious. It's *amazing* here! So, anyway, what time is it there?"

I glance around the room, but not finding a clock I just shrug and say, "Um, early. You?"

"I have no idea, but probably afternoon. I went to this

amazing club last night—did you know you don't even have
to be twenty-one to go to a club or drink here? I'm telling
you, Ever, *this* is the life. These Italians really know how to
live! Anyway, well, I'll save all that for later—for when I get
back—I'll even reenact it for you and everything, I promise.
But for now, the cost of this call is already giving my dad a
coronary, I'm sure, so I'll just get to it and say that you need
to tell Damen that I stopped by that place Roman told me
about and—*hello?* Can you hear me—are you there?"

"Um, yeah, I'm still here. You're breaking up a little, but,
okay, you're good." I turn my back to Damen and move several steps away, mostly because I don't want him to witness
the horrible mask of dread that's displayed on my face.

"Okay, so anyway, I stopped by that place Roman was going
on and on about, in fact, I just left a few minutes ago—and,
well, I gotta tell you, Ever, there's some really freaky stuff in
there. And I mean *really freaky*. Like, someone's got lots of explaining to do when I return."

"Freaky—*how*?" I ask, feeling Damen's presence hovering
right behind me now, his energy shifting from relaxed to
full-scale alert.

"Just—*freaky*. That's all I'm gonna say about it, but—*crap*—
can you hear me? I'm losing you again. Listen, just—*ugh*—
anyway, I sent some photos via e-mail, so whatever you do,
do *not* delete it without seeing them first. Okay? *Ever? Ever!*
Stupid—damn—phon—"

I swallow hard and press *end*, feeling Damen's hand on my
arm when he says, "What did he want?"

"He sent me some photos," I say, voice low, eyes never
once leaving his. "Something he really wants us to see."

Damen nods, arranging his features into an expression of

determined acceptance, as though the moment he's been waiting for has arrived, and now he's just anticipating the fallout,
to see how I react, to see how much damage has been done.

I click to the *home page*, then over to *mail*, watching as the
little connecting swirl goes around and around until Miles's
e-mail is displayed. And then, the second it pops up, I just
hold my breath and tap it—my knees going all wobbly the
very moment I see it.

The picture.

Or rather, the picture of the painting. Photography wasn't
yet invented back then, wouldn't be invented for several hundred more years. But still, there it is, flaunted before me, and
there's no mistaking it's him. *Them.* Posing together.

"How bad is it?" he asks, body perfectly still as his eyes
graze over me. "As bad as I expected?"

I glance at him, but only for a second before I'm focusing
back on the screen, unwilling to tear my eyes away. "Depends
on what you were expecting," I mumble, remembering how I
felt that day in Summerland when I spied on his past. How
sick, how completely green with envy I was, when it got to the
part where he hooked up with Drina. But this—this isn't
anything like that. In fact, not even close. Oh sure, Drina is
stunning—Drina was *always* stunning, even at her ugliest and
most vicious she was breathtaking, or at least on the outside
anyway. And I'm sure no matter what decade she was in, be it
the era of bustles or poodle skirts, I'm sure she was stunning
then too. But the fact is, Drina's gone, so gone that the thought
of her, the *sight* of her, doesn't really bother me anymore. In
fact, it doesn't bother me at all.

What bothers me is Damen. The way he stands, the way
he gazes at the artist, and how—how arrogant and vain

and, well, *full of himself* he is. And even though he carries a trace of that outlaw edge that I like, this isn't quite so playful as what I'm used to. It's a lot less *let's-ditch-school-and-bet-at-the-track* and a lot more *this-is-my-world-and-you're-just-lucky-I-let-you-live-in-it*.

And the more I gaze at the two of them, Drina sitting demurely in a straight-backed chair, hands folded neatly in her lap, dress and hair adorned with so many jewels and ribbons and shiny things, it'd look ridiculous on anyone else—while Damen stands behind her, one hand resting on her chair, the other hanging by his side, his chin tilted, brow arced in that cool, haughty way—well, there's just something about him—something about that look in his gaze that's—well—almost cruel, ruthless even. Like he'd be willing to do whatever it takes, whatever the cost, to get what he wants.

And even though he's made plenty of mention of his "before picture" of his former, narcissistic, power-hungry self—it's one thing to hear about it, it's quite another to see it so clearly displayed.

But even though there are three more portraits attached, I only give them the most cursory glance. Miles is only interested in the fact that Damen and Drina were captured on canvas hundreds of years ago, and that in each passing portrait, some of them painted centuries apart according to their plaques, they somehow manage to remain young, beautiful, and eerily unchanged. He could care less about Damen's demeanor, the way he carried himself, the look in his eyes—no, that was my surprise.

I hand the phone to Damen, seeing the way his fingers tremble ever so slightly when he takes it from me, glancing quickly through the pictures before handing it right back. His voice low and steady as he says, "I've already lived it once, I really don't need to see it again."

I nod, dropping the phone back in my bag, taking too long to place it, obviously avoiding his gaze.

"So, now you've seen him. The monster I used to be," he says, his words going straight to the heart of me.

I swallow hard, dropping my bag onto the thickly woven rug, a priceless antique that should be in a museum some-where, not used for this sort of daily wear. His strange choice of words reminding me of my conversation with Ava—everyone has a monster, a dark side, *no exceptions whatsoever*. And even though most people spend their whole lives determined to bury it, force it down deep, I guess if you've lived as long as Damen, you're bound to confront it from time to time.

"I'm sorry," I say, suddenly realizing I am. It hardly matters where we've been. It's where we are now that counts. "I—I guess I wasn't expecting it and I was a little taken aback. I've never really seen you like that."

"Not even in Summerland?" He looks at me. "Not even in the Great Halls of Learning?"

I shake my head. "No, I mostly fast-forwarded through all of those parts. I couldn't bear to watch you with Drina."

"And now?"

"And now—" I sigh. "I'm no longer bothered by Drina—just you." I try to laugh, try to lighten my mood, but it doesn't quite work.

"Well, if I'm not mistaken, I think that's what you'd call progress." He smiles, pulling me into his arms and holding me tightly to his chest.

"And Miles?" My eyes graze over his face, the slant of his

brow, the square of his jaw, my fingers scratching at the swath of stubble that grows there. "What are we going to tell him? How do we ever explain this?" My hesitation, my fleeting rejection of the old him, now vanished for good. Our past may shape us, but it doesn't define who we become.

"We're going to tell him the truth." He nods, voice firm, as though he really does mean it. "When the time comes, we'll tell him the truth. And with the way things are going, it won't be much longer now."

THIRTY

"Okay, so now, what I want you to do is to focus on feeding your energy. Cleansing it, lifting it, accelerating it to greater and greater speeds. Think you can do that?"

I squinch my eyes shut and concentrate. The accelerating part's always been the hardest for me. Remembering when Jude tried to coach me to do the same thing so I could see Riley again. But no matter how hard I tried, my energy remained just stagnant enough, just bogged down enough, just muddled enough, to pick up on the thoughts and images of a smattering of earthbound entities, and not the ones who've crossed over, the ones I wanted to see.

"With every intake of breath I want you to imagine a beautiful, healing, shimmering white light filling you up, starting at your crown and drifting all the way down to your toes. And then, with each exhale, I want you to im-agine all that leftover negativity, any doubts, anything that serves the word *can't* leaving you for good. Imagine it as a thick, mucky, clumpy, clotted stream of gray drudge if you want—that always seems to work for me." She laughs, her voice like a smile.

I nod, and since my eyes are closed, I can only imagine the twins are nodding too. Their approach to Ava is pretty much the same as their approach to Damen—complete and total idolization, willing to do whatever she says. And while they weren't too thrilled about *The Book of Shadows* being banished from their lesson plan, even after I shared my own cautionary tale of magick gone wrong, showing them just how astray things can go when the intent gets a bit clouded and good judgment is overruled by obsession, they wasted no time in pointing out that *they'd* never be as stupid as *me*. Would *never* practice any kind of ritual on a dark moon. Would only try to manipulate matter and never the actions of another human being. But Ava held firm, which is why we're all back to energy cleansing and meditating again.

And even though I'm going along with the plan, picturing the white light streaming all the way through me, while banishing the negative crud that tends to build up inside— even though in just a few weeks of doing this I've already seen a tremendous difference in the way that I look, feel, and, almost more important, in the way I can manifest and communicate telepathically with Damen again—even though I know that taking part in this group meditation only serves my own best interests and will help steer me toward the ultimate destination I want to reach—even despite all that, my mind keeps wandering back to yesterday at the beach, when I took the day off from work to hang out with Damen.

We spread our towels out next to each other, so close the edges overlapped. Adding a mountain of unread magazines by my side, a customized, newly manifested surfboard by his (since the old one broke to pieces in the unfortunate cave collapse from a few weeks back), along with some chilled bottles of elixir, and an iPod we passed back and forth but mostly I listened to. The two of us determined to enjoy the summer we had both anticipated but had yet to experience. The two of us looking forward to a long, relaxing day at the beach, just like any other couple.

"Surf?" he said, rising from his towel and grabbing hold of his board.

But I just shook my head. As far as surfing goes, it's better for everyone if I just stay put and watch from afar.

So I did. Watching as he headed off toward the water, raising my shoulders and shifting my weight onto my elbows as he moved across the sand so swiftly and effortlessly, I wondered if anyone else was as mesmerized by the sight of it as I was.

My gaze still focused on him as he dropped his board into the ocean and began to paddle out, turning what was once a series of pretty ho-hum, semi-flat waves into a succession of near perfect barrels. Fully content to ignore my magazines and iPod in favor of watching him, until Stacia came up beside me, tucked her long, newly highlighted hair back behind her ear, hitched her designer beach bag higher up on her shoulder, and lowered her sunglasses onto her face as she said, "Jeez, Ever, *white much?*"

I swallowed hard, breathed in and out, blinked a few times, but that's it. I gave no indication of having seen or heard her. I was determined to ignore her, determined to act as though she was invisible to me, and keep Damen in focus.

She stood beside me, making little *tsking* sounds of disgust as she harshly looked me over, but it wasn't long before she tired of the game and moved on, shuffling down the sand and settling in somewhere near the water but still within perfect viewing distance of me.

And that's when I let myself do it. That's when I went against everything Ava has taught me about empowering myself by tuning her, and everyone else like her, out, in favor of my own, more positive, upbeat soundtrack. That's when I let her words replay in my head as my eyes raked over my body and agreed she was right. Even though just a few minutes before I'd felt good about the way I looked, thrilled that my formerly unhealthy, emaciated body was now nicely filled out again, there's no getting around the fact that I was white—*glaringly* white—a white that definitely required the wearing of sunglasses and that could only be described as *pasty*. And when you factor in the light blond hair and the white bikini—the truth is, it wasn't pretty. I may as well have been a ghost.

And I was so far gone by that point, so convinced of her negative view of me, it took a whole, long session of those deep cleansing breaths Ava's so fond of to get rid of it. But even so, I wasn't willing to let it go completely, and I watched as she and Honor whispered back and forth, watched as Stacia laughed loudly, dramatically tossing her hair all around and swiveling her head from side to side, continually checking to see who was noticing her but always coming back to me, smirking, eye rolling, shaking her head in disgust, and pretty much doing whatever she could to show me just how revolting she found me. And even though it would've been easy enough to tune in, focus my quantum remote, and hear all the words that were and weren't being said, that's when I decided to stop.

Even though I was definitely tempted, especially after

knowing all about Honor's plans to overthrow Stacia, and stage her own senior-year social coup—not to mention her "amazing," well, according to Jude anyway, progress in his Psychic Development 101 class, catching on so quickly and easily, mastering so many techniques he's switched to one-on-one sessions where he tutors her exclusively—but still, despite all that, I didn't do it. Didn't eavesdrop. Figuring I'll be getting plenty of that when school starts again. Instead, I switched my focus to Damen, enjoying the way he maneuvered through the water so gracefully, so elegantly, the way he practically glistened in the sun. A startling arrangement of bronzed skin, smooth rounded muscles, and jaw-dropping good looks as he came out of the water, board tucked under his arm, and headed for me.

Immune to Stacia's hard, glinting stare, her high-pitched, saccharine-sweet greeting as he passed, dropped his board onto the sand, and trailed large drops of salty wetness onto my belly as he bent down to kiss me. Ignoring the way she watched so intently, so closely, not missing a beat as he settled in beside me and kissed me again, that veil of energy hovering between us, keeping us safe, but invisible to them.

Or, at least that's what I thought, until I lifted my head to see the way Honor was looking, mostly at *him*. Her gaze reminding me of Stacia's—lingering, longing, but also, or at least in her case anyway, filled with a great deal of *knowing and seeing* as well.

And when her eyes met mine, and I saw the smile that formed on her lips, a smile that flashed and vanished so quickly, I wondered if I really had seen it. Left only with a lingering sense of dread as I turned away from her and back toward Damen—

"Ever? Yoo-hoo?" Ava calls, as Romy giggles and Rayne mutters under her breath. "Are you still with us? Still enjoying your cleansing breaths?"

And just like *that,* my memory of the beach collapses and I'm back in Ava's house again.

I shake my head, my gaze meeting hers as I say, "Um—no, I guess I got a little distracted."

But Ava just shrugs, she's one of those nice teachers, there are no demerits in her class. "It happens," she says. "Anything we can help you with?"

I glance at Romy and Rayne, shaking my head when I say, "No. I'm good."

Watching as she lifts her hands high overhead, stretching from side to side, leisurely, languorously, as she looks at me and says, "What do you think? You want to give it a try?"

I press my lips together and shrug. Not sure if I'll get in but ready to give it a go.

"Good. I think it's time." She smiles. "Would you like company, or would you rather go it alone?"

I glance at the twins, seeing the way they study their feet, the pictures on the walls, the hem of their dresses, anything but me. The last couple attempts to get them to Summerland have failed, and not wanting to risk making them feel badly again, I say, "Um, I think I'll go it alone, if that's okay with you."

Ava looks at me, her gaze holding mine for a moment before she presses her palms together, bows her head, and says, "Have a safe trip, Ever. Godspeed."

Her words still echoing in my head as I bypass the vast fragrant field and land smack in front of the Great Halls of Learning. Brushing myself off as I rise to my feet, feeling ready, cleansed, totally and completely whole again, and hoping whoever's in charge of admittance will agree.

Hoping the ever-changing façade will make itself visible to me.

I clamber up the steps, unwilling to waste even a second, unwilling to allow any time for doubt to move in. Gazing up at the grand building before me, the imposing columns, grand sloping roof, and gasping in relief as it begins to shimmer and change. Transforming itself into all of the world's most beautiful, sacred places, as the doors spring open for me.

I'm in!

I'm back.

Making my way across the shiny marble floors, past the long line of tables and benches that house row after row of spiritual seekers. Each of them hovering over their square crystal tablets, each of them searching for answers. And suddenly, I realize I'm not so different from them, we're all here for the same reason—we're all on some kind of quest.

So I close my eyes and think:

First of all, thank you for giving me a second chance and allowing me back. I know I messed up for a while there and got a bit off track, but now that I've learned a few things, I promise I won't mess up again—or at least not like that. But still, the truth is, my quest hasn't changed. I still need to get that antidote from Roman so that Damen and I can—well—be together. And since Roman is the key—the only one who has access to it, I need to know how to handle him, how to approach him in a way that'll get me what I need but without—well, without manipulating him or—or casting spells—or getting caught up like that again. So, um, I guess what I'm trying to say is, I need to know how to approach him. I don't really know where to go from here, and, well, if you could help me with this, provide some kind of clue, show me whatever it is you think I need to know in order to deal with him in just the right way—well, I'd really appreciate it.

I hold my breath, hold perfectly still, aware of a distant *whir*, a soft, swirly sound whooshing around me, and when I open my eyes, I find myself in a hall. Not the same hall as before with the infinite runner and the hieroglyphic Braille on the wall, this hall is wider, shorter, more like a walkway that takes you to your row of seats in an indoor stadium or concert hall. And when I get there, when I reach the end, I see that I am in a stadium, a sort of indoor coliseum, only in this particular one, there's only one seat, and as it just so happens, it's reserved just for me.

I settle in, unfolding the blanket beside me, and placing it onto my lap. Gazing around at the walls, the columns, all of it appearing old, crumbly, as though it was built long ago, back in ancient times, and wondering if I'm expected to do something, make the first move, when a colorful, shimmering hologram appears right before me.

I lean toward it, squinting at an almost hallucinatory image of a family—the mother pale, feverish, flat on her back and wracked with great pain, screaming in agony, begging for God to just take her, not even getting a chance to hold the son she's just birthed before her wish is granted, she heaves her last breath, and moves on. Her soul traveling upward, onward, as her baby, the tiny, kicking, newly born baby is cleaned and swathed and handed to a father who's too busy grieving for his dead wife to pay him any notice.

A father who never stops grieving for his wife—and who blames his son for her loss.

A father who turns to drink to numb the pain—and then to violence when that fails to work.

A father who beats his poor young son from the time he's old enough to crawl, until the day when, in a drunken stupor, he starts a fight with someone much bigger and stronger, a fight he cannot win. His battered, bloodied body, left in an alleyway, beaten beyond repair, but still smiling his last breath, when the sweet release he's sought all along finally arrives. Leaving behind a hungry, abandoned child that soon becomes a ward of the Church.

A child with smooth olive skin, large blue eyes, and a golden crop of curls that could only belong to Roman.

Could only belong to my nemesis, my enemy, my eternal antagonist whom I can no longer hate. Whom I only feel pity for after watching how, younger than the others and small for his age, he struggles to fit in, to please, to be noticed and loved, only to go from being an overlooked, ignored, and abused son, to everyone's servant, everyone's favorite whipping boy.

Even when Damen makes the elixir and urges them all to drink to spare them from the ravages of the Black Plague, Roman is the last to be served. Having completely overlooked him until Drina brought him forward, insisting the last drops be saved for him.

And even though I make myself stay until the end, watching hundreds of years of his growing resentment toward Damen, hundreds of years of his love for Drina being denied again and again, hundreds of years of him becoming so strong, and so accomplished, he can get anything or anyone he wants except the one thing he wants the most—the one thing I robbed him of forever—even though I watch all of that—I didn't need to.

The beast was born six hundred years ago, when his father beat him, when Damen overlooked him, when Drina was kind to him. Sure he could've lived differently, made better choices, if only someone would've shown him the way. But you can't give away what you don't have.

And when the hologram ends, when the images disappear, and the lights go dim, I know what to do.

Without being told, I know exactly how to proceed.

So I rise from my seat, give a silent nod of thanks, and make my way back to the earth plane.

THIRTY-ONE

When I pull into the drive and park, I'll admit to a fleeting but still major feeling of trepidation. My mind spinning with questions like: *Should I really be doing this? Will I even get a chance to do this? Or will she toss me right out like last year's Emo look?*

Realizing I won't know until I try, I take a moment to calm myself, to get centered, to summon my strength from within, and fill myself with that bright, radiant, healing light just like Ava taught me to do. Tapping my amulet just under my dress once for good measure, I hop out of the car and head for the door. Having no idea if she even still lives here now that she's super-charged, infinite, with the whole world at her feet, but figuring it's the best place to start.

"Hi." I smile, peering over the housekeeper's shoulder, relieved to see that from here anyway, everything seems to look pretty much the same, which means it's in its usual state of chaos and disorder. "Is Haven here?" I add, my voice hopeful, as though willing her to say *yes*.

She nods, opening the door even wider and motioning up toward Haven's room as I bolt up the stairs, following the wave of her fingers and allowing no time for turning back or second-guessing as I stand just outside the door and knock twice.

"Who is it?" she calls, clearly annoyed, as though the last thing she wants is a visitor. And when I tell her it's me, well, I can only imagine how *that* goes over.

"Well, *well*," she purrs, cracking the door just enough to confirm it, her eyes really raking me over without letting me in. "The last time I saw you—you were trying to—"

"Attack you." I nod, figuring I'd surprise her by admitting it, openly, freely, with no holding back. "About that—" I start, but she's not about to let me finish.

"Well, actually, I was going to say, *seduce my boyfriend*. But yeah, come to think of it, the only one you got physical with was *me*." She smiles, but it's not the nice, happy kind, nope, far from it. "So tell me, Ever, what brings you here? Eager to finish the job?"

I look at her, keeping my gaze as open and honest and direct as I can when I say, "No, not at all. I actually came here hoping to put an end to all this—to explain and call a *truce*." Wincing at my use of the word, remembering the last time I used it with Roman and how it didn't go over so well.

"A truce?" She lifts a brow and cocks her head. "You? Ever Bloom? The girl who pretended to be my best friend, stole my crush right out from under me—um, hel-*lo*, Damen?" she says, shaking her head in response to my look of confusion. "If you'll remember, I called dibs on him long before you, but still, you just dove right on in and scooped him right out from under me, which, fine, whatever, it all worked out in the end, I guess, *but still*. And then, even after all that, once you seemingly have everything a person could ever want, apparently that just isn't enough for you and so you decide to go after Roman too, because apparently one smokin' hot immortal just isn't enough. Oh, and you're so single-minded in your quest, you decide you'll try to kill me if that's what it takes to get to him. But now, you've suddenly suffered a dramatic change of heart, leading you to just show up at my bedroom door and ask for a truce? Is that right? Is that what's really happening here?"

I nod. "Basically, but there's a lot more to it than that, something you need to know. Because the truth is, I tried to put a spell on Roman—a spell that would make him do my bidding and give me what I want. Only it totally backfired and ended up binding me to him in a way that—well, in a way I still don't fully understand." I scrunch my nose and shake my head at the memory of it. "But that's the only reason I did what I did. *I swear.* The magick took control and I wasn't in my right mind. It wasn't really *me* that was doing those things—or at least not entirely." I shake my head. "I know it sounds crazy, and it's not all that easy to explain, but it's like I was being compelled by a force outside myself." I look at her, willing her to believe. "I wasn't in charge."

She looks at me, head tilted, a single brow lifted. Smirking as she says, "A *spell*? You seriously expect me to believe that?"

I nod, carefully holding her gaze. Willing to confess the whole sordid tale, whatever it takes to get her to trust me again. But not here. Not in the hall. "Listen, do you think maybe I could—?" I gesture toward the inside of her room.

She frowns, eyes narrowed to slits as she takes her time to consider. Opening the door just wide enough for me to squeeze through when she says, "Just so you know, you make one move I don't like and so help me God I will take you down so fast you won't even know what hit—"

"Relax," I say, plopping onto her bed just like the old days, only this is nothing like the old days, not even close. "I'm feeling very nonviolent today, I assure you. In fact, I'm feeling very nonviolent pretty much every day from now on, and I have no intention of going after you in any way. All I want is peace and the return of your friendship, but failing that, I'll settle for a truce."

She leans against her dresser, arms folded tightly across the black leather corset she wears cinched over her antique lace dress. "Sorry, Ever, but after all we've been through, it's just not that easy. I have no reason to trust you, and I'm gonna need a little more assurance than that."

I take a deep breath and run my hand over her old floral bedspread, surprised she hasn't changed it by now. "Trust me," I say, looking at her. "I get it, I really do. But, Haven"—I pause, shaking my head and starting again—"the truth is, I can't stand what's happened to us. I miss *you*. I miss our friendship. And I hate knowing it's partly my fault."

"*Partly?*" She balks, rolling her eyes and shaking her head. "Um, excuse me for saying so, but don't you think that statement would be a little more accurate if you admitted to *all of it* being your fault?"

I look at her, look her straight in the eye when I say, "Fine, I'll concede to most of it, but certainly not *all* of it. But, Haven, the point is—while I don't like Roman—and believe me I have my reasons—I get that he's your boyfriend, and I get that no matter what I say about him I can't change your mind, so I'm not gonna try. And I know you find that hard to believe, especially after what you saw the other night—but the thing is—well—like I said before, that wasn't really *me*."

"Oh right—it was that pesky *evil spell*." She shakes her head and rolls her eyes, but I don't let that stop me.

"Listen, I know you don't believe me, and I know how crazy I probably sound right now, but I think that considering the circumstances, you of all people should know that the craziest-sounding things are often true."

She looks at me, mouth twisted to the side, a sure sign she's not just discarding but actually considering my words.

"We're on the same side, you and I—and I hope that in time, you'll see that too. Trust me—I'm not trying to stand in the way of your happiness. And I would never try to steal someone you wanted for yourself—despite how it may have looked. I just—well, I'm just hoping there's still some way for us to be friends again, some way to mend our friendship, in spite of all that's happened. I mean, I know it won't be the same. I hardly expect it to be after all we've been through, and I know you're really busy with your job, and hanging out with—um—those other immortals . . ." I say, temporarily forgetting their names.

"Rafe, Misa, and Marco," she mumbles, clearly annoyed.

"Yeah, them. But still, school's starting up in a few weeks, and Miles will be back soon, and I thought maybe, I mean, not every day if you don't want, but maybe every now and then, we could all sit together at lunch. You know, like we used to."

"So, it's a lunchtime truce?" she says, her eyes a kaleidoscope of tortoiseshell swirls fixed firmly on mine.

"No." I shake my head. "It's an *all the time* truce. I'm just hoping it'll extend to the occasional lunch too."

She frowns, picking at her cuticles, which, I know for a fact, are not at all ragged because immortals do not get hangnails. I also know it's an excuse to avoid me, avoid my gaze, make me wonder and wait while she takes her time to consider my words.

"It can never be like it was," she finally says, lifting her gaze to meet mine. "And not just because of everything that happened with Roman—which was seriously messed up, by the way. But the real reason we can't go back is because I'm different now—and the thing is, I *like* being different. I don't want to go back to the way I was. I don't want to be that sad, pathetic loser ever again."

"You were never pathetic or a loser—just a bit sad at times," I say, but she quickly waves it away.

"Besides, so much has changed—maybe too much—I'm not sure I can get past all of that."

I nod. I realize this too but still hope that she can.

"And yeah, Misa, Rafe, and Marco are cool and all, don't get me wrong, but other than our immortality, and our work at the store, we really don't have all that much in common, you know? I mean, we have totally different backgrounds, totally different references, they've never even heard of most of my favorite bands, which really kind of bugs me."

I shrug *and* nod, like I get it, totally and completely get it.

"And even though I never really felt like you and I had all that much in common either, I did always feel like you sort of *got* me, you know? Like maybe you couldn't exactly relate to me, but still, you accepted me, you didn't judge me, and, well, it meant a lot—or it meant *something,* anyway."

I press my lips together and wait for the rest, knowing she's far from done yet.

"So yeah, I've missed you too." She looks at me, shrugging when she adds, "It'll be nice to keep at least one friend for the rest of eternity. But are you sure we can't turn Miles too?"

"No!" I blurt, before I realize she's joking.

"Jeez, do you ever *unclench*?" She laughs, uncrossing her arms and dropping onto her leopard beanbag chair in a heap of leather and lace, spreading her dress all around her before resting her head against her hand. "Could help with the acting stuff though—he'd definitely snag all the best roles."

"And that's good for how long?" I look at her. "Trust me, even in Hollywood people would start to notice how he never aged a day over eighteen."

"Didn't seem to hurt Dick Clark."

I squint, having no idea who that is.

"America's Oldest Teenager? *New Year's Rockin' Eve?*"

I shrug, still no bells.

"Whatever." She laughs and shakes her head. "Anyway, I have this theory that there's a whole lot more of us than we think, actors, supermodels—I mean, seriously? How do you explain some of them?"

I shrug. "Luck, good genes, plastic surgery, and lots and lots of Photoshop." I laugh. "That's how I explain it."

"Well, between you and me, Roman's not always all that forthcoming with the details. He tends to hold a lot back."

No kidding.

"This one time, when I asked him just how many more of us were out there, and how many he himself turned, he just turned away, mumbled some childish nonsense about that being for him to know and the rest of the world to find out, or something like that. And no matter how much I bugged him, that's all he'd say. Just kept repeating that over and over until I got so annoyed, I dropped it."

"That's what he said?" I ask, trying to keep the alarm out of my voice but not entirely succeeding. "He said it's *for him to know and the rest of the world to find out*?" I gasp, not liking the ominous sound of it. Not liking it at all.

Haven looks at me, attempting to backtrack when she sees my expression, hears the way my voice rises, and realizes she might've gone just a tad too far. That her loyalties no longer extend to me and are definitely balanced in Roman's favor. "Or maybe he said for *me* to find out? That's how the saying goes, right?" She lifts her shoulder as her fingers pick at the lace on her sleeve. "Well, anyway, it's probably better not to talk about Roman since I love him and you hate him and if we want to be friends we're going to have to exist in a Roman-free zone, right? We're going to have to agree to disagree."

A Roman-free zone—how lovely! But that's just what I think, what I say is entirely different.

"Do you love him?"

She looks at me, looks at me for a long moment, before she dips her head and says, "I do. I really, really do."

"And is it—*reciprocated*?" I ask, doubting Roman's even capable of loving anyone, especially seeing how it was never shown to him, never really offered in any real or lasting way, according to what I saw. And it's pretty hard to give something you've never experienced yourself. Even what he felt for Drina wasn't love, or at least not the real kind anyway. It was more an obsession with something just out of reach, like a shining, glittering object that you yearn for but can never quite touch. Exact same feeling he's trying to duplicate with Damen and me. Only it won't work. With or without the antidote he'll never win that one. What Damen and I share goes much deeper than that.

"Honestly?" She looks at me. "I really don't know. But if I had to guess, then I'd say, *no*, he doesn't—doesn't love me at all. I mean, even though he keeps his feelings under wraps, usually pretending like he doesn't even have any—sometimes—sometimes he goes off on this—well, I call it his dark jag—where he locks himself in his room and won't talk to anybody or come out for hours—and, well, I have no idea what he's doing in there. And even though I try to respect it, try to let him have his space, I'm still really curious. Though, I figure, if I hang on long enough, he'll finally learn to trust me, let me in, and"—she shrugs—"change all of that."

I look at her, amazed by how composed she is, acting far more self-assured than she ever did before.

She gazes down at the strategically shredded black leggings she wears under her dress, fingers picking at one of the holes when she says, "You know, Ever, in every relationship, there's always someone who loves more, right? I mean, last time, with Josh, it was him. He definitely loved me far more than I did him. Did you know he even wrote a song about me after we broke up, in an attempt to get me back?" She lifts her brow and shakes her head. "It was pretty good too, and I was flattered for sure, but it was too late and I'd already moved on to Roman who I clearly love more. He just agrees to hang out with me, and we have a good time, and it's not like there's any other girl on the scene—well, other than you—" She looks at me, her eyes narrowed in a way that makes me cringe, but just as quickly she laughs and waves it away. "But the point is, no matter what you think, no matter how it may look from the outside, the truth is, it's never really equal. That's just not the way it works. There's always the *pursued* and the *pursuer,* the cat and the mouse, that's just how it goes. So, tell me, Ever, who loves more in your relationship—Damen or you?"

The question catches me off guard, even though it's pretty obvious it was coming. But when I see the way she pauses, head tilted to the side, fingers twirling a random chunk of hair, patiently waiting for me to respond, I end up mumbling a bunch of jumbled nonsense that finally results in, "Well, um, I don't know. I never really thought about it, I guess. I mean, I never even really noticed, for that matter—"

"Really?" She shifts onto her back and gazes up at her star-spangled ceiling that I know from experience glows in the dark. "Well, I have," she says, gaze still focused on the constellation overhead. "And just so you know, it's Damen, not you. Damen's the one who loves more. He'd do anything for you. You're just along for the ride."

THIRTY-TWO

I wish I could say Haven's words didn't bother me. That I was able not just to refute it but to plead a case so convincing she was instantly swayed to my side. But the truth is, I didn't do or say much of anything. I just shrugged, pretending to brush it off, as she blasted a series of songs from her iPod I'd never even heard before, by bands I didn't even know existed, and we flipped through a pile of magazines, the two of us hanging out in the same way we used to. Just like old times. But that's just how it seemed on the surface. Deep down, we both knew things were entirely different.

Then after I left, while I was hanging at Damen's, Haven's words kept replaying in my head, asking me which of us loved more. And to be honest, they've pretty much stayed with me today as well. All through my breakfast with Sabine, I wondered, all through shelf restocking and register ringing at the store, I asked myself was it me or him? Even through all three back-to-back readings that "Avalon" was scheduled for, including the one I'm finishing now, the question kept repeating in my head.

"Wow, that was—" She looks at me, eyes wide with wonder. "That was truly, truly, *truly* remarkable." She shakes her head and reaches for her purse, face wearing a blend of excitement, doubt, and a longing to believe—the usual post-reading look.

I nod, smiling politely while gathering up the deck of Tarot cards I spread out for show but don't really use. It's just easier to have some kind of prop or tool—keeps it more remote and detached that way. Most people get pretty freaked by the idea of someone being able to peer straight into their heads and listen in on all their deepest thoughts and feelings, never mind how one brief touch can reveal a long and complex history of events.

"It's just—you're so much *younger* than I expected. How long have you been at this?" she asks, slinging her purse over her shoulder as her eyes continue to study me.

"Being psychic is a gift," I say, even though Jude specifically asked me *not* to say that, figuring it would discourage potential students from signing up for his psychic development class. But since the course has pretty much fizzled down to just him and Honor, I really don't see what harm it could do. "It knows no age limit," I add, mentally urging her to quit gaping at me and move it along. I've got plans, somewhere to be. My evening carefully designed down to the minute, and if she lingers much longer, she'll seriously mess with my agenda. But seeing a look of skepticism start to creep in, I tell her, "That's why children are such naturals at it, they're open to all the possibilities. It's only later, when they discover how society frowns on these things that the desire to be accepted takes over and they shut it all out. What about you? Didn't you have an imaginary friend as a kid?" My gaze moves over her, knowing she did because I saw it the moment I touched her.

"Tommy!" She gasps, hand clamped over her mouth, surprised that I knew, surprised that she just blurted that out.

I smile, having already seen it myself. "He was real to you, right? Helped you through some hard times?"

She looks at me, eyes going wide as she shakes her head and says, "Yes—he—well—I used to have nightmares." She lifts her shoulders and gazes around as though embarrassed to be confessing all this. "Back when my parents were divorcing, well, everything was so unstable, financially, emotionally, and that's when Tommy appeared—and he promised to help me get through it, to keep all the monsters away—and he did. I think I stopped seeing him around the time I turned—"

"Ten." I rise from my seat, a visual indication that this session is over and she should do the same. "Which, to be honest, is a little older than most, but still, you didn't need him anymore and so he—went away." I nod, opening the door and gesturing her into the hall where she'll hopefully head on over toward the register and pay.

Only she doesn't head for the register. Instead, she turns to me and says, "You have *got* to meet my friend. Seriously. She'll *flip*. She doesn't really believe in this stuff, in fact, she made fun of me for coming, but we're having dinner later, a double date, and, well—" She pauses to glance at her watch, grinning at me when she says, "Well, actually, she should be here now, if not soon."

"I'd love to." I smile like I really do mean it. "But I have to be somewhere and—"

"Oh, that's her over there! Perfect!"

I sigh and gaze down at my feet, wishing I could use my manifesting skills to make people pay up and disappear—or at least just this once anyway.

Sensing my plans are about to be pushed back even further, but having no idea how much further until she cups her hands around her mouth and calls out, "Sabine! Hey, over here, I've got someone you've just *got* to meet!"

My whole body goes cold. Frozen, solid, and cold. Like: *Hello, iceberg, meet the Titanic* kind of cold.

And before I can stop it, before I can do anything about it, Sabine is heading right toward me. At first not recognizing me as *me,* and not because I'm wearing that black wig, because I'm not, I gave that up a long time ago when I decided it made Avalon look like a freak, but because I'm pretty much the absolute last person she ever expected to see. In fact, she's still squinting and blinking even after she's standing right before me with Munoz at her side, who, by the way, looks just about as panicked as I feel.

"*Ever?*" Sabine gazes at me as though she's just awoken from a very deep sleep. "Wha—" She shakes her head as though to clear it of cobwebs and starting all over again. "What on earth is going on here? I don't understand."

"Ever?" Her friend glances between us, her eyes squinched, darting, suspicious. "But—but I thought you said your name was *Avalon?*"

I take a deep breath and nod, knowing it's all over now. My carefully crafted life of lying, hiding, and secret hoarding has resulted in *this.* "It is Avalon." I nod, avoiding Sabine's gaze. "But, it's also Ever—depending."

"Depending on *what*?" my client squawks, as though she's been personally and deeply offended and wronged. Her aura suddenly flaming, wavering, as though she doubts not only me but everything I just spent the last hour telling her, no matter how spot-on my predictions were. "Just who the heck are you?" she says, looking at me as though she's about to report me to—well, she hasn't decided yet—but someone, someone will get a report, that's for sure.

But Sabine's back on her game, her voice calm, collected, and just a tad attorney-like, when she says, "Ever's my niece. And apparently she has *a lot* to explain."

And just as I'm about to do just that—well, not explain exactly or at least not in the way that she wants—but still, just as I'm about to say something that'll hopefully calm everyone down and put an end to all this, Jude makes his way over and says, "Everything go all right with your reading?"

I glance at my client, Sabine's friend, knowing that with my energy now so improved, so super-charged with the cleansing and healing meditations Ava's been putting me through, it was one of my best readings ever—and yet I failed to predict this. But also *seeing* how reluctant she is to pay for it now, now that she knows me as her friend's juvenile delinquent niece who moonlights as Avalon, the Shady Psychic Reader, I don't even give her the chance to respond, I just jump in and say, "Uh, no worries, this one's on me." Jude squints, his eyes darting between us, but I just nod firmly and add, "Seriously. No worries. I've got it covered."

But while that seems to settle the client, if not Jude, it doesn't do much for Sabine whose aura is in an uproar and whose eyes are severely narrowed on mine. "Ever? Don't you have something to say for yourself?"

I take a deep breath and meet her gaze. *Yeah, I've got plenty to say but not here and not now. There's someplace I need to be!*

And I'm just about to say something to that effect, only nicer, gentler, in a way that won't piss her off any more than she already is, when Munoz jumps to my aid and says, "I'm sure you two can discuss this in the morning, but for now, we really should go. We don't want to risk losing our reservation after it was so hard to get."

Sabine sighs, conceding to the wisdom in Munoz's argument but still unwilling to let me off the hook quite so easily. The words coming from behind clenched teeth when she says, "Tomorrow morning, Ever. I expect to see you first thing in the morning." Then, seeing the expression on my face, she adds, "No buts."

I nod, even though I've no plans to make that appointment. If things go the way I plan, then tomorrow morning I'll be about as far from that kitchen table as it gets. Instead, I'll be sprawled out in a suite at the Montage with Damen beside me, the two of us finally fulfilling those long-ago plans . . .

But it's not like I'm about to tell her that, so instead I just nod and say, "Um, okay." Well aware that as a trial attorney, she always insists on a verbal response, that way the meaning can't be twisted or misconstrued. And just when I think that the worst is over—or at least for now anyway, she insists I apologize to her friend—as though I committed some crime against her. But even though I know I'll pay for it later, that I won't do.

Instead, I just look at her and say, "None of this changes what I told you in there." I gesture toward the back room.

"Your past, *Tommy,* your future—you know what I said is true. Oh, and about that *choice* you have coming up?" I glance between her and her date. "Well, as much as you may doubt me right now, you'd still be wise to heed my advice."

I glance at Sabine, watching as her aura flares up in a bout of anger that's just barely subdued by the presence of Munoz's arm slipping tightly around her waist. Winking at me conspiratorially, he turns her away from me and out the door as their friends follow behind.

The second they're gone Jude looks at me and says, "Dude, that was some seriously bad mojo that just went down in here. I feel like I should smudge the place with some sage to help clear it out." He shakes his head. "What gives? I thought you'd told her by now?"

I look at him. "Are you kidding? You saw what just happened. That's exactly the kind of scene I was hoping to avoid."

He shrugs, counting up the cash in the drawer as he says, "Well, maybe it would've gone better if you'd warned her, if she hadn't felt so sucker punched when she walked in and saw you were working here—giving *readings* no less."

I frown, scrounging around in my wallet for the money I owe him for the pro bono reading I just unwittingly gave.

"You sure you wanna cover it?" he says, refusing to take it when I offer it to him.

"*Please.*" I thrust it at him, seeing his brows lift and knowing he's about to insist otherwise when I add, "And keep the change too. Think of it as payment for all the—*bad mojo*—I caused. Seriously." I wave it away. "If that hadn't happened, who knows, she might've become a regular, so, you know, just look at it like payment for all that future lost revenue."

"I'm not so sure you lost her," he says, shoving the money

in the bank bag and slamming the register shut. "If you gave her as good a reading as I think, she'll find her way back, or at least tell some friends, who'll come out of curiosity if nothing else. That sort of thing's pretty tough for most people to resist. You know, straitlaced lawyer takes in scam artist niece who, unbeknownst to her, spends her spare time moonlighting as an insanely accurate psychic reader—could be a book or, at the very least, a movie of the week."

I shrug, taking a moment to touch up what little makeup I wear, peering into my small, handheld mirror when I say, "About that—"

He looks at me.

"I think my days as Avalon are over."

He sighs, clearly disappointed.

"I mean, don't get my wrong, I really have enjoyed it, and today, well, up until the fiasco anyway, I felt like I was starting to get really good at it—like I was able to reach people—help people—but now—well, maybe it's time to bring Ava back on board. Besides, school's about to start up and—"

"Are you quitting?" He frowns, obviously not thrilled with the idea.

"No." I shake my head. "No, I just, well, obviously I'll need to cut back, and I don't want to cause you any more problems than I already have."

"No worries." He shrugs. "I've already put Ava back on the schedule, figured you'd have to cut back your hours anyway, but, Ever, you can start up again anytime, the clients love you, and I—well—" His face flushes. "I've been very impressed with your performance as well. As an *employee*." He pinches the bridge of his nose, shaking his head and sighing when he adds, "Man, I'm about as far from smooth as it gets."

But I just shrug, wondering who's more uncomfortable here, him or me.

"So, any idea what you're gonna tell her tomorrow?" he asks, desperate to move on to something else.

"Nope." I drop my lip gloss into my bag and snap the bag shut. "Not a clue."

"Well, don't you think you should think about it? Come up with some kind of plan? You don't want to get caught before you've even had a chance to drink your first cup of joe, do you?"

"I don't drink coffee." I shrug.

"Fine, elixir, whatever." He laughs. "You know what I mean."

I heave my purse onto my shoulder and glance at him. "Look, don't get me wrong, I love Sabine. She took me in when I lost everything, and in return, I've done nothing but make her life a living hell on an ongoing basis. And while I'm perfectly willing to come clean, if for no other reason than the fact that after all this, she deserves to hear the truth, or at least *some* semblance of the truth—it won't be tomorrow morning. Not even close." And even though I try not to smile when I say it, I can't help myself. When I think of my plan, my fail-safe, foolproof plan, my whole face lights up.

For now, all of my energy, all of my light, all of my *good mojo*—as Jude puts it—needs to be saved up and channeled exclusively toward Roman. I've got to extend my love, peace, and goodwill toward him because approaching him this way is the only way I can win. The only way I'll ever get what I want.

If there's one thing I've learned through all this, it's that resistance never works. Fighting the war against what I *don't* want only serves to manifest that very thing. And that's why Roman's power over me weakened when I appealed to Hecate—because I stopped obsessing about it for five minutes and it started to deteriorate as a result. So, with all this in mind, I think it's safe to assume that by pouring my energies into what I *do* want—peace between us and the rogues along with the antidote to the antidote—well, it can only result in a win.

So, when I go to him tonight, it won't be as an enemy, as someone who plans to connive and fight to get what they want. Instead, I'll approach him as my higher self—the purest, clearest form of me.

And then I'll offer him the chance to rise up from the depths and meet me on that very same level.

And I'm so lost in my thoughts, so lost in the excitement of my plan, at first I don't even hear Jude when he says, "Where you headed?" Squinting at me, his psychic radar on its highest alert.

But I just look at him, unable to keep the smile from my face when I say, "I'm going to go do something I should've done a long time ago." Pausing when I see the way his head tilts, the way his brow creases, the way his aura wavers and flares, and wishing I had time to stick around and reassure him, tell him it'll all be okay. But I don't, I've wasted enough time already. So, instead, I just look at him and say, "Don't worry. This time, I know what I'm doing. This time, everything's gonna be different. *You'll see.*"

"Ever—" He reaches toward me, hand clawing at the air before falling empty at his side.

"No worries." I shrug. "I know exactly what to do. I know

how to handle Roman now." I nod, taking in his thick tangle of dreadlocks, seeing how the last few weeks of summer surf have lightened them to a sun-bleached blond. "I know exactly how to fix it, exactly how to proceed," I add, seeing the way he tilts his head, leans back on the stool, and rubs his chin thoughtfully. His malachite ring glinting before me, nearly the same shade of green as his tropical gaze, which is narrowed, assessing, tinged with more than a slight bit of worry. But I just ignore all of that. Just brush it right off. For the first time in a long time I finally feel powerful, sure of myself, and I won't allow room for anyone to plant even the smallest seed of doubt. "I went to the Great Halls of Learning—" I pause, knowing he needs more convincing than just my nodding head and confident word. "And—well, let's just say I got a good lead. A *very* good lead." I press my lips together and hike my purse higher onto my shoulder, knowing I should probably leave the conversation right there.

He looks at me, rubbing his hand over the front of his T-shirt, fingers tracing the black and white yin yang symbol as he tilts his head and says, "Ever—I'm not so sure you should go that route again. I mean, if you'll remember, last time you went face-to-face with Roman it really didn't work out all that well, and I really don't think enough time has passed for you to try it again. At least not so soon."

I lift my shoulders, his words glancing over me like oil meeting water, having no effect whatsoever, which, from the expression on his face, only seems to worry him more. "Noted," I say, tucking my hair behind my ear. "But here's the thing—I'm doing it anyway. I'm going in. One last time. So to speak."

"When? Now? Are you serious?" He looks at me, brows merged, gaze locked on mine in a way that gives me pause for concern.

I square my shoulders and fold my arms across my chest, meeting his gaze when I say, "Why? You planning to follow me so you can try to stop me?"

"Maybe." He shrugs, not even pausing when he adds, "I'll do whatever it takes."

"Whatever it takes to—*what* exactly?" I cock my head, challenging him with my gaze.

"Keep you safe. Keep you from *him*."

I take a deep breath and look at him, and I mean *really* look at him. Starting from the top of those dreadlocks and moving all the way down to his waist where, because of the counter, my view of him ends. "And why would you do that?" I finally say, gaze returning to meet his. "Why would you even think of trying to interfere with my plan? I thought you wanted me to be happy—even if that means my being with Damen? Or at least that's what you told me."

He rubs his lips together and shifts on his seat, a move so awkward, so clearly uncomfortable, I feel bad for saying it. I went too far. Just because we've spilled our hearts in the past, sharing more than we probably should have doesn't mean I have the right to question him or to exploit what he told me. Doesn't mean I should insist on an answer when the question obviously pains him. But still, something about the way he just shifted, not just physically, but energetically too, leaves me wondering, guessing—leaves me just the tiniest bit unsure . . .

I turn, heading for the door as he follows behind, around to the alleyway out back where we've both parked our cars.

"I'm meeting up with Honor later—you want to drop by? You can bring Damen if you want, I won't mind."

I stop and look at him.

"Well, I might mind, but I'll put on a good show—scout's honor." He raises his right hand.

"So, you're hanging with Honor?" I say, watching as he opens the driver's side door of his old black Jeep and climbs in.

"Yeah, you know, your friend from school, the one who came to your birthday party?"

I start to tell him that she's not my *friend,* that from what I saw that day on the beach, the energy she gave off, she's probably anything but—but when I see the expression on his face, see the amusement that creases his brow, I decide to keep it to myself.

"She's not so bad, you know?" He inserts his key and starts the engine in a series of sputters and spurts. "Maybe you should give her a chance?"

I look at him, remembering what I said to him that very first day, before I even really knew him, long before I knew about us. Something about him always falling for all the wrong girls and wondering if he's falling once again. But when I see the way his gaze shifts, the way his aura sparks and flames, I know that that wrong girl is still me. Honor's not even in the game. And I'm not sure what bothers me more—the realization of that or the sudden flood of relief that it brings?

"Ever—"

He gazes at me in a way that halts my breath. His face so conflicted, it's clear he's struggling with what comes next, but in the end he just squints, rubs his lips together, and takes a deep breath when he says, "You gonna be okay? You sure you know what you're doing?"

I nod, climbing into my car, feeling more confident and empowered than ever before. The darkness is gone, conquered by light, and there's no way this can go wrong. Closing my eyes and bringing my engine to life, then looking at Jude as I say, "Don't worry. This time, I know what I'm doing. This time, everything's gonna be different. *You'll see.*"

THIRTY-THREE

When I get to Roman's, it's quiet.

Just as I'd hoped.

Just as I'd planned.

When Haven told me she was going to a concert with Misa, Marco, and Rafe, I knew it was the perfect opportunity to catch Roman on his own, undisturbed, so I could approach him in a peaceful, reasonable manner and calmly plead my case.

I stand outside his door, taking a moment to close my eyes and be still. Drawing my attention deep down inside myself, unable to find even the slightest trace of the monster in there. It's as if by letting go of all my anger and hatred for Roman, I've deprived the dark flame of the oxygen it needed to survive—and I am what's left in its place.

And it's only after I've knocked a few times and he still fails to answer that I let myself in. Knowing he's in there, and not just because his cherry red Aston Martin is parked in the drive but because I can *feel* him, *sense* his presence, but oddly enough he doesn't seem to feel or sense mine or surely he'd already be here.

I head down the hall, peeking into the den, the kitchen, through the window to the detached garage in the back, and when I see that it's dark, with no sign of him, I head for his bedroom, calling his name and moving much louder than necessary, preferring not to surprise him or catch him in the middle of something embarrassing.

Finding him lying on the middle of a large, elaborate, canopied bed, one with so many drapes and tassels it reminds me of the ones Damen and I enjoy in our Summerland version of Versailles. Clothed in an unbuttoned, white linen shirt and faded old jeans, his eyes shut tight, with a pair of earphones clamped to his head, and a framed picture of Drina clutched to his chest. And I stop, wondering if I should maybe just turn around and leave, catch him another time, when:

"Oh, fer chrissakes, Ever, don't tell me you knocked the bloody door down again?" He sits up, tossing the earphones to the side and carefully placing the photo of Drina back in the drawer of his nightstand. Seemingly not the least bit embarrassed at being caught in such a private, sentimental moment. "This whole act of yers is gettin' a little overplayed, don'tcha think?" He shakes his head and rakes his fingers through those golden waves, pushing them back into place. "Seriously, darlin', can't a bloke get a little privacy around here? Between you and Haven—" He sighs and swings his bare feet to the floor as though he's about to stand, only he doesn't, he just remains sitting like that. "Well, I'm feelin' a little tapped out—you know what I mean?"

I look at him, knowing I probably shouldn't say it, but I'm far too curious to let it go. "Were you—were you *meditating*?"

I squint, never having pictured him as the type to go in, go deep, and try to connect to that universal force.

"So what if I was, mate? So what if I was?" He rubs his hands across his brow, then turns to me when he says, "If you must know, I was trying to find Drina. You know you're not the only one around here with—*abilities*."

I swallow hard, already well aware of that, already guessing the answer to my next question when I ask, "And—*did you see her*?" Willing to bet that he didn't, especially knowing what I know about the Shadowland.

He looks at me, face bearing a fleeting expression of pain when he says, "No. I didn't. Okay? Satisfied? But someday I will. You can't keep us apart forever, you know? Despite what you've done—I've got every intention of finding her."

I take a deep breath, thinking: *Oh, I hope not. You are* not *going to like it there*. And feeling terrible for the times I tricked him into thinking I was her—even though I wasn't in the driver's seat when it happened.

But I don't say that. In fact, I don't say anything. I just continue to stand there, collecting my thoughts, my words, myself, waiting for just the right moment to begin.

"Roman, listen, I—" I shake my head and start over, telling myself I can do this, summoning my strength from somewhere down deep when I look right at him and say, "This isn't what you think. I'm not here to seduce you, or play games with you, or taunt you, or try to get something from you, or at least not in the way that you think. I'm here to—"

"To get the antidote." He picks his feet up off the floor and plops them back down on his rumpled bed. Arms folded, blocking his chest as he leans back against his silk-covered headboard and squints. "I'll say one thing, Ever, you're persistent if nothing else. How many more times are you planning to do this? Every time you come over here you have a new plan of attack, a new agenda in mind, and yet, every single time you fail to make the score even though I've provided you ample opportunity to do so. Makes one wonder if you really do want it. Maybe you only *think* that you want it, but your subconscious won't allow it, since it knows your real truth. Your *deep—dark—*truth." His eyes glint on mine, wanting me to know that he knows about the monster, and just how amusing he finds it. "And, sorry, luv, but I have to ask, how does Damen feel about all these little visits of yours? I reckon he can't be too pleased about that, or the fact that Miles is about to become privy to yet another one of his secrets. He's got many, you know. Secrets you haven't even yet begun to uncover—stuff you can't even imagine—"

I nod, calmly, sincerely, refusing to let his words get to me. I'm just not that girl anymore.

"So tell me, does he know you're here now?"

"No." I shrug. "He doesn't." But when I think of the text that I sent him, just before I got out of my car and made my way in, I know it won't be long until he does know. As soon as he comes out of the movie with Ava and the twins, he'll check his messages, see my plans to meet him at the Montage, and he'll know. But for now, nope, not a clue.

"I see." He nods, his eyes grazing over me. "Well, at least you took the time to clean yourself up. In fact, you're looking better than ever—radiant—kind of *glowy* even. Tell me, Ever, what's your secret?"

"Meditation." I smile. "You know, cleansing, centering,

focusing on the positive—stuff like that." I shrug, continuing to stand my ground as he erupts into a bout of shoulder-shaking, eye-squinching laughter.

Allowing the hysterics to die down when he says, "That ol' Damen's got you trekking the Himalayas too, eh?" He tilts his head and takes me in. "That ol' bugger, he never learns. And a lot of good it does him."

"Well, excuse me for saying so, but weren't *you* just meditating?"

"Not like that, luv. No, not like that, I wasn't." He shakes his head. "You see, my way is different. I was reaching out to *one person* in particular—not calling upon some made-up, universal, all-is-one nonsense. Don't you get it, Ever? This is it. Right *here,* right *now.*" He pats the rumpled sheets beside him. "*This* is our paradise, our heaven, our nirvana, our Shangri-la—whatever you want to call it." His brow shoots up as his tongue wets his lips. "This is *it.* And I mean that both figuratively *and* literally. It's all we got, and you're wasting your time seeking anything more. Now, granted, you've got plenty of time to waste, I'll give you that, but still, it's such a shame to see the way you choose to spend it. That Damen's a bad influence, I tell you." He pauses, as though taking a moment to consider. "So, what do you say? Shall we try it again? I mean, you come here looking like that, and, well, seeing as I heal quickly and all, I'm apt to forgive you for the last time, let bygones be bygones and all that. Just don't try any fast moves or make me think you're Drina again and we're good to go. You've pulled some cold stuff the last few times, though, funny thing, I think it just made me like you even more. So, what do you say?" He smiles, tossing a pillow aside to make room for me as he cocks his head, flashes his tattoo, and gazes at me in that mesmerizing way.

But this time, it doesn't work. Even though I move toward him, toward the anticipatory gleam in his eye, it's not for the reason he thinks.

"I'm not here for that," I say, watching as he shrugs, like he couldn't care less either way.

Head bent forward, inspecting his perfectly buffed and manicured nails when he says, "Then just what are you here for? Come on, get on with it already, Haven'll drop by eventually, soon as her concert is over, and I don't think either of us needs a scene like that again."

"I've no plans to hurt Haven." I shrug. "I've no plans to hurt you either. I'm merely here to appeal to your higher self, that's all."

He gapes, eyes searching my face for the joke he's sure that I'm hiding.

"I know you have one. A higher self. In fact, I know all about you. I know all about your past, how your mother died in labor, how your father beat and then abandoned you—I know it all—I—"

"Bloody hell," he says, blue eyes wide, voice so soft, so stunned, I almost missed it. "Nobody knows about that— how the hell did you—?"

But I just shrug, the *how* doesn't matter. "And after knowing all that, I find that I can no longer hate you. I just don't. It's not in me."

He stares at me, eyes narrowed, full of skepticism. Returning to his usual bravado when he says, "Of course you do, luv, you *love* to hate me, that's just what you do. In fact, you love to hate me so much, I'm all you can think about."

He smiles, nodding as though he's onto me, like he's known all along.

But I just shake my head, perching on the edge of his bed when I say, "While that used to be true, it's not anymore. And the only reason I came here is to tell you how sorry I am for what happened to you. I really, truly am."

He averts his gaze, clenching his jaw and kicking at the blanket when he says, "Well, you bloody well shouldn't be! There's only one thing you have to be sorry for, luv, and that's what you did to Drina. All the rest—you can spare me. I'm not the least bit interested in your misguided alms for the poor, destitute, and downtrodden. I don't need your sympathies, darlin'. In case you haven't noticed, I'm no longer that kid. Surely you can see that, Ever, just look at me." He smiles and spreads his arms wide, inviting me to take a good long look at his undeniably, glorious self. "I'm at the very top of my game. Have been for centuries now."

"And that's just it." I lean toward him. "You view it all as one big game—as though life is the board and you're the piece that always needs to stay three steps ahead of all the others. You *never* let your guard down, *never* allow yourself to get close to anyone—and you have no idea how *to love* or how to *be loved*, since love was never given to you. I mean, sure you could've made different choices, and there's no doubt you should've, but still it's kind of hard to offer what you've never had, what you've never experienced for yourself, and I forgive you for that."

"What is this?" He glares at me. "Amateur hour? You gonna send me a bill for your ridiculous psychobabblings? Is that it?"

"No," I say, my voice quiet, my gaze fixed on his. "I'm just trying to tell you that it's over. I refuse to fight you anymore. I choose to love you and accept you instead. Whether you like it or not."

"Show me," he says, back to patting the bed again. "Why don't you just crawl on over here and show me the *love*, Ever?"

"It's not that kind of love. It's the *real* kind. The unconditional kind. The nonjudgmental kind. *Not* the physical kind. I love you as a fellow soul who inhabits this earth. I love you as a fellow immortal. I love you because I'm tired of hating you, and refuse to do so any longer. I love you because I finally understand what made you the way you are. And if I could change it, I would. But I can't—so I choose to love you instead. And my hope is that my acceptance of you will spur you on to do something good too, but if not—" I shrug. "At least I can say I tried."

"Bloody hell," he mumbles, rolling his eyes as though my words do nothing but pain him. "Somebody's been drinking the hippie juice!" He shakes his head and laughs, settling down and looking at me when he says, "Okay, Ever, you love me and forgive me. Bravo. Well done. But here's the news flash—you still don't get the antidote, okay? You still love me? Or you back to hating me again? Just how deep *is* your love, Ever—to quote a song from the seventies that I'm sure you've never heard of." He drops his hands onto his lap, leaving them open, relaxed. "I feel sorry for your generation. All that crap music you listen to. You should hear the band Haven went to see— The Mighty Hooligans? What kind of a piss-poor name is that?"

I just shrug. I know an avoidance tactic when I see one, but no matter how hard he tries, I refuse to be swayed off course like he wants. "Your choice," I say. "I'm not here to ask you for anything."

"Then what are you here for? What's the point of this little visit of yours? According to you, you're not looking for the antidote, you're not looking for a good shaggin' even though it's bloody obvious you're desperately in need of one. You just waltz on in here and disrupt my privacy so you could tell me you love me? *Really, Ever?* Because I'm sorry to say it, but I find that all a bit hard to *digest*."

"Of course you do," I say, completely unfazed. This is pretty much exactly what I expected, it's all moving along just as I planned. "But that's only because you've never experienced that before. Six hundred years and you've never known a moment of real and true love. It's sad. Tragic really. But it's hardly your fault. So, for the record, *this* is what it feels like, Roman. *This* is what it looks like. I just want you to know that, despite all you've done, I forgive you. And because I *forgive* you, because I *release* you, you can't get to me or hurt me anymore. If you never give me the antidote—well, Damen and I will work around it, because that's what soul mates *do*. That's what true love *is*. It cannot be broken, it cannot be chipped away, it's eternal, everlasting, and it can weather any storm. So if you're determined to continue like this, I just want you to know you'll get no resistance from me. I'm done with all that. I've got a life to live—how about you?"

He looks at me, and for a brief moment, I know I've got him. I see the flash in his eye, the blip of understanding that the game is now over. That it requires two players, and one just dropped out. But then, just as quickly, it's gone and the old Roman's returned, saying, "Come on, darlin'—you serious with all this? You mean to tell me you plan to spend the rest of your immortal life settling for a chaste bit of hand-holding? Hell, you can't even do that—despite the energy condom you've made—it's nothin' like the real thing now is it, luv? Nothin' like *this*."

And before I know it, he's beside me, his hand gripping my leg, gaze deep, intense, locked on mine as he says, "I may have never known the kind of love you're blabbering on about, but I've had plenty of the other kind—*this* kind." His fingers inch higher. "And I'm telling you, darlin', in a pinch, it's just as good if not better. And I can't stand the idea of you missing out."

"Then give me the antidote and I don't have to miss out," I say, smiling sweetly, making no attempt to remove his fingers from my flesh. That's what he wants me to do. He wants me to freak out and resist. To throw him against the wall. Make a menace of myself. The usual routine. But not this time. Nope. This time I've got too much to prove. Too much to lose. Besides, I'm about to show him just how boring the game can be when only one decides to play.

"You'd like that, wouldn't you? To win this one?"

"It's a win-win, wouldn't you say? You do something nice—something nice will be done for you—it's karma. It's a ripple effect. It's no fail."

"Oh, back to that, are we?" He rolls his eyes. "I say, that Damen bloke's really done a number on you."

"Maybe." I smile, refusing to rise to his bait. "Or maybe not. You never know until you try it, right?"

"What? You think I've never done anything nice?"

"I think it's been a while. You're probably a bit rusty by now."

He laughs, throws his head back and laughs, but he doesn't remove his hand, no, it stays right there, smoothing my thigh.

"Okay, Ever, theoretically speaking, let's say I did do this one small thing for you. Let's say I did give you the antidote that would allow you and Damen to shag your little hearts out. Then what? How long do I have to wait for this so-called good karma to boomerang back at me? Can you tell me that?"

I shrug. "From what I've seen, you can't force karma, it works on its own terms. All I know is, it works."

"So, I'm supposed to just hand over something to you, something you desperately want, and risk getting nothing in return? That hardly seems fair darlin', so maybe you should reconsider, maybe there's something you can give to me." He smiles, sliding his hand much higher, way higher, *too high*. And when he gazes into my eyes, trying to overpower me, lure me into his head like he used to—it doesn't work. I remain right where I am, rooted in place.

And yet, that simple act alone has spawned an idea, one that might move this along even quicker than I hoped, and get me to the Montage, where I told Damen we'd meet.

"Well," I say, doing my best to ignore the feel of his fingers splayed across my thigh. "If you won't trust karma, will you at least trust *me*?"

He looks at me, head titled, Ouroboros tattoo flashing in and out of view.

"Because, come to think of it, I *do* have something to give you. Something I know for sure that you want. Something that only *I* can give you."

"Well, bugger that!" He smiles. "*Now* we're talkin'. I knew you'd come around eventually, I knew you'd see the light." He scoots even closer, grips my leg tighter.

But I just continue to sit there, breathing steadily, evenly, aware of the light still shining inside me when I say, "It's not that—it's—it's something much better than that."

He squints. "Aw, now don't be so hard on yerself, darlin'. First time's always a wash. I promise we'll have plenty of goes for you to improve your skills and get better."

And even though he laughs when he says it, obviously wanting me to laugh too, I don't. I'm still thinking about what I just said, this new plan now forming in my head. Knowing it won't be exactly what he expects, and may cause him to hate me even more, but still, it's the only way I can think of to get him to connect—well, if one can actually connect with a lost soul, that is . . .

"Let go of my leg." My eyes gaze into his.

"Ah, bugger!" He shakes his head. "See, I knew you were full of it—you're nothing but a tease, Ever, you know that? Nothing but—"

"Let go of my leg and take hold of my hands instead," I say, my voice calm, determined. "Trust me, you have nothing to lose, I promise you that."

He hesitates, but only for a moment before he does as I ask. The two of us sitting cross-legged on the bed, my bare knees pressed against his, his hands gripping mine, the whole scene reminding me vaguely of the binding spell that started this mess.

Only this is nothing like that.

Nothing at all.

I'm about to take a huge leap of faith. I'm about to share something with Roman that'll definitely result in his handing over the antidote. Looking him straight in the eyes when I say, "Your argument is flawed."

He squints.

"Your argument. About there being nothing but the here and now. If you truly believed that, then why were you trying to connect with Drina? If you truly believe that there's nothing beyond this, the earth plane, where we sit now, then exactly what is it you were trying to connect with?"

He looks at me, obviously flummoxed when he says, "Her essence—her—" He shakes his head, tries to let go of my hands, but I just grip his tighter. "What the hell is this?" he asks, clearly unhappy with me.

"It doesn't end here, Roman. There's more, *lots* more. More than you could ever imagine. *This,* what you see here—this is all just a tiny little blip on a much bigger screen. But I have a feeling that despite what you say, you already sense that. And because you already sense that, you're open to it. And so, with that in mind, I'm wondering if we can maybe broker some kind of deal."

"I *knew* it!" He laughs and shakes his head. "I *knew* you hadn't given up. Never say die, Ever, right?"

But I just ignore it, forging ahead when I say, "If I take you to Drina, if I show you where she rests, will you give me the antidote?"

He drops my hands, his face blanched, shocked, clearly struggling to steady himself. "You putting one over on me?"

"No." I shake my head. "I'm not. I'm really not. I swear."

"Then why are you doing this?"

"Because it only seems fair. You give me what I want most, and I'll give you what you want most. You may not like what you see, you'll probably even end up hating me—but I'm willing to take that chance. And I promise you, I'll give you the whole, unobstructed view. I'll hold nothing back."

"And—what if you give me what I want and I *still* don't give you the antidote? What then?"

"Then I misjudged you." I shrug. "Then I walk away with nothing. But I won't hate you, and I won't bother you again. But I think you'll definitely believe in karma once you experience the effects of an action like that. So—you ready?"

He looks at me, looks at me for a long moment, weighing, considering, until he finally nods, his gaze holding steady on mine when he says, "Wanna know where I keep it?"

I swallow hard. My breath quickening.

"It's right here." He reaches over to his nightstand, opens a drawer, pulls out a small, jewel-encrusted, velvet-lined box and retrieves a slim glass vial filled with an opalescent liquid that looks an awful lot like elixir—except that it's green.

And I watch as he waves it before me, seeing it sparkle and shine, hardly able to believe that the answer to all of my troubles is so small and contained.

"I thought you said you didn't keep it here," I say, my mouth gone suddenly dry as I take it in—seeing it shimmering before me.

"I didn't. Not 'til after the other night. Before that, I kept it at the store. But this is it, luv—a single serving with no recipe card on file—the full list of ingredients exists only in here." He taps the side of his head and eyes me carefully. "So, we have a deal, right? You show me yours—and I'll give you mine." He smiles, slipping the antidote into his shirt pocket and gazing at me when he says, "But you first. You hold up your end of the deal. Take me to her—and the happily ever after is yours."

THIRTY-FOUR

"Close your eyes," I whisper, grasping Roman's cold hands in mine, our knees pressed tightly together, our faces so close I can feel the chill of his breath on my cheek. "And now open your mind. Ridding it as best you can of all extraneous thoughts. Just empty it out—let it go blank—drop everything and just—*be*. Got it?"

He nods, squeezing my fingers even tighter. So focused on this, wanting so badly to see where Drina now lives, it's heartbreaking.

"Now, I want you to enter my mind. I'm going to lower my shield and allow you in, and—I'm warning you, Roman—you may not like what you see, you may become extremely angry with me, but I want you to remember I'm holding up my end of the deal, okay? I never said you'd like it, I only said I'd take you to where she is." I open one eye to see him nod once again, "Okay, so now—come in—slowly find your way in and—you with me?"

"Yes," he whispers. "Yes—it's so—*dark*—*so*—I can't see a thing—and I'm falling—so fast—so—where—?"

"It'll end soon—just hang in there," I coax.

His breath quickens as the chill of it, a cloud of cold fog, hits my cheek. "It's—it's stopped—the fall—but it's still so dark—and so—I'm—*suspended*—and—alone—*so alone*—but I'm not—someone else is out there—*she's* out there—and—oh, God—Drina—*where are you*—" He grips my hands tighter, so tight they're about to go numb, his breath shallow, ragged, his body dripping with the sweat of his efforts as it collapses onto mine and he's swept away by the events unfolding in my head—his head—a breathless tour of the Shadowland, the infinite abyss, the final resting place for all immortal souls—including ours.

Mumbling a string of words so softly I can't make them out, I only know from the tone that they're agitated, disturbed, fretful, as he hovers in the darkness, clawing and grasping, desperately seeking her. His forehead pushed against mine, nose pressed to my cheek, lips resting so near, all of his energy and strength focused on *her*.

And that's how Jude finds us.

That's what he sees.

Roman and I together, sweating on his sheets, our bodies pressed tightly together, clutching at each other, both of us so lost in the vision, we don't see him, don't hear him, until it's too late.

Too late to stop him.

Too late to undo what he does.

Too late to rewind and go back—back to how it was before—when I was so close—so close to getting what I want.

And before I know it, I'm wrenched from Roman's grip, as

Jude lunges on top of him, fist headed right toward the center of his torso, immune to my scream.

My agonized: *"Noooooo!"*

The sound of it filling up the room, and repeating over and over again.

Scrambling to get up—to pull him off—to stop him from going any further—but it's too late. As fast as I am—I can't beat him—I got a late start—I was thrown off my game—and Jude's already there.

Already on top of Roman.

Already slamming his fist into his sacral center.

His weakest chakra.

His Achilles' heel.

The center of jealousy, envy, and the irrational desire to possess.

The collection of needs that drove Roman for the last six hundred years.

Instantly turning him from glorious golden boy to pile of dust.

I leap onto Jude, grab him by the shoulders, and fling him to the other side of the room, hearing a dull crack as he lands against the dresser, but not bothering to look back. Focusing on only one thing, Roman's white linen shirt glittering with tiny shards of glass as a dark green stain spreads across its front.

The antidote.

The vial for the antidote now smashed—destroyed in the struggle—and taking my hopes along with it.

And now, with Roman gone, his soul headed for the Shadowland, there's no way to ever retrieve it.

"How could *you*?" I turn, eyes blazing on Jude. "How could

you *do* such a thing?" Watching as he struggles to stand, face blanched, hand rubbing at his back. "You've destroyed *every-thing. Everything!* I was so close—so close to getting the antidote—and you wrecked it! *Forever!*"

Jude looks at me, hands on his knees, brow merged, struggling to catch his breath when he says, "Ever—I—I didn't mean to—" He shakes his head. "You have to believe me. I thought you were in trouble—you *looked* like you were in trouble! You didn't see what I saw—you were—he was all over you—" He shakes his head. "And it seemed like you were struggling—internally, like you couldn't handle it, couldn't fight your attraction to him. And that's why I came. That's the only reason I'm here. I knew where you were heading when you left the store and I didn't think you were ready to try this again. And when I got here just now—and saw you like that—well, I didn't want it to end up like that last time and so—I just—I—"

"And so you *killed* him?" My eyes gape as my throat goes dry. "You used *everything* I shared with you against me, and you *killed* him?"

He shakes his head and stands before me, his T-shirt torn from when I grabbed him and flung him across the room, his aura flaring in distress as he fiddles with the green malachite ring on the hand he used to kill Roman with. "You're always going on and on about how bad he is—how evil—how he runs an evil tribe of rogues—and how because of the spell you cast, you can't seem to resist him. You came to *me* for help. You confided in me first—*not* Damen. You chose *me*, Ever, whether you like it or not! And all I wanted to do was to save you—from Roman—from yourself. That was my only intention—to look after you—to take care of *you!*"

"Was it?" I narrow my gaze, as a new idea begins to take shape. "Was that *really* your only intention? *Truly?*"

"What are you talking about?" He squints, rubbing his lips together, trying to decipher my words.

"You know exactly what I'm talking about," I say, body trembling with fury, outrage, and defeat, as I clutch Roman's shirt, his antidote-stained shirt. "You did this on purpose." I glare at him, having no real proof that it's true, but still, once the words are out there, spoken aloud, the idea begins to gain strength and build, so much so that I quickly repeat it, venturing even further when I add, "You did this on purpose. This is no *mistake.* You knew exactly what you were doing when you came here. So, is this it then? Is this how you figure you'll win the game of four hundred years? Is this your big move? Robbing *me,* the girl you supposedly *love,* of the one thing I want most in this world? Ensuring that I'll never, ever get to be with Damen? Is that how you're playing it, Jude? You honestly think that this'll make me give up on my soul mate and choose *you?*"

I shake my head and gaze down at Roman's shirt, my heart sinking when I look at the stain that runs across it, when I think of Roman's sad, pathetic life, and what's now become of his soul. Knowing I was so close, *so close,* to reaching him, to making a difference, to getting what I want—and now *this.*

Everything lost in an instant.

"*Ever—*" Jude pleads, the sting of my words conveyed in his voice, in his eyes, as he moves toward me, his hands reaching, but I won't let him get close, won't let him touch me. "How can you even *say* that?" he asks, finally stopping, conceding defeat. "I *do* love you. You know that. I've loved you for centuries, it's true. But I didn't intentionally set out to do this—to keep you from Damen in this way. You mean too much to me to ever do that, I value your happiness, like I told you before. And when you *do* finally make your choice, choose between us, I want it to be fair. This time, I'm determined that it be *fair*."

"But I've already chosen," I say, my voice now a whisper. I just don't have it in me to fight anymore. Rising from the bed, still clutching the shirt, when Haven comes in and catches me like that.

Eyes blazing as she surveys the scene, instantly filling in the blanks and putting the pieces together when she sees Roman's shirt in my hand.

"What've you done?" she says, voice so low, so menacing, it sends a chill down my spine. "What the *hell* have you done?"

She snatches the shirt, grasping it against her lace-covered chest as her eyes rake over me, assuming I'm to blame, and ignoring Jude when he tries to step in and assume full responsibility.

"I should've known." She shakes her head, eyes narrowed to slits. "Should've known all along—when you came over to my house and tried to play nice—you weren't even the least bit sincere—you were using me, playing me, pumping me for information—trying to see when I'd be gone, so you could get him alone and then—and then *kill him*."

"It's not what you think!" I cry. "It's not like that *at all*!" But no matter how many times I repeat it, it doesn't penetrate. She's made up her mind, about me, about Jude, about everything that's happened here tonight.

"Oh, it's exactly what I think." She glares, hands clutching her shiny, black leather-clad hips. "*Exactly*. And trust me,

Ever, you won't get away with it. Not this time. You're done interfering in my life. You're done robbing me of the people I hold dear. This is war. *Absolute war.* I'm gonna make your life so miserable, you're gonna *wish* your only problem was that you can't touch your boyfriend. Cuz make no mistake—you've never seen anything like I've got coming for you." She lifts her brow and flashes her teeth. "And Jude?" She spins on her heel, acknowledging him for the first time since she arrived. "You're gonna wish you were immortal, because after tonight, there's no way you'll ever be able to withstand what's headed your way."

THIRTY-FIVE

"So, it worked," Damen says, his voice sounding soft, far-away. "It really did exist."

I take a deep breath and gaze down at my knees, my feet curled up on the soft leather seat, remembering how he found me just as I was leaving Roman's, Jude following behind, as Haven continued to scream a full litany of threats from the door. Arriving at the scene just seconds after the movie let out. Not even bothering to stop by the Montage where I'd planned for us to meet, sensing there was trouble from the moment he read my message.

I nod, gazing up at my house and remembering that triumphant moment when it all came together—when the antidote was as good as mine. Only to have it all fall apart.

Our dreams snatched right out from under us in one hor-rible instant.

I shake my head and sigh, knowing tomorrow morning I'll have to face Sabine. Have to come clean about my job, my psychic abilities, my moonlighting as Avalon—and reminiscing about a few hours earlier when I thought that was the worst of my problems.

"It really and truly did work," I say, meeting Damen's gaze, not just wanting but *needing* for him to believe it. "He had the antidote, he showed it to me and everything. It was so—*so small*—just this tiny glass vial filled with sparkly, green liquid." I shrug. "And then he stuck it in his pocket and—" I swallow hard, no need to relive the rest. Not verbally anyway. Not when the scene keeps replaying again and again in my head.

He frowns, having already viewed it almost as many times as me. "And then Jude busted in." He sighs and shakes his head. Gaze grim, jaw clenched in a way I've never seen before. "Why did you trust him? Why'd you confide our weaknesses—our chakras—how to get to us? Why would you do something like that?" He looks at me, desperate to understand.

I swallow hard, swallow past the big, dry lump now blocking my throat, thinking: *Well, there it is—the blame I've been seeking all along. He's finally judging me—but this time, it's more for what Jude's done than what I've done.*

But when I look at him again, I see that isn't it. He's simply trying to make sense of it all. But still, I just shrug and say, "It's my fifth chakra. My weak link. I suck at discernment, misuse information, and, apparently, trust all the wrong people in place of those who've been faithful all along." I peer at Damen, knowing he requires more, deserves more, bowing my head as I add, "And the truth is, he caught me in a weak moment—" I pause, remembering just how weak that moment truly was—how close I came to crossing the bridge that leads to the other side. And though I told Damen all about the magick, and how I turned to Jude before him, I failed to tell him that part, mostly because I was too ashamed. "An *incredibly* weak moment." I sigh. "What can I say?"

Damen turns, his leather seat squeaking, as he looks at me. "And here I was hoping you'd learn to trust me enough to turn to *me* in weak moments, *not* Jude." His voice so quiet, so solemn, it breaks my heart to hear the words spoken out loud.

I close my eyes and lean back against the headrest, feeling the threat of tears as I whisper, "I know. I should've told you. But despite all your assurances, despite what you told me, I just didn't believe it—*couldn't* believe it. I didn't think I deserved it. And, Damen, if you think you know the worst of it, well, think again. I'm afraid it gets much worse—"

I turn, turn until I'm facing him, and press my palms flat against his cheeks. Aware of the energy veil now dancing between us, allowing for that *almost* feel of his skin, and knowing this is it—this is as good as it ever will get. I'm all out of options—*we're* out of options. Roman is dead and he took the antidote with him. Then I take a deep breath, close my eyes, and share *everything*. Every single horrible and humiliating moment revealed—flowing from my mind to his. Airing the unedited version, that awful night with Roman when I almost lost my virginity, followed by the scene at the Bridge of Souls—every horrible second revealed in all its high-definition, degrading glory. Knowing he deserves to know the truth about me—what I was, where I've been—and who I am now. The whole sordid journey.

And when it's over, he just shrugs, covering my hands with his as he says, "There's nothing there that changed my mind about you. Not one single thing."

I nod, knowing that's true. I finally get it. What true and unconditional love really is.

"Ever," he says, voice urgent, gaze fixed on mine, "you need to reframe how you see yourself and the choices you've made."

I squint, not quite understanding.

"What you view as these huge glaring mistakes—well, they aren't mistakes at all. The reality is nothing like you've chosen to see it. You think you've done this terrible thing by feeding me Roman's elixir, when the truth is—*you saved my life!* You spared me from the Shadowland! I wouldn't have lasted 'til Romy got back, despite the magick circle Rayne made. I was hovering in and out of consciousness. Not quite here, not quite there, and if you hadn't've done *what* you did *when* you did—if you'd refused to let me drink—well, I would've perished and my soul would've been lost, stranded, left to drift in darkness and solitude for all of eternity."

I look at him, my eyes wide, never having thought of that. I'd been so busy beating myself up, focusing on how we can no longer really touch in the way that we want, I failed to realize I'd actually spared his soul from that infinite abyss.

"And another thing"—he reaches for my chin, the *almost* touch of his fingers causing a rush of warm tingle—"you actually got through to Roman! And you succeeded not by trickery or calculated cunning but by appealing to his deepest sense of humanity—a humanity the rest of us failed to see in him and were sure didn't even exist. But you were able to go deeper than that, to see what we couldn't. You saw the promise in the person we'd all written off. Do you have any idea how amazing that is—how proud that makes me?"

"But what about turning Haven?" I whisper, remembering her threat and having no doubt she plans to make good on it.

"Did I not make the same choice when I saved you?" he asks, lips at my ear.

"But you didn't know about the Shadowland. I did, and I condemned her soul." I shrug, pulling away to get a better look at his face.

But he just shakes his head and pulls me back to him. "I know I told you to do otherwise, but if it were me in your position, I would've done the same. Where there's life, there's hope, *right*? At least, that's been my motto for the last six hundred years."

I lean against him, pressing my head into the hollow of his shoulder as I gaze up at the house, seeing the light in Sabine's room go off and squeezing Damen's hand when I say, "Romy and Rayne were right. You know, about the magick. That used for selfish and nefarious reasons it'll result in karma that comes back times three."

We shift, our gaze meeting as the air hangs heavy between us.

"The first was when I was forced into that situation with Haven and I changed her—turned her into an adversary bent on destroying me. The second was my attraction to Roman— the dark flame that burned inside me. And now—and now *this*—Roman—the death of his soul and along with it, the death of the antidote." I look at him. "I mean, that is the three, *right*? Or was my attraction to him just me? A monster of my own making, a shadow of me that already existed and now there's still another one out there—somewhere—waiting for just the right moment to boomerang back at us? Something we won't even see coming until it's too late?"

I fight to catch my breath, suddenly overcome by panic,

the foreboding feeling that it's not over yet, there's more out there, and it's headed our way.

Soon comforted by the feel of his strong arms holding me tightly, his tingle and heat, and the knowledge that there's now a brilliant, white light shining inside me. And because of it, because of everything I've been through, I'm now strong enough to meet it—my karma, my destiny—in whatever form it may take. . . .

Damen's warm breath at my ear, echoing my thoughts when he says, "Either way, we'll ride it out together. That's how it is with soul mates. That's just what they do."

ACKNOWLEDGMENTS

As always, huge, sparkly, confetti-strewn thanks go to:

Bill Contardi—what can I say? You are the absolute BEST! Thanks for all your hard work on my behalf!

Marianne Merola—thank you for helping to spread The Immortals throughout the world!

The St. Martin's Team—including but certainly not limited to: Matthew Shear, Rose Hilliard, Anne Marie Tallberg, Katy Hershberger, Brittney Kleinfelter, Angela Goddard, and more . . .

My family and friends—you know who you are! Thank you for all the love and support and for dragging me away from the computer just when I need it the most—I appreciate you more than you know!

Sandy—the Patron Saint of Blue Hippos—you rock my world!

And, of course, my readers—not only do you make it all possible—you make it fun and worthwhile and an absolute thrill—I can't thank you enough!

THE IMMORTALS

NIGHT STAR

The unmissable new novel from

Alyson Noël

Coming soon!

A selected list of titles available from Macmillan Children's Books

The prices shown below are correct at the time of going to press. However, Macmillan Publishers reserves the right to show new retail prices on covers, which may differ from those previously advertised.

Alyson Noël

The Immortals: Evermore	978-0-330-51285-5	£6.99
The Immortals: Blue Moon	978-0-330-51286-2	£6.99
The Immortals: Shadowland	978-0-330-52051-5	£6.99

Elizabeth Chandler

| Kissed by an Angel | 978-0-330-51149-0 | £6.99 |

Meg Cabot

The Mediator: Love You to Death & High Stakes	978-0-330-51950-2	£6.99
The Mediator: Mean Spirits & Young Blood	978-0-330-51951-9	£6.99
The Mediator: Grave Doubts & Heaven Sent	978-0-330-51952-6	£6.99

All Pan Macmillan titles can be ordered from our website, www.panmacmillan.com, or from your local bookshop and are also available by post from:

Bookpost, PO Box 29, Douglas, Isle of Man IM99 1BQ

Credit cards accepted. For details:
Telephone: 01624 677237
Fax: 01624 670923
Email: bookshop@enterprise.net
www.bookpost.co.uk

Free postage and packing in the United Kingdom